THE TERROR OF THE GRAVE

The thunder rumbled again and lightning flashed as Judd stood at the lip of the grave, staring down. The man had been large, long hair, beard, no shirt, but a leather vest partially covered his dirt-caked upper torso. Hanging from either side of the vest, two metal crosses stuck to the surface, glued there by mud.

Judd felt he had to drag the body out of the grave. Little by little, he moved the hulk of the man up and away from the bike. Then, jumping from the grave, Judd grabbed the dead man's hands and pulled, inching him up and out of the earth.

When the feet cleared the lip, Judd stopped and turned him over. His scream mixed with the next roll of thunder when he saw the gaping wound in the dead man's neck. Partially clotted, filled with mud and dirt, the neck looked as if it had a second mouth, full of earth and grinning broadly at Judd.

JOHN TIGGES

AS EVIL DOES

LEISURE BOOKS  NEW YORK CITY

For
Jaime,
Tony and Koji,
my three grandsons

A LEISURE BOOK

Published by

Dorchester Publishing Co., Inc.
6 East 39th Street
New York, NY 10016

Printed in the United States of America

PART 1
Death

Fear and trembling are come upon me: and darkness hath covered me.

Psalms 54:6

1

Thin pencil-like beams from the late morning sun pierced the gloom of the trees, projecting tiny spots of light onto the shadowed floor of the woods. The two girls, contrasts in appearance, wended their way through the brush and rotting vegetation. The leader, a dark-complexioned young woman, her black lion-mane hair flowing out and away from her triangular face, reveled in her communion with nature. She stopped, waiting for her companion to catch up. Cindy Wellington brushed the hair back from her high forehead and turned, a smile spreading across her firm mouth.

"Come on, Tami," she chided, "we haven't got all day, you know. We *do* have to leave for school this afternoon."

"I know, I know," Tami Castle said, puffing as she reached Cindy's side. "I didn't realize I was so out of shape. Criminy, one year away from gym class and volleyball and I'm down the tubes as an athlete."

"I told you you should have gone out for something when we enrolled a year ago." Cindy punched her friend on the arm. That first year in college had gone like a week at a slumber party. They had studied, but it seemed as if the flow of college life had caught them up, sweeping them along until the first two semesters of their advanced education were behind them. They had returned to the state university in the middle of August and had come home to Rushton for the three-day Labor Day weekend. Before having to return to school, they had decided on a quick walk in the woods to Morrison Creek, where they had picnicked and necked with boys and waded and swum throughout their high school days.

"I guess I'll just have to do something about it," Tami said, motioning with her head for Cindy to take the lead once more. "Do you think Judd will mind that we took off like this?"

"He shouldn't. After all, we can come home just about any weekend we choose."

"Only if there isn't a football game to go to," Tami reminded her. "You know, I really envy you your relationship with Judd."

"He's really super, isn't he?" Cindy said, picturing her brother in her mind. Ever since their parents had died four years before, he had taken over, being both father and mother as well as a loving brother. She knew there wasn't a thing he wouldn't do for her, and she felt exactly the same way about him.

"He's a hunk, all right. If it weren't for Peggy Dixon, I think I'd go for him myself." Tami wolf-whistled softly behind Cindy. "When are they going to be married?"

"Judd's made that perfectly clear. Not until I finish college. He doesn't want the responsibility of my tuition and a new wife at the same time."

"I guess I can understand that." Tami stopped. "There it is. The meadow."

The girls stood still for a moment, drinking in the sight of the open green dotted with wildflowers and low bushes. Songbirds chorused from the trees overhead, as if announcing the girls' arrival at the grassy glade. Tami bent down, brushing her designer jeans free of tiny burrs and clinging grass and leaves.

"Come on, Miss Perfect," Cindy said, "we don't have all day to get to the creek." She struck out into the meadow and had gained a half dozen steps on her friend when she stopped. "What's that?"

"What's what?" Tami asked, coming alongside her.

"Listen." She held up her hand as if admonishing Tami not to make a sound.

A gentle breeze washed over them, bringing the sound of the birds from the trees behind them, along with the balmy quiet of the countryside.

"I don't hear anything." Tami turned to face Cindy, a quizzical expression crossing her oval face.

"I must be hearing things," Cindy said, turning to resume walking.

"What was it?"

Cindy shrugged.

"What did it sound like?"

Cindy shrugged again. "It sounded sorta like bees or insects of some kind. I really don't know."

For an instant, Tami's face clouded. Overhead, a liquid-clear, azure sky canopied the countryside from horizon to horizon. "Listen."

Cindy stopped. "What is it?"

They both listened intently. Then Tami smiled, sheepishly crinking her icy blue eyes. "I guess I wanted to hear it, too. I don't hear anything. Do you?"

Cindy shook her head, her hair billowing out.

Tami relaxed, turning away to continue walking. "You know, if I had a brother like Judd, I guess I'd be just about the happiest person in the world. Being an only child isn't all it's cracked up to be."

Cindy grinned. Tami Castle had everything she'd ever wanted or desired. Her parents were wealthy and important to the community of Rushton. For the last six years, Brad Castle had been mayor, and the city had prospered under his leadership just as he had for himself. "I know you've told me that before, but why would you want a brother? I'd think that if you could have your choice, you'd choose a sister."

"I've already got a sister, more or less, in you," she said with a smile. "But you and Judd have such a neat relationship. Really, I'm jealous."

"Don't be. I'll share him with you whenever—" Cindy held up her hand again, calling for silence. "Now do you hear it?"

Tami cupped one hand behind her ear, hoping to better catch the sound on the breeze. "Yeah, I hear it. It does sound like bees or hornets or some such insect. I wonder—" Her voice trailed off when the sound decrescendoed into nothing and evaporated on the ether.

"It might be trucks on the highway," Cindy offered.

Tami shrugged. "I don't know. It could be. But if it is, why haven't we ever heard it before when we were out here? Besides, today is Labor Day. Would there be that much truck traffic on a holiday?"

"I don't know." Hunching her shoulders, Cindy continued walking. "Well, let's not let something that dumb spoil our day."

They headed toward a small rise in the center of the meadow, a gentle wind from behind them ruffling the tall grass. The buzzing sound, much louder, much deeper and noisier, seemed to come at them from all directions. The girls stopped once more.

"What is that?" Cindy asked, facing Tami.

Tami slowly turned in a circle, trying to pinpoint the source of the strange sound. "I—I don't know. It sounds like bees or something, but it's so loud. If that's what it really is, I don't think I want to meet up with bees that can make that loud a noise. Come on." Tami started at a half run toward the small hill in the middle of the middle of the meadow.

Then the first motorcycle flew over the top of the hillock, followed by another and another until more than two dozen of the roaring machines spewed onto the meadowland across from the startled girls. One by one they fell into line behind a Harley-Davidson ridden by a huge, bearded man in a vest, his beefy arms effortlessly handling the bike as it bounced across the uneven ground of the meadow.

Cindy reached out for Tami and they encircled each other with their arms. "I—I hope they go on and don't bother us," Tami said loudly to be heard over the cacophony of the machines.

"Maybe they don't see us," Cindy said, watching the motorcycles lining into a single file that weaved across the open space.

Then the leader turned his bike, once everyone was behind him in line, and roared straight at the huddling girls. Like a tribe of Indians attacking a wagon train, the file of bikes formed a circle, surrounding Cindy and Tami. It slowly pulled in closer and closer. The girls half expected to hear the men whooping war cries, but when they looked at the faces of the riders, they shuddered, their pulses racing, at the lack of expression on each face. The circle pulled tighter and tighter until the front wheel of each motorcycle was separated by a mere inch or two from the back wheel of the machine in front of it.

The large bike carrying the leader and a woman passenger, the first which had flown over small hill, pulled out of the circle formation and ground to a halt in front of the women. By some unseen signal the others braked, and when the machines revved up, the din pounded on the girls' ears in undulating waves of sound until it grew to a deafening pandemonium. As if one mind, one hand, controlled each throttle, the thirty motors turned off as one.

The following silence crushed in on the strange group. Cindy held her breath, not knowing what to expect next. Tami, her pointed chin jutting out, shook loose from Cindy's embrace and walked toward the leader.

"Who are you?" she demanded.

The leader threw his head back, laughter erupting from his bearded face. As suddenly as he had laughed, he stopped, staring from behind mirrored sunglasses at the white-haired young woman confronting him. His fleshy cheeks swelled up above the hair line of his beard until his glasses moved. Taking off the red beret with the words "Light Bearer's Chosen" embroidered in white letters on it, which sat cocked to one side on his head, he bowed and said, "And who the fuck are you?"

Tami stopped in her tracks. Cindy reached out for her to return and when she did, the two embraced again, huddling together.

Cindy studied the man Tami had challenged. His beefy body seemed to ooze strength, and she thought of him as a tree springing from the earth, rather than as a human being. Long dark-brown hair, thinning at the top, cascaded down to his shoulders in thick waves. After he plopped the red beret back in place, she noticed he wore no shirt, only a leather vest from which two metal Maltese crosses dangled on either side. His worn jeans had patches with cabalistic designs sewn onto them. A star, a red devil's head, the numbers 666, and an inverted cross stretched down the faded blue pants legs. Heavy boots balanced him and the machine without effort.

"Well," he snorted, "who the fuck are you?"

Tami, catching her breath, stepped forward once more and said, "I happen to be the mayor's daughter and—"

He threw his head back again, laughing loudly. The rest of the gang followed suit, and their forced laughter grated on Cindy's and Tami's ears. Cindy could feel cold sweat running down the sides of her body.

"Hey, Bull," one of the members shouted to the leader, "what are we going to do with these two lush plums?"

"We?" Bull said quietly, evenly.

"Ah—you, Bull, you. What are you going to do with them?"

"That's better, Gordo," Bull said,

turning to stare malevolently at the speaker, a short, overweight man.

Gordo turned away, his face flushed.

"I don't know," Bull said, turning his attention back to the two girls. "What do *you* two think we should do with you?"

"You'd better let us go, and let us go right now," Tami said, her voice shaky but defiant.

"Oh, I don't think I can do that. Not right away, at least. Can we, Cow?" He turned to the woman riding behind him.

"Whatever you say, Bull."

He laughed. "See! I guess I can't let you go *right now*. What would my people think? That their leader is afraid of some chicken-shit mayor?"

Bright sunlight flashing from his sunglasses, he glared at Tami, who wilted under his perusal before fleeing to Cindy's side.

"What about your little cunt-friend there. What's she got to say for herself? Or do you do all the talking, you blond cock-sucker?"

Cindy and Tami cringed under the filthy assault but said nothing. Why infuriate these degenerates? Maybe if they were lucky, the gang would simply let them go and there'd be no further complications other than a bad dream and an even worse memory—both of which would dissipate in time.

"Well, speak up. What are you two cock fuckers doing out here in the woods without protection of some sort?"

"We—we—" Cindy coughed to clear her throat. "We don't need protection."

"Oh?" Bull asked, tilting his head to one side. "Did you hear that, guys? They don't need protection. Well, Little-Tits, just who the hell is going to protect you from us?" He dug the little finger of his right hand into his ear and dug viciously.

The women in the group snickered and the men guffawed at the threatening joke.

Cindy looked at Tami, who had tears welling in her eyes. "What are we going to do, Cindy?" Tami whispered.

" 'What are we going to do, Cindy?' " Bull mimicked. "Is that your name, Little-Tits? Cindy?" He took off the sunglasses and glared at the girl.

"Ye-yes!" she said, too frightened to do anything except tell the truth.

"So, tell me, Cindy Little-Tits, what are you and Blondie there doing out here in the country by yourselves?"

"We—we ju—just wen—wen—went for—for—for a—a—a walk." Why wouldn't her voice work properly?

"See? You never know who you might run into when you go for a walk in the woods. You might run into the Big Bad Wolf. Or a bunch of horny fuckers—like us!" Bull paused, studying the terrified girls. "Want to have a little party?"

"A—a—a par—party?" Cindy and Tami said together.

"You know. All of us will fuck the both of you," Bull said, his eyes twinkling at the prospect.

Tami unleashed a flood of tears, and Cindy bit her tongue to fight the scream she felt building within her. What could they do? Could they run? The motorcycles would overtake them in seconds. Besides, even if they could manage to get away into the woods, what would prevent the men on the motorcycles from following on foot and catching them that way? Still, they had to do something, and do something now—before anyone grabbed them. Cindy shuddered at the prospect of any one of the men touching her, much less holding her or— She wanted to throw up, but that might prove to be their undoing. They had to do something.

Grabbing Tami's hand, Cindy broke into a run, charging at the only open space in the surrounding fence of motorcycles. Both girls dashed through the opening, toward the woods some one hundred twenty yards away.

The gang, taken off guard, watched for a second or two as the girls ran headlong toward the trees.

"After them!" Bull shouted, kicking

his engine over. The roar was joined by one, then two, then three, then all of the motors as they coughed and caught life. Roaring after the girls, who were less than a third of the way to the haven of the forest, the leader caught up to them and paced them, keeping abreast of Cindy who was in the lead. Tami, puffing, fell back several yards behind her friend.

"Don't get too winded, you won't be worth a fuck," Bull said laughing.

Realizing the futility of running, Cindy slowed until she dropped to her knees, then fell face down in the lush, green meadow grass. Tami dropped beside her. The bikes circled the downed women for a moment while Bull towered over them on his bike, peering down.

"Shit, I don't see why you want to leave so soon," Bull said, "the party ain't even started yet. Besides, you two are the guests of honor. That's a bitch of a way to act—trying to run out on the party we want to give for you. Cow?"

The woman behind him got off the bike and approached Cindy and Tami. Her large breasts, untethered by anything other than a vest similar to Bull's, swung freely. "Come on, you two cunts, get up. We ain't got all day. You'd be surprised how long it takes to have thirty guys fuck your bones."

"Wait! Wait a minute," Tami cried.

"What do you want? Money? I can get money. Just tell us—what do you want?"

"We want you, Blondie," Bull said. "We want you without your clothes on. We want you layin' down—without your clothes on. We want you layin' down, without your clothes on—with your legs spread wide open in an invitation to be fucked. Ain't you ever been gang-banged before? Hell, it's really somethin'. Ain't it, Cow?"

"Best time I ever had," she said, laughing.

"Then why don't you do it and let us go?" Cindy asked, forcing the lump in her throat to go away. Perhaps they could reason with these people. After all, she had never heard of thirty men doing it to one woman before—or two, for that matter. The whole idea seemed unreal.

Bull rammed his little finger into his right ear again, wiggling it about as he reamed it free of wax. When he pulled it out, he flicked the offending drainage away with his thumbnail.

Cindy gasped at the size of the nail that extended an inch and a half beyond the tip. She looked at the rest of his fingers. The nails were all normal length. Why was the one nail so long? Then it dawned on her. He used it to snort coke. She had seen something like that in a movie or on TV.

A man, smaller than Bull, called out,

"What are we going to do, Bull?"

"Don't get impatient, Buckshot," Bull called. "You'll get your turn—dirty thirty—if you behave. Otherwise, you might just get to watch and not get a taste of these young cunts."

"Let's get on with it," Buckshot persisted. "I'm horny."

"Fuck one of the mamas then. Don't bother me with your sex needs, you underfed asshole." Bull glared at the man.

"Where do you want to do it?" Cow asked.

Bull forced a smile for the benefit of his "wife." "Not out here in the open. Too exposed, if you know what I mean."

"How about the woods?"

"Go for it," he said tersely.

Cow motioned for one of the other women to help her, and "Mary Queen of Sots" stumbled off her perch behind "Jack the Ripper" and approached Cindy and Tami. Cow looked around the group and called one other woman to help control their captives. "Sweet Rosie O'Lay" jumped from the bike on which she had been a passenger and came over.

"We'll take 'em into the trees," Cow said simply.

Mary and Rosie bent down, each one grabbing the wrist of one girl, and unceremoniously pulled them to their feet.

Cindy's legs felt like rubber bands.

This couldn't be happening. It was a dream. Any second, she'd awaken and find herself in her own bedroom. It had to be a dream. Things like this didn't happen. Not in real life. Where was Judd? Judd? Why wasn't Judd here to help her?

"*Judd!*" she screamed at the top of her voice. Rosie, who held her wrist, twisted her arm up behind her back. Her mind racing, Cindy could think of nothing she could do. The pain in her arm and shoulder tore at her. The woman's mouth, close to her own face, puffed its fetid breath, and Cindy wanted to throw up. A rotten stench mixed with stale beer and garlic pierced her nose, assaulting her senses. Oh, God, where was Judd? Why didn't he come? Why didn't she wake up? This dream was getting out of hand.

Cindy and Tami resisted as best they could. But the two gang "mamas" pushed them toward the trees and the conceal-ment they would offer.

"Just what the fuck are we going to do?" Buckshot asked again.

"I thought we'd have a trial or maybe some games to see who gets to fuck them first—after me," Bull said, claiming his right as leader to sample any new woman himself before anyone else did. While the members' wives were off limits to such overtures, the lesser mamas were fair game to any member—male or female.

"A trial? Games?" Buckshot squeaked. "Why don't we just get on with the fucking?"

"Quiet, Buck*shit*!" Bull yelled, following the women who steered the kicking and squirming Cindy Wellington and Tami Castle into the woods. One by one, the motorcycles followed until the only things left in the meadow were the green grass, the flowers, and an occasional bird flying overhead.

2

When the women dragging Cindy and Tami stopped, the two captives thought they had never seen such a dark, foreboding section of the woods. Thickly leafed branches barely permitted the sunlight to penetrate, allowing only a thread of light here and there to seek and find the ground.

"That's far enough," Cow yelled from behind.

Mary and Rosie threw the girls to the earth. Cindy sensed their situation was hopeless. They were going to be raped. What had Bull called it? *Gang-banged?* The woman he called Cow apparently had had it happen to her and she seemed to have enjoyed it. But had she been taken by force or had the woman done it willingly?

Cindy turned enough to look at Tami. Her normally icy blue eyes rolled, terror-stricken and red from crying. Mary, who had held Tami, had applied an arm hold to her, and now, while rubbing her stretched shoulder, Tami wept uncontrollably. Cindy's arm hurt as well, but she had a higher threshold of pain than her friend.

"What—what are they going to—to do?" Tami whispered hoarsely, once she stopped attending her arm.

"I don't know," Cindy lied. Why tell Tami what she thought was about to happen? Why panic the girl? She'd find out soon enough. If she did tell Tami, perhaps she would begin yelling and screaming and the gang would do something more than rape them.

"Shut up, you two!" Cow snapped at them. "You'll have plenty to talk about once this party is over." She grinned wickedly, her white teeth contrasting with her swarthy skin. Her black eyes sparkled as she perused one, then the other, of the girls. Ruffling her own shoulder-length hair in a mocking gesture with one hand, she threw open her vest, exposing her breasts from the scant protection of the leather covering. Each of her nipples, standing erect and taut, held a golden ring that had been pierced through the viable flesh.

"Tie 'em up," Bull ordered when he

pushed his way through the gang surrounding the captives. "Put 'em up there," he said, pointing to a low hanging branch on a nearby tree.

Cow, Mary, and Rosie picked Cindy up, and when Bull offered a leather thong to his wife, she took it, binding Cindy's wrists in front of her, and left a long tail dangling below. Mary took the leather rope and threw it over the branch, pulling hard.

Cindy's arms jerked upward over her head, and when Mary continued pulling, Cindy stretched until her feet barely touched the ground. Satisfied, Mary tied the thong, holding the girl in place. The same was done to Tami, who screamed from the pain in her shoulder.

"Shut up, cunt," Rosie growled at Tami. "You ain't had nothin' happen to you to make you cry out like that. Not yet—at least!" She laughed, and the gang joined in, while she pumped her hips at the two girls.

"Okay, now," Bull said, raising his voice so that everyone could hear him. "These two bitches have been known to walk through woods and fields without proper protection. Any biker who rides the roads knows that that is stupid and breaking the law. Right?"

"Right!" the forty-five members chorused together.

"Bullshit!" one man growled and

stepped from the crowd.

"Get back there, Buckshot." Bull glowered at the man, slowly taking off his mirrored sunglasses.

"Jesus Christ! If we're going to fuck 'em, let's get on with it. All this shit of trails and games is for the fuckin' birds. I say we fuck 'em and fuck 'em now."

Cindy fought back the urge to scream while Tami merely stared at the barbarous people surrounding her. They were going to be raped and there was nothing they could do about it. And there was no one who could help them even if they could yell loud enough to be heard by someone. It would take an army to rescue them and there just wasn't anyone or anything around that could help them.

"I'm not going to hold a fuckin' vote on this, Buckshot. Goddamnit, get back there where you belong. We'll get around to fuckin' 'em. Don't worry about it."

"Shit, I'll blow my wad in my pants unless you get movin' on it."

One of the women stepped forward. "Shit, Buckshot, you pump ten, twelve times and you blow your nuts. Why don't you go jack off and let Bull get on with it?"

Everyone except Cindy and Tami and the man called Buckshot laughed uproariously.

"Yeah, a great lover you ain't!" Mary Queen of Sots bellowed the accusation and the laughter grew.

Several of the women went over to the two girls hanging from the tree branch. ''Want to see what you're going to get?'' one of them asked looking at the men, and tore Tami's expensive blouse, exposing her breasts.

Wolf whistles and catcalls rose from the gang.

The same woman moved closer to Cindy, reaching out her hand to pull away her blouse.

''Don't,'' Cindy managed weakly.

''Fuck you!'' the woman said, tearing the material away.

Cindy's dark-skinned breasts stood upright, the brown aureoles colored more deeply than normal. Cindy closed her eyes. Shame. Humiliation flooded through her. She remembered when Chuck Allen had opened her blouse once, to play with her breasts. It had felt good. She hadn't minded that he looked at them. She liked Chuck. He liked her, then. Although they hadn't gone all the way that time, they had done it later. But, shortly after graduating from high school, Chuck had enlisted in the Air Force and was gone. They had had no formal arrangement and both were free to date. Why? Why, of all thoughts to pass through her mind, was Chuck Allen and his fondling her breasts reliving itself now?

Rosie O'Lay stepped forward and rolled Cindy's nipples between her fingers. "She'll be ready in a minute, fellas!" she cried, and the whistles and calls came again.

"Let's get on with the trial to see what sort of punishment these two little sluts get," Bull called out.

"Fuck your trial," Buckshot said, stepping forward and shoving Bull.

A gasp went up from the gang. No one ever confronted the leader, much less made a swipe at him the way Buckshot had just done. Not unless there was a challenge to be made. And certainly Buckshot was no match for Bull.

"Are you crazy, man?" Bull asked quietly, his voice even and deadly sounding in its softness.

"No, I ain't crazy, 'Man'! I'm just fuckin' pissed off and fed up with the way you're runnin' this gang. Fuckin' trials! Fuckin' games to determine who goes second to his fuckin' royal highness, here!" Buckshot's thin, scraggly goatee quivered as he spoke, emphasizing his slack jaw line. He frowned when Bull didn't react immediately. "Well?" he persisted.

Without a word or warning, Bull's huge fist shot out, clipping Buckshot on the side of the face. Buckshot fell backward, but the blow had not been square and he kept his feet.

"Do you want to challenge me for the leadership of the Light Bearer's Chosen?" Bull growled, pulled himself to his full six-foot-four-inch height.

Buckshot did the same, falling four inches short of Bull. "You're goddamned right I do. You ain't no leader, you asshole."

Another gasp went up from the crowd.

"Right here. Right now, fuckhead!" Bull reached behind his back, loosening the bike chain he wore around his middle.

Buckshot stepped back and reached inside his pants, pulling a similar chain from his pants leg. Swinging it slowly to and fro, he said, "Any time you're ready, you fat faggot!"

Without warning, Bull whipped the chain over his head straight at Buckshot's head, but the smaller man leaped to one side, flailing out with his chain at Bull's legs.

The tip of Buckshot's weapon ripped across the back of Bull's calf but inflicted no real damage. Bull pulled his chain back, to find Buckshot circling him, his pop-eyes staring at Bull's middle, his chain in constant motion.

Bull charged Buckshot sending the chain at his adversary's head again but missed. Buckshot, frowning, deep lines forming between and over his protruding eyes, leaped away even farther than his first jump had carried him when Bull tried the second time. The flab hanging on his arms jiggled and his foot caught a tree root just as Bull came at him again. This time, when he tried to avoid the murderous chain coming at him, he stumbled backward almost losing his balance. The tip of Bull's weapon sizzled through the air, catching Buckshot's T-shirt at the neck line and slicing it wide open to the man's waist. His fleshy pectorals bounced up and down as he fought to regain his balance, and when he did, he sent his own chain toward Bull. It caught the leader on the side of the head, gashing it open. Blood poured down the side of his face, making a ruddy, grotesque mask of Bull's scowling countenance.

The crowd fell back, making room for the fighters, urging them on with shouts of encouragement. Buckshot took up a position in front of Cindy, knowing that Bull would be hesitant to swing at him for fear of injuring the girl before everyone had had her.

"Get away from her!" Bull shouted.

Buckshot only grinned, his mouth fighting to turn up at the corners from its natural half frown. "Fuck you, 'Big Man'!" He leaped forward just as Bull charged him, and both brought their chains whistling through the air at the same time. Each man's chain struck the wrist of his adversary, wrapping around once, slicing the skin open. Both men dropped their chains, and Bull enfolded the smaller man in a bear hug. Buckshot brought his thigh up, forcing it into Bull's crotch, and the large man grunted, releasing his foe.

Lashing out with his right foot again, aiming it at Bull's groin, he missed, and Bull grabbed it, upending Buckshot. When Buckshot hit the ground, Bull viciously kicked him in the stomach, doubling him over. Another kick, aimed at his head, missed, and while Bull fought to regain his own balance, Buckshot struggled to his feet and threw himself at Bull.

Grappling, the two men fell to the ground, rolling over and over toward the crowd of people. The crowd quickly separated to make room for the two men, who rolled into some heavy brush. After the undergrowth swallowed them, they stopped, Bull on top of Buckshot, both arms wrapped around him in another bear hug. He pulled his arms together, tighter—tighter.

Buckshot, his arms caught along his body, could feel with his hand the switch-blade knife in his pocket. Could he get it out? He moved his fingers a half inch, then another and another until his fingertips poised over the opening. He fought for his breath as Bull's constricting arms pulled closer. He had to get it out and get it out now or Bull would knock him out with the suffocating hold. With the last drop of his strength he brought his knee up, smashing Bull's testicles against his pelvis, and jammed his hand into his pocket as the man on top of him released his hold, screaming in pain. Bull fell back rolling on the ground, holding his crotch. Like a panther leaping on his prey, Buckshot flew through the air, releasing the sheathed knife blade at the same time, and landed full on Bull's side. Pulling Bull's head back by the thick, wavy hair, Buckshot ran the keen edge of the blade over his exposed throat, slitting it wide open.

Bull instantly relaxed, a gurgling sound bubbling from the huge mouthlike wound grinning through the beard. He tried speaking, his eyes rolling at Buckshot, but only a muffled sucking of air gurgled in the stillness. Blood spurted up like a fountain as Bull's heart pumped the life from his body through the crimson aperture.

Buckshot stared at the man dying. He had never killed anyone before and stood, fascinated by the dying man's gyrations and sounds.

"Hey? What's going on in there?" someone yelled from outside the thicket, breaking the quiet of the gang since Bull's scream. The crunching of brush drowned out Bull's dying rasp, and when the first of the gang stepped in, he saw the huge man lying on his back, arms outstretched, his eyes sightlessly glaring at nothing, the grinning wound no longer pumping blood.

"Jesus Christ! Buckshot's killed Bull!" Gordo cried.

"G'wan! You're shittin' us, right?"

"No shit! Bull's dead. Buckshot slit his throat. Come on in and see for yourself if you don't believe me."

One by one, the male gang members filed into the thicket and stared.

"Now what do we do?" one of them asked.

At first there was no sound, no response, other than the occasional bird singing from some distant branch and the gang's own heavy breathing.

"I guess we bury him," Mule said simply, his perpetual sneer emphasizing the sarcasm of his terse statement.

"Right!" someone agreed.

"What do you think, Buckshot?" Mule asked.

"Huh?" Buckshot looked up for the first time since the gang members had come into the thicket. "What did you say?"

"I asked you what you thought," Mule repeated.

"About what?" Buckshot shook his head trying to clear his thoughts. By gang law, he should be the new leader. But would the gang accept that?

"About burying Bull. You killed him. That makes you the new leader, right?" Mule looked from one gang member to the next, expecting their acquiescence.

Buckshot slowly nodded his head. Then one by one the other members of the Light Bearer's Chosen nodded, agreeing with the gang rule.

"Yeah. Bull was a pretty good leader, wasn't he?" Buckshot asked, hoping to appease anyone in the crowd who might have thought it wrong for Buckshot to have beaten Bull in the fight.

Nods of agreement rippled through the circle of bikers.

"Well, goddammit, he should be given a leader's burial then. Where's Cow?"

Cow stepped into the brush and looked at her dead husband. "You're going to make a piss-poor leader, Buckshot. Bull was ten times—shit—twenty times the man you'll ever hope to be. But I gotta go along with the rules. You killed him. That makes you the leader. Bury the poor sonofabitch. With his 'hog'! Y'hear?"

"Of course it'll be with his hog. Christ a'mighty! How do you think he'll get around in the other world without it? Geezus! I ain't that fuckin' dumb!"

"Let me ask you somethin' then," Cow said. "Do you know all the rites and prayers that Bull said to the Light

Bearer?''

Buckshot nodded quickly. What if he didn't? Right now, he didn't want to get into any sort of argument over the dumb rituals and prayers that the Chosen Ones performed and prayed four times a year.

''You, Mule, and three or four others pick Bull up. How many spades we got?''

''I'll get them,'' Blaster said, trudging off toward the bikes parked in among the trees that surrounded the small clearing where Cindy and Tami still hung from the tree branch.

''Mary, you 'n Rosie watch these two fucks hanging here,'' Buckshot said, nodding toward the girls. ''We'll be back and take care of them as soon as we get done burying Bull.''

Mary and Rosie nodded. While two of the men walked Bull's Harley-Davidson and four of them carried the slain leader, Buckshot led the funeral entourage through the trees, looking for a suitable burial site. After walking some five hundred yards through the dense under-growth and brush, Buckshot stopped at the sight of a small hillock rising four feet or so in the center of a small clearing. Trees surrounded the tiny hill spotlighted by the sun through the opening above.

''Here,'' he said. ''We'll bury him in that hill over there. Start digging.''

With the camping spades in hand,

twelve of the men stepped forward and attacked the soil, throwing shovelful after shovelful to the side.

Rosie looked at Cindy and Tami, both of whom were almost unconscious. "Why don't we get 'em ready for the men?"

"Hey, why not," Mary agreed. "That way we can have a little fun ourselves until they get back."

She stepped up to Tami, who stared at her through half-closed eyes. The pain had long since passed, and her arms, if they were still attached to her body, were completely numb and she was unable to account for them by feel alone. Nor could she turn her head far enough to see if they were still there.

Mary tore the rest of Tami's blouse off and undid the button of her designer jeans. "Pretty nice. Y'know, they might just fit me," she said, stripping them from Tami's slim hips.

Taking off her own worn jeans, Mary slipped into the purloined ones and snapped the button after zipping the front. "Well, what do you think?" she asked, turning in a circle for Rosie's benefit.

"Not a bad fit. Shit, she can do without them. She probably got a pisspot full of them at home." Rosie, who had been bedded by every member of the gang, both male and female, pulled Cindy's top from her and stroked her small breasts. "Christ, they're hard. Not soft and floppy like mine and yours."

Mary reached up, fondling Tami's breasts. "Yeah. Hers are hard, too. Sure's a fuckin' shame to get old like you'n me!" Mary laughed. "How old are you, Rosie?"

"Thirty."

"Yeah. Real fuckin' old. Just like me. I'll be thirty next month. No. This month. It's September, ain't it?"

"Yeah," Rosie said, licking Cindy's breasts, sliding her tongue toward her navel.

When the hole was deep enough, two of the men jumped in to lower the motorcycle into the grave. When it was in position, they eased Bull's body down, which in turn was seated on the bike.

They placed his hands on the handlebar grips, and when the first man jumped out, the second hesitated and reached out toward the Maltese crosses hanging from Bull's vest. He undid the pin holding it and was about to pin it to his shirt when Buckshot stepped to the edge of the hole.

"What the fuck are you doing, Blaster?" he demanded, kicking dirt at the man.

"Just takin' a souvenir. That's all."

"Put it back. Christ a'mighty, don't

you know nothin'? It's a sin and sacrilege to take anything off'n the dead—especially one of our own. You want that Light Bearer comin' down on you an' us, go ahead—take it. Pin it on yourself and I'll cut your fuckin' throat when you get up here. 'Sides, it'd be nice for Bull to have company on the other side."

Blaster quickly pinned the cross back on Bull's vest and clambered out of the grave.

While the men shoveled the dirt back into the hole, covering Bull and his motorcycle, Buckshot moved to the head of the grave, facing Bull.

"All things will die at one time or another. We don't know when, but as long as we kiss Lucifer's ass and do something for him every once in a while, he'll look after his chosen ones—us. Bull's time was up when he ran into a more stronger force—me—and now I'm the leader of the Light Bearer's Chosen. Take Bull, Lucifer, he's a good biker and will do whatever you want done. Bull, take care of yourself and obey Lucifer!"

Without another word, Buckshot turned and walked off the small hill. Cow fell in behind him, and the others followed their new leader back through the trees toward the clearing where Cindy and Tami waited.

3

The line of unkempt men and their women filed through the trees, silent in their final respect for their dead leader. Bull's widow, Cow, followed the murderer of her husband, an impassive expression gripping her face.

When they neared the small clearing where they had left Sweet Rosie O'Lay and Mary Queen of Sots guarding Cindy and Tami, Buckshot, the new leader, stopped, holding up one hand. When the procession stopped, he faced Cow.

"Cow, do you want to be my woman?"

Her eyes darted from side to side before settling on the slack-jawed man who had killed Bull. "Jesus Christ, you asshole, I'm in mourning. Ask me later."

Buckshot nodded and turned, entering the clearing. The people who had helped bury Bull gathered around Buckshot, slapping him on the back, offering their congratulations.

"Nice going, Buckshot."

"Way to go, pardner."

"Lead us the right way, Buckshot."

"Congratulations."

"You're our new 'man'!"

Pulling away from the well-wishers, Buckshot went over to the two girls hanging from the tree branch. "Are they all right?" he asked the two women who guarded them.

"Sure. We been licking 'em a little to get 'em ready for you, Buckshot," Mary said, grinning, only to display a gap in the middle of her top row of teeth. She hiccuped and blew her whiskey-laden breath toward the new leader.

"They're fine," Rosie agreed.

"Cut 'em down," Buckshot ordered, loosening the top button of his faded jeans. The only sound accompanying the falling bodies was his zipper being pulled down. The rest of the gang gathered around the two prostrate girls.

"Roll 'em over," Buckshot said quietly, and knelt down nearest Cindy.

She looked at him, her eyes glazed with the pain coursing through her shoulders and arms. What did that strange-looking man want? What was he going to do? She turned away, unable to look directly at him any longer because of his close-set pop eyes, fleshy cheeks, and thin goatee. His sparse hair fell on either side of the leather cap he wore, and if Cindy hadn't hurt so much, she might easily have laughed at the grotesque figure. When she saw the ring of weird faces hovering around her and the man, the episode in the meadow crashed back to the fore of her consciousness.

They were going to rape her.

She struggled to move, desperately wriggling backward, head-first away from the man the gang was calling Buckshot. Her head bumped something, and she looked up to see a woman peering down at her. It was the woman who had big breasts with gold rings piercing her nipples, and wore nothing over them but a leather vest. An evil grin twisted her mouth, and Cindy felt lost. She might as well have been dead for all the compassion she expected to find on the faces above her.

"Don't—don't—please don't!" she managed to whisper, her voice sounding strange to her, as if someone else had spoken.

Where was Tami? Was she all right? Maybe Tami had gotten away. If she had, she might be calling for help. But from where? Where could she call for help out here in the woods?

Her eyes widened as Buckshot crawled nearer her. Oh, God, he was so ugly and scrawny and filthy-looking. When he got as close as he could before lying on her, she caught his body odor and gagged. He smelled as bad as he looked. His penis, jerking spasmodically in front of him, held her attention for a brief second. Did he have any diseases? Would he make her pregnant? Would they kill her and Tami if Tami hadn't gotten away? Why would they leave witnesses behind? Tears flooded from her eyes, down the sides of her face, toward her ears. *Please God, let me die, right now. Let me die!*

Buckshot reached out one dirty, blood-stained hand, touching her breasts—first one, then the other.

"They're little but they're firm," he said chuckling, before spreading her legs apart.

Cindy pulled them together again, but Buckshot roughly pushed them apart and looked at the faces of the bikers surrounding him.

"Hold her legs," he ordered, and two women stepped forward, grasping Cindy's ankles.

Guiding his penis into her, he pushed hard, bringing a cry of pain from Cindy. She wasn't a virgin but she hadn't had that much experience.

"*Geezus Christ!*" Buckshot guffawed.

"I think I got me a virgin here."

A murmur went through the gang, and Cindy closed her eyes as Buckshot began his animalistic pumping. She bit her tongue, deep sobs ripping at her.

It seemed to take forever for the man to finish. Someplace, off in the distance, Cindy could hear someone counting.

"Ten. Eleven. Twelve. Thirteen."

Buckshot shuddered, and Cindy could feel his hot sperm flooding into her.

"See. Thirteen times and he's finished," a woman's voice cried out from the gang.

Laughter bubbled around the ring of faces for an instant, and Buckshot pulled away from his victim, standing. "Who said that?" he demanded.

"I did," the woman said, stepping forward.

"Go find a log and fuck yourself, Rat-face," Buckshot snarled at the woman with the prominent nose, buck teeth, and pinched-together face.

"Where's the other one?" Buckshot asked, turning to the two women who had guarded Cindy and Tami.

"Over here," Mary said, pushing aside two men before pointing to the ground where Tami lay, her white-blond hair disheveled and caked with dirt, partially covering her face.

Buckshot's penis hung limp. "Get me

ready," he ordered Mary and looked at Rosie to help. The women dropped to their knees and began fondling their new leader. In several minutes he was ready and he stepped toward Tami.

Cindy turned her head, barely able to see through the legs surrounding Buckshot and Tami, but she could make out the face of her friend, turned to one side, staring into space, right at Cindy, but not seeing anything. Tami didn't move, didn't resist, didn't fight in any way. Cindy turned away, unable to watch her friend being violated—raped.

When Buckshot finished, this time without a count from Ratface, he stood and slipped into his jeans. "Okay, line up."

The men fell into two lines, one near Cindy and the other near the unmoving Tami. Cindy looked up. The fat man standing over her dropped his black and red plaid jeans, pulled out his undersized penis, and knelt. Drops of saliva clung to his heavy beard as he lowered himself onto her.

Cindy turned away. She had to think of something else or go mad. What could she think about? Judd. Of course. Her brother. What was he doing? Painting. He had just begun painting the picket fence that surrounded their home. Their home—their house that held so many happy memories for her. Her parents. She sobbed. They were dead. Killed by some drunken driver as they came home from grocery shopping one winter evening four years before. God, how she had cried. And how Judd had been there, ready to embrace her and help her through the traumatic event. She had been only fifteen at the time, and while Judd, who was ten years her senior, tried, there were certain things she couldn't talk about with him even though he had offered. That was when he called on Peggy Dixon, whom he had just begun dating. Peggy filled in for Judd whenever Cindy had a question dealing strictly with woman-type problems, and for that she loved Judd even more. He was able to admit when he fell short and didn't feel the least bit inferior or insecure in having to ask someone else to help him out.

Cindy recalled the Christmases they had celebrated both before and after their parents' deaths. Happy times. Good times. Loving times.

The hardware store—their father's business—flashed into her mind. Judd had been out of college for a year and a half when their parents died and was able to step in and take over the business without it losing a beat. Judd was established. He had his own business. He had a beautiful girlfriend in Peggy Dixon, and it was all because of Cindy's college that the two of them hadn't yet married. But they would be as soon as she graduated.

Cindy opened her eyes and saw the round, pimply face of a stranger close to hers. His breath was awful. Who was he? What was he doing there? She felt numb. As if someone had given her a hypo that took away all feeling from her body. She could feel movement. The man on top of her was pumping up and down and his motion carried through, affecting her. But why couldn't she feel anything?

Closing her eyes, she saw her high school and the college campus at the state university. She had friends in both places, students who were her friends and teachers who had taken an interest in her. What would they think if they could see her now? She opened her eyes a slit to see the pimply-faced man pulling away from her and another man, coarse-looking with a salt-and-pepper growth of beard that appeared to be several weeks old, coming down on her. He roughly grabbed her face and kissed her full on the lips, jabbing his tongue into her mouth.

"Hey, look at the lover. Ol' Dirty Thirty is going to make love to her," someone shouted. "Come on, people, this should be interesting."

What was going on? Who had called

out like that? Who was this man—what was his name? What was he going to do to her? His mouth tasted terrible. Sour. Unclean. Tobacco. Old tastes that had not been cleaned away for a long time. He rammed his tongue into her mouth again, and she wanted to gag but found she couldn't. Why couldn't she gag? She felt him moving—slow at first—then the tempo mounted until he was pumping just like all the rest. She felt detached from her body. In one sense, she could feel everything, although in a remote, distant way, while in another fashion, she seemed to be watching a movie or TV program—it was happening to someone else.

She turned her head. Tami was lying in the same position as she had been earlier. How much time had passed? How long had it been? Seconds? Minutes? Hours? She had no idea how much time had gone by since they first encountered the gang of bikers.

Why didn't Judd come and help her? Wasn't that his job? He had to be mother and father as well as a brother to her. She had no sisters. Well, none that were real. She and Tami had a sisterlike relationship and they shared everything. Everything. Everything? She opened her eyes and turned her head toward Tami. A man was on top of her. They—they were—he was having sex with Tami. But Tami looked as if she wanted nothing to do with him. Her head still faced Cindy. Her eyes were two icy blue pools of space. She saw nothing. Cindy turned her head back to the grizzled man on top of her. He was raping her. From deep within her, she felt a primeval scream building, and when it reached sufficient growth on its own, she opened her mouth and screamed—long—loud.

"Shut her up," the man said as he finished with Cindy.

One of the women kicked at Cindy's head but managed only a glancing blow.

"Is that it?" Buckshot asked, looking around the faces of his gang. When no one answered, he said, "Anybody want seconds—or thirds for those 'animals' who already had seconds?"

Again, there was no response.

He walked over to Tami. She still had not moved since Buckshot had raped her. "Are you all right?" he asked.

No answer.

"Shit!" Buckshot kicked her in the stomach and turned to Cindy. "How about you, Cindy Little-Tits?"

Cindy struggled to answer. What could she say? *We're fine, thank you. You can go now. Don't worry about us.* She managed to nod weakly and Buckshot turned away for a moment.

What would happen next? The irony of the situation suddenly hammered at her.

What was she going to college for?—a degree in sociology. She wanted to be a case worker—one who helped people who were caught up in certain circumstances that tried even the most patient person's better qualities. From what sort of social background had these people come? Were they underprivileged? She remembered an assignment she had had her first year in college about dropouts in which several instances were cited. Motorcycle gangs had been one. Were motorcycle gang members underprivileged? Were these the type of people she was slated to work with and help?

A new batch of tears formed and flowed down the sides of her face. Perhaps if she just could get to her feet, she might be able to point out to them the wrong they had committed against her and Tami.

"Aren't you going to pray over them, Buckshot?" one of the other men said.

"Why the fuck should I? They ain't members of the Light Bearer's Chosen. Those prayers we say to Lucifer are for us and us alone. No outsiders get 'em."

"And all you're goin' to do is kill 'em?" the same man asked.

"You got it, Jack," Buckshot said shortly and turned back to Cindy.

The conversation had registered, but she felt as if she might be dreaming—or that the voices were talking about someone else.

Standing over Cindy for a long moment, Buckshot hauled one foot back, kicking her hard in the stomach.

Her head swam, multicolored lights popping off and on as a dark curtain fell over her line of vision. Where had everyone gone? She heard another kick but felt nothing and knew it had been Tami who had been kicked when the girl moaned. Cindy's eyes glazed, then slowly cleared. Turning her head, she saw Tami and the man called Buckshot leaning over her. Something was in his hand—something that glinted in a shaft of sunlight that dared penetrate the gloomy woods.

Buckshot brought his hand down in an arc, and Cindy screamed when she saw the knife slicing toward Tami's throat. It made no sound as it slit the soft skin. Blood pumped out slowly, almost lethargically. Buckshot stood and turned toward her. What could she do?

Reaching down, he grabbed her thick hair, twisting her head back, exposing her throat and neck.

She saw the blade coming toward her and, strangely enough, felt nothing when the razor-sharp edge severed her skin, the muscle and the jugular vein.

Weak. She felt weak. She wanted to scream but heard only a bubbling, slurping sound whenever she tried. But that was too much effort. She should do something—something before she died. But what? Pray?

Oh, my God, I am heartily sorry for having offended Thee—

"Come on," Buckshot said, wiping the bloody blade on the grass and folding it back into the handle.

The gang members turned away, one by one, fascinated by the dying girls as they bled to death. They mounted their motorcycles, and the peaceful quiet of the inner woods was shattered by the motors as they roared to life. Buckshot, the new leader of the Light Bearer's Chosen, headed out first, followed by Mule and the others. When the sound of the thirty bikes died in the distance, a bird, startled away from its perch over the small clearing by the din of the gang leaving, settled back onto the branch and broke into song.

Beneath the limb, Cindy and Tami lay, dead.

4

Bruce Springsteen finished belting out his latest hit, his voice booming from the transistor radio lying next to the paint can at Judd Wellington's right knee. Judd smoothed out the paint he had just applied to the last picket on the fence before squeezing the brush along the top of the container. Finished. At last. He hated painting the picket fence, had hated it ever since he first did the job sixteen years ago when his father gave him that responsibility in exchange for the final payment on his bicycle. Still, he could hardly expect Cindy to paint it. And he would never think of hiring anyone to do the relatively simple task. It was just so blasted tedious. But at least he was finished with it for another two or three years.

When he turned off the radio, he sensed the presence of another close to him.

"Well, Judd, I see you've done it again." The voice belonged to Zella Ludinger, his next-door neighbor.

He looked up, grinning. "What's that, Zella?"

"Just look at my grass. All splattered with little white drops of paint. Are you trying to kill my lawn?"

Getting to his feet, Judd picked up the can of paint and the radio. "Oh my God, Zella, I did. I'm sorry. Tell you what, if your grass dies, I'll give you the seed from the store, free of charge."

"Why can't you be more careful?"

"You know, I never thought of it, but I've got some splatter-free paint down at the store. I should have used that, shouldn't I?" His eyes twinkled merrily when he faced the woman.

No more than four feet eleven and, if she were dressed in her heaviest clothing, maybe a hundred pounds, Zella Ludinger returned the smile. "It looks real good, Judd. So does the house ever since Bill and Tom finished painting it last spring. You sure keep the place looking real good. Your folks would be proud."

"I guess they would, Zella. Sorry about your grass."

"Posh! I was only fooling. You know that, Judd."

"Sure, I know that. Did you enjoy the long weekend?"

'Isn't any different than any other three days of the week for me. Ever since I quit working and sold my beauty shop, one day seems just like the next. How 'bout you?"

"I worked all weekend. First at the store until Saturday night. Then I cleaned the basement yesterday and—"

"Instead of going to church?" She clicked her tongue.

"I go enough. But I don't know when else I'd get some of these jobs finished— especially since Cindy's going to college now."

"How's she doing?"

"Just fine. Say, what time is it?"

"It was just past four-thirty when I came out to hassle you. Why?"

"Cindy should have been back by now. She and Tami went out to Morrison's Creek for a walk."

"What time did they go?" Zella looked up into his tanned face that suddenly frowned over with concern. She brushed a wisp of white hair out of her eyes.

"That's just it. They left this morning around ten. They were going to go out there and then leave for State when they got back here."

"Oh, I wouldn't worry, Judd. They're fine. Worry's for somebody my age. When you quit work and don't have anything to do, that's when you worry about anything and everything."

"I suppose you're right. I've got to get cleaned up and get over to Peggy's."

"When are you two going to get married and make an honest woman of her?" Zella's eyes, although round naturally, crinkled at the prospect of young love and marriage.

"Not till Cindy's finished at school. 'Bye, Zella. See you." Judd turned away without waiting for the old woman to say anything else. The last thing he needed right now was a long-drawn-out conversation with his neighbor. He liked Zella. She had been like a mother to him and Cindy when their parents had died. But then, shortly after the tragedy, and once the awful shock had worn away, he had taken over and merely used Zella for a sounding board whenever he felt he needed a little motherly input to his thinking. Peggy Dixon, on the other hand, had been more than helpful whenever Cindy hit him with a question that only another woman could answer. And for that—the two women to whom he could turn in the event of an informational crisis—he was more than thankful.

But unless he got cleaned up and over

to Peggy's, she'd be up in arms—especially if her picnic dinner was ruined because of his delay.

The thought of Cindy bobbed to the surface of his mind again. Where was she? Why had they changed their plans? What was it she had said that morning when Tami bounced into the kitchen?

"We're going to go for one last walk out to Morrison's Creek, Judd. You don't mind, do you?"

"Mind? Why should I mind?" he had asked.

"We'll be leaving for school right after noon—when we get back. It's just so darn nice outside. The next time we get home will probably be Thanksgiving and then it'll be too cold and bleak to go hiking through the woods and meadow."

"Hey, it's no problem. I've got to paint the fence today anyway. Are you driving out or walking all the way?"

"We're taking Tami's car to the bridge. Then we'll walk the rest of the way."

"Just be careful," had been his last words to them when they raced out of the kitchen and to Tami's Cordoba parked in the driveway.

After cleaning the brush and resealing the paint can, Judd wiped his hands free of any paint with a rag and hurried to the house. Shucking off his paint clothing, a T-shirt and cut-off jeans, he took off his old tennis shoes and, clad in nothing but his jockey shorts, raced from the mud room through the house to his bedroom.

When he finished showering, Judd toweled off and dressed. Had he understood the girls correctly? They *had* said they were coming back before leaving for school. They *had* said they would leave shortly after noon. Pulling his robe around him, he crossed the hallway to Cindy's room. Her suitcase was still on her bed, open. Of course they were coming back. He glanced at the digital alarm clock on the nightstand when he returned to his room. Five-oh-one.

Maybe they had gone to Tami's home for a while. Cindy should have called him if that's what they'd done. Picking up the phone after looking up the Castles' telephone number, he waited patiently for someone to answer. After ten rings he hung up. Where could Mayor Castle and his wife be? With the girls? Hardly. More than likely, they were at some Labor Day function, doing their political thing. He'd try them again in a little while.

After he finished dressing, he called Peggy.

"No, they're not here," Peggy said when Judd asked her.

"Gee, I wonder where they could be," he said after a few seconds pause.

"Don't be such a worry wart, Judd.

What time are you coming over? I'm almost ready for you."

Changing his mood, Judd said, "I'm ready to leave right now. I just wanted to call ahead to see if they were there. I'll write a note to Cindy and be right over. 'Bye."

By six-forty-five, Judd and Peggy had eaten the steak dinner she had grilled on the balcony of her apartment. Judd, quieter than usual, had hardly said anything while they ate. While Peggy cleared the table of the dishes, he stood.

"I've got to do something. This is driving me crazy—not knowing."

"Come on, Judd. Cindy's a big girl. Besides, Tami was with her. They're fine. I'm sure." She faced him, her brown eyes unblinking.

Judd pulled away from her reassuring hand when she laid it on his arm.

"Maybe," she continued, "they came back, got her suitcase, and took off." Taking the last items from the table, she walked in her determined way to the kitchenette, her auburn hair flashing red highlights.

Shaking his head, Judd said, "I doubt that very much. I left a note in the kitchen and one in her suitcase. I told her where I was and that she should call here as soon as she got home."

Peggy came out of the kitchenette, taking off her little apron, and hung it on the back of her chair. "What are you going to do?"

Judd stood and for a moment hesitated before answering. "I think I'll drive out to the bridge and see if I can find Tami's car. Maybe they had trouble. I should have driven out there before. I don't know what I was thinking."

"I'll come with you," Peggy said, moving around the table.

"I would like you to, but I think you should stay here just in case they come back to my place, find the note and call here. Do you mind? I'll only be gone twenty minutes if I don't find anything. If I'm not back by then, you'll know I found them and that there's something wrong with Tami's car." He waited while she mulled over his reasoning, wondering if she'd understand. It hardly seemed likely that there would be something wrong with Tami's Cordoba, because it was barely two years old—a gift from her father on graduation from high school. But then, something *could* be wrong with it.

"Okay," Peggy said in a moment. "Hurry back. I'll wait." She closed the intervening space with two strides, throwing her arms around his neck, and kissed him on the mouth.

"I'll hurry," he said and left.

When Judd reached the bridge, his face fell when he saw the white car parked well off the road. Tami's Cordoba. He parked his Toyota pickup next to it and got out. The car was locked. Peering into the trees that bordered the road next to Morrison's Creek where the highway crossed it, Judd waited a few seconds. Then, cupping both hands around his mouth, he called, "Cin—dy! Tami!" He waited, the sound of his voice evaporating in the dusky light. Nothing. He called again. Nothing. As still as it was, he felt certain that if they were within half a mile of the road, they would hear his call. Where could they be?

Now what should he do? He'd found the car. Locked. Apparently undisturbed. Should he go into the woods and search? He looked around. It was practically dark. He'd find nothing. Not by himself. He needed help. A lot of help.

Jumping back into his truck, he spun the wheel and pulled out onto the two-lane highway.

"There've been no calls," Peggy said, after Judd closed the door to the second-floor apartment.

"Damn! I was hoping they'd had trouble, hitched a ride into town, and were over at my place or at the Castles'. I'd better try calling there again." Picking up the telephone book, he looked up the number and dialed it.

"Castle's," Rod Castle said.

"Mr. Castle? This is Judd Wellington. Is my sister Cindy there by chance?" he asked, holding his breath after asking the simple question.

"I—I don't think so, Judd. I thought they were going back to school this afternoon."

"They were supposed to," Judd said, and quickly explained everything that had happened or not happened since the girls had left their houses earlier that day.

"I see," Rod Castle said after digesting the information. "Have you called the sheriff's department? Or the police?"

"I guess I was waiting for someone to suggest it. I didn't want to sound like a worry wart. Do you think I—we should?"

"Well, it's highly unusual, to say the least. Why don't you call the sheriff's department and sound out the procedure in a situation such as this, and I'll call the police. I don't think they'll be able to do much at this time, simply because the car is out in the county. But I'll find out more information there than you can, Judd. Besides, it'll save time if we each make a call."

Judd hesitated. "I'll get right back to you after I call the sheriff." He hung up.

"Is he concerned?" Peggy asked.

"Of course, he's concerned," Judd said tersely. Grabbing the book he looked up the sheriff's number. "I'm sorry, honey. I'm just worried."

Peggy moved closer to him. "I understand."

"Sheriff's Department," the nasal voice twanged on the phone.

Judd explained the purpose of his call and waited.

"We don't move on nothing like that until twenty-four hours have passed, Mr. Wellington. Why don't you plan on coming in tomorrow when the full staff is here and make your report then. By that time, I'm sure your sister will have come home. She's probably out with her boyfriend or somebody like that."

"She wasn't alone. Tami Castle was with her. Tami's car is parked out by the highway bridge over Morrison's Creek. I went out there."

"Tami Castle?" the man asked.

"Yes. Mayor Castle's daughter."

There was a long pause on the other end before the deputy's voice sounded again. "You see, Mr. Wellington, the problem is Labor Day. See, there's a lot of picnics and celebrations throughout the county today and we're spread pretty thin right now. I suppose we might be able to put together some sort of search party, but tomorrow would be a lot better."

"I think we'd better do something tonight. I'll call Mayor Castle and we'll meet at the sheriff's office."

"How long will that be?"

"We'll be there within thirty minutes." Judd hung up.

"How are things in the hardware business, Judd?" Rod Castle asked amiably after they shook hands.

Judd wanted to scream at him to stop playing politics. His sister was missing and so was the mayor's daughter. This was no time to let politics or anything else interfere. He prayed that Rod Castle would be a parent first and mayor second.

"They're fine, Mayor. Let's go inside."

When they entered the sheriff's department, they found fifteen men, flashlights and search lanterns in each one's hands.

"Mr. Mayor? How are you?" Sheriff Jerry Kane asked, thrusting out his hand. "And you're Judd Wellington?" He turned his attention to Judd.

Judd merely nodded in acknowledgment and waited to see what would happen next.

"Can you give me a brief description of your daughter, Mayor Castle?"

"She's about this tall," Rod began, holding his hand up to his nose.

"About five-seven," the sheriff said, jotting the information into a notebook.

"She'd weigh about one-twenty or so, I guess. White-blond hair."

"Natural or dyed?"

"Natural. Like her mother's."

"What was she wearing?"

Rod shrugged.

"I can answer that," Judd said. "I saw both girls this morning. Tami was wearing jeans and a white blouse. Sandals. Cindy, my sister, was wearing jeans and a red-and-white checked blouse. She had tennis shoes on."

Turning his attention to Judd, the sheriff said, "How tall is your sister?"

"About five-six. Dark complected; long, thick, dark brown hair—it's almost black. Dark brown eyes. She weighs about one-ten or so. I—"

"That'll be fine for now, Mr. Wellington," the sheriff said quietly. "Now where was it they were supposed to have gone?"

"They were going to Morrison's Creek for a short walk before they returned to State University this afternoon." Judd studied the sheriff. He was tall and lanky, and when he walked he seemed to fulfill the role of law man from a different era than the one in which he found himself enforcing the law.

"Wasn't there something about a car?" he asked, turning to his deputy.

"I went out there," Judd said quickly. "I found Tami's car parked and locked."

"Did you touch anything?" the sheriff asked, a slight edge to his voice.

"Just the car handle on the driver's door. Other than that, I called both their names several times and then came back into town. That's when I called Mayor Castle."

"I think I'll notify the Highway Patrol to meet us out there. Art?" he said turning to the deputy behind the desk. Art picked up the microphone and radioed to the state law enforcement officer assigned to Rushton's south area.

"Everyone here follow me out to Morrison's Creek Bridge," Kane said. "Double up so there aren't so many vehicles parked along the road. And when you park, make sure you *are* off the road. Understand?"

The gathered men nodded, mumbling their answers, and the group moved for the door.

Judd remained silent as they rode through the night toward the bridge. Mayor Castle did not talk much either, other than to answer the sheriff's questions. Judd prayed silently the entire time it took to reach the bridge. When the sheriff pulled off the road, he parked behind Tami's car. Judd's legs felt rubbery when he got out of the sedan after the sheriff opened the door. He noticed there weren't any handles on the inside, and for a fleeting second he felt a twinge of claustrophobia when he realized he couldn't get out if he wanted to.

"Ed," the sheriff said, addressing one of his deputies, "you stay here and watch the car. Make certain no one touches it. Call Downer's and have them send a truck out to tow it into the county garage. You go with it and make certain nobody touches it until we dust for prints."

"Right," Ed Walley said, taking up a position close to the car after radioing into town to Downer's Garage.

"All right, men," the sheriff said, "let's fan out and form as long a line as possible with the number of people here. Keep at least a ten or fifteen-foot space between you and the man on either side of you. Sweep the ground with your lights. If you see anything, don't touch it. Just call out, and I'll come a-running. Understand."

A murmur ran through the men again, and Judd took up the position between the sheriff and Rod Castle. Just as they were about to step into the woods, the Highway Patrol car that had been summoned pulled up.

The sheriff turned, calling out to the patrolman to watch the site along the road and to keep the traffic moving. He didn't want any blocked highways.

"Did you see any of the bikers that were in the area today, Sheriff?" the patrolman called from his car as he got out.

"I saw one but they were from up Dumont way. The 'Over-Forty Harley-Davidson Bunch.' I know that group. They're all solid citizens who like to ride motorcycles. What else was around?"

"There were two others, but they kept moving and didn't give any trouble."

The sheriff turned to Judd. In the eerie half-light that surrounded them from the flashlights, Judd could see that the lawman was asking with his expression if the girls might have gone with a gang of that type.

"I know what you're thinking, Sheriff," Judd said. "Neither Cindy nor Tami are the type of girl to want to ride a motorcycle or want to associate with the kind of person who rides with some sort of gang."

"All right. Which way do we go?" He waited for Judd to answer.

"There's a spot back there where kids go for picnics and making out. I think that's where they were heading. It's real pretty there and—"

"I know the spot," the sheriff said. "The one on the other side of the meadow?"

"Right?"

"The best we can do tonight, under the circumstances, is walk and hope we find them and that they're all right. Otherwise, if we don't find anything, we'll have to launch a full-scale, intensive search tomorrow with helicopters and the whole works." The sheriff started walking, and, like a reluctant wave, the men moved into the woods and the night.

The trees closed in on them, and despite the lack of breeze, branches seemed to move of their own accord whenever the men shot a beam of light toward a tree and then away again. On occasion, a man would stumble on the blackness and let out a garbled curse, but other than that, there were no sounds except those of sleeping birds, suddenly disturbed.

Like so many fingers, the beams from flashlights swept back and forth as the line of men stretching more than two hundred feet moved through the raven shadows of the night. Then, when the trees thinned, Judd knew they had reached the meadow that separated the woods lining the road from the trees that bordered the creek where it curved away from right angles to the road and paralleled the old two-lane highway some eight to nine hundred yards distant.

Judd flashed his light onto his wrist to check the time. Almost nine-fifteen. "Shouldn't we be calling their names,

Sheriff?''

"Probably a good idea, Judd," he said, cupping his free hand around his mouth. "Ci—i—i—n—n—nde-e-e-e! Ta—a—a—a—m—e-e-e-e!''

In seconds, the other searchers joined in, and the calling took on an unearthly sound in the dark as the line of men crossed the meadow toward the far stand of trees. When they neared the small hill that was almost centered in the meadowland, they continued up and over it. As they passed the downhill side, Judd stopped, his beam of light fixed on something that froze his attention.

"What is it?" the sheriff asked, hurrying to his side.

"Looks like a tire track of some sort. See it?" Judd said, crouching to run his finger above the imprint that stood out in a small bare spot in the long grass.

"We'll have to come back another way to make certain no one steps on this and send someone out here with plaster to make a mold. Of course, we don't know when the track was made. It might be important and it might not. We can't take any chances, though." He tore a sheet of paper from his notebook and fixed it under a small rock to mark the area.

The line continued its way toward the dark trees that were beckoning to them from the edge of the grassy plain. Once they passed through the trees, they came to the parklike area that had witnessed so many picnics and late-night parties. They found nothing.

"All right, men," the sheriff said, "let's move another two hundred feet or so south and then we'll sweep back toward the highway. If we don't find anything when we get back, I hope I can count on all of you helping tomorrow when we come back. Move out."

The men searched as they went, and at the word of the sheriff, they turned and resumed their light-sweeping of the darkness. While they walked, the names of the two missing girls being called more infrequently, Judd thought back to the picnic area. He had taken girls there when he was in high school. The flat ground on both sides of the meandering creek seemed to almost have been planned by someone, rather than just being a flattened area caused by some quirk of nature. There were times in the past, before television and the frantic pace of life in which most people found themselves caught up, that the natural park had served as a family outing spot. But that had been before Judd's time, and he had only heard stories from his parents and from people like Zella Ludinger.

When the members of the search party reached the meadow again, they continued on their way, flicking their lights from side to side, finding nothing. Then the trees swallowed them once more. They had gone no more than a hundred feet or so when one of them men called out.

"Over here, Sheriff! I've found them."

"Thank God," Judd said and instantly stopped, a glacial chill slowing through his body. If the man found them, why hadn't the girls answered the calls of their names? Were they all right? Maybe they were sleeping. But why?

Judd snapped out of his bewilderment and followed the sheriff, who had gained several steps on him. Running to catch up, he stopped short when the sheriff did. Most of the others who had been to Judd's right had already gathered, standing in a half-circle, their flashlights trained on the ground.

Pushing his way around the sheriff, he stopped and screamed.

When Rod Castle came into the group, he stopped, speechless, as Judd dropped to his knees, wailing, "Oh, my God! Oh, my good God!"

PART 2

From Beyond
the Grave

5

The stink of garbage, urine, stale beer,
and exhaust fumes seemed bonded to the
interior of the Holmes Warehouse by the
sweet, overlaying smell of marijuana.
Campsites set up within the main room
lined both long walls, each with a motorcycle parked nearby. Bull, in one of his
shrewd bursts of energy, had put enough
money together to rent the barnlike
building for two months and then had
coerced the owner into allowing them to
stay there. As Bull had put it at the time,
"to guard the premises against pilferers
and burglars."

Charcoal braziers, littered with
graying coals, marked the front of each
assigned area. The gang members,
jealous of their own individual territory,

lived by a strict set of rules.

But the gang was not happy and a pall of insurgency hung over the Light Bearer's Chosen. Not since Bull had been killed in the fight with Buckshot had the bikers felt normal. No one had confronted the new leader with the state of mind under which the members labored.

Gordo, his fat body spread out in a deck chair, stared into space, seeing nothing but witnessing the past as it unfolded before his imagination. Bull had been murdered. There was no questioning that fact. It was merely the law of the jungle that had permitted Buckshot to take control. Buckshot was no leader. Everyone in the gang, probably even Buckshot himself, realized that. But no one wanted to change the rules. Not at this time. Why should they? Wasn't the premise of the gang simply to shock the regular community by doing what they wanted, where they wanted, whenever they wanted? The Light Bearer's Chosen reveled in their peculiar position in society, believing that they were above and beyond any written laws as they applied to others. So they had their own set of rules, which included selecting their leaders by the oldest known law: kill or be killed. And Buckshot had managed to cut the throat of Bull—Bull who had been a real leader.

"Hey, Gordo," the tall, thin man said, coming up to Gordo's campsite.

Gordo snapped out of his revery and looked up. "Snake," he said, acknowledging the new arrival's presence. "What's up?"

"Same." Snake lay back on the dirty floor, his T-shirt exposing both arms that carried tattoos of writhing snakes. "Sure's a mess, ain't it? Got any 'shit'?"

"What's a mess?" Gordo magically produced a cigarette from beneath the chair, handing it to the man.

Snake's head motioned to one side in the direction of Bull's old campsite, the one that Buckshot had deemed proper for him to take over as the new leader.

"Yeah," Gordo said, nodding his head. "But what you want to do 'bout it?"

Snake shrugged, dragging on the cigarette. "I don't want the job. But I sure as hell could cut Buckshot's balls out and hand 'em to him without even working up a sweat."

"Assuming that he's got balls." Gordo managed a gruff laugh at his own comment. "Think you could have whipped Bull and taken over?"

Snake shook his head and sucked more smoke into his lungs before it dribbled from his nostrils. He smiled foolishly and giggled.

"But Buckshot did. That makes him

the leader."

"I know that. But what has the sono-fabitch done since then to prove he's a leader. He ain't brought one red fuckin' cent in. Christ, Bull was always thinkin' up ways to make a buck. Even if it was only breakin' a leg for a couple a hundred. Shit. We gotta eat and drink and smoke up, don't we?"

"Yeah, I know." Gordo stood up. "But that's not what bothers me."

Snake propped himself up on his elbows and said, "What does? Fuckin'?" He grinned, displaying the gap between his eyeteeth that gave his mouth the resemblance of a poisonous viper.

Gordo shook his head. "There's plenty of that around here."

"What, then?" Snake stood.

"The two girls our dumb leader saw fit to snuff."

"Oh, yeah. I almost forgot. I heard some of the others talking about that, too. You think that's goin' to be trouble?"

" 'Goin' to be'?" Gordo asked. "Where were you the day the 'man' showed up?"

Snake turned to him, a puzzled look twisting his oval face. He stared at Gordo in the unblinking way that had first gotten him his nickname before he adorned his body with various tattoos of snakes. "What the fuck you talkin' about?"

" 'Bout a week after he sliced their

throats, the 'man' shows up here, askin' questions."

"Nobody said a word to me. What happened? Where was I?" Snake thought for a minute and butted the joint. "Oh, yeah. I had a job for a couple of days over in Bakerston. Guardin' a guy's 'old lady' while he went off with his girlfriend for a fuckin' fling. Made three hundred bucks."

"D'you tell Buckshot?"

"Fuck no. That asshole would have taken it all and claimed that he had thought of the job and gotten the money and everythin'. Anyway, what happened?"

"They had casts of a tire track. Didn't match any of the hogs here. But I think I know whose hog it was."

Snake's faced paled. "Did it match mine?"

Gordo shook his head, his jowls flapping. "Naw. I recognized the tread. It matched a couple of others but the tread was different depths. I think it probably was from Bull's."

Snake visibly relaxed. "Well, shit. That's no problem, then, is it. He and his hog are buried."

"Yeah, but what if they ever find him? That could put all of us there where the girls were put away."

"What the fuck you worryin' about? Shit, we'll just mount up and ride away. The 'man' and his laws don't apply to us.

We got our own. Right?"

Gordo nodded slowly.

"So what did Buckshot tell the cops?"

"About what?"

"About where Bull is?"

"Shrugged his shoulders and said he didn't know."

"And they bought that?"

"Not until Mule told 'em that Bull had told him he was just takin' off. That he was fed up with the gang and leadin' us 'n all."

"Did they buy that?"

"Not until a couple of others said that he told them the same thing."

"Shit. Then we ain't got nothin' to worry about, have we?"

Gordo didn't say anything.

"Well?" Snake persisted, wanting some sort of affirmation to his conclusion.

"Buck*shit* is goin' to have to shape up and start usin' his fuckin' head or he's goin' to get all of us in hot water."

Priscilla Puss called over from the next campsite, "What are you two talkin' about?"

"Fucking your hairy twat, Puss," Gordo said, laughing.

"Your place or mine?" she asked, coming over.

Gordo told her about their conversation, concluding with, "What have you heard?"

"Pretty much the same. Most everybody I talk with seems to think that Buck-shot's no leader. That he'll fuck up and get all of us in trouble. What are we goin' to do?"

Gordo and Snake shrugged.

"Christ, we ain't no fuckin' saints," Gordo wheezed, lowering himself back into the lawn chair. "Face it, most of the 'regulars' look on the Chosen and other bikers like we got the plague or herpes or fuckin' AIDS or somethin'."

"Yeah, but the same honest John Citizen type will look us up if they want somebody roughed up, rubbed out, or scared to death. Right?" Snake looked first to Gordo and then to Priscilla, whom he eyed up and down drinking in the woman's chunky body. Her breasts peeked from behind the open blue work shirt she wore hanging over her cut-off jeans. "You wanna fuck, Puss?"

"Sure, why not," she said, extending her hand to Snake, who took it and allowed her to lead him to the campsite next to Gordo's.

Gordo shook his head. No wonder the gang wasn't concerned if the men carried their brains in the heads of their peckers and the women let the guys pump precious ounces of their thinking matter into the mamas' bodies. He turned his attention away from the writhing couple on the floor not ten feet away from him.

Snake wasn't that imaginative, nor was Priscilla Puss. If she got humped five or six times a day, it seemed to keep her quiet.

Across the building, Gordo caught site of Buckshot standing up at Bull's old campsite. Buckshot had taken it over, giving up his own meager spot at the end of the building when they returned to the warehouse that Monday after he had deposed Bull for the leadership. Gordo couldn't help wondering why Cow had gone along with the new leader. Bull had looked like a real man—big, powerful, well muscled, solid as a stout tree. Buckshot, on the other hand, was flabby. His chest looked almost like a woman's, his fat jiggling whenever he took a step. The way the man strutted, he probably thought that he appeared powerful. Maybe that was why he wore sleeveless T-shirts that showed the huge upper arms. But Gordo knew for a fact that Buckshot's arms were more fat than muscle.

Cow was the problem. Was she that hard up for a fuck? Or was she the type who wanted to be with power, no matter who the power might be? That was probably the answer. Gordo didn't give a good, swift shit about any of it. As long as he had some booze and "shit" to smoke or "coke" to snort and a woman to fuck whenever he wanted, he didn't give a care about anything else.

Gordo turned away when Cow and

Buckshot started toward him. Why would they want to come over to him? Maybe they could read minds. That was stupid.

Closing his eyes as if he were asleep, he watched them approach through half-opened eyes.

"Wake up, Gordo." Buckshot kicked him in the foot when he stood over him.

Gordo feigned waking up. "Huh? What's up, Buckshot?"

"Look." He pointed to his jeans.

Gordo's eyes widened when he saw the same cabalistic patches and designs that Bull had had on his pants. The goat's head. The inverted star. The numbers "666" embroidered above each knee. "D'you take up sewing, Boss?" Gordo smothered the laugh he felt building at his joke.

"Cow here did it. Pretty nice, huh? She's gonna teach me the rites, too, aren't you, Cow?"

She nodded, placing her hands on her hips. The leather vest she wore was spread open and her bare breasts thrust out, the ring-pierced nipples and aureoles staring at Gordo in a defiant way.

"In fact," Buckshot continued, "we're goin' to have a rite. Tonight. We gotta get the gang goin'. For the last two weeks, we've been sittin' on our asses doin' nuthin'. Tonight, we pray to Lucifer and we get on the move again. Pass the word."

Gordo smiled. Maybe Buckshot would

prove to be a leader after all. It had been Bull, with Cow's prodding, who had turned the gang to worshiping Lucifer, and the tide of the gang's luck seemed to have turned at the same time. None of them believed in any religion, but until it was proven different, Lucifer and the rituals that Cow had introduced through Bull would suffice.

"Okay, Buckshot. Tonight it is." Gordo struggled to his feet and set off to tell everyone in the building.

A small fire, its flames dancing in one of the charcoal grills, served as the only illumination other than the nine candles on the table made of packing crates, centered in the huge warehouse room. Cow, completely naked, lay on the improvised altar, while Buckshot stood over her.

Rosie O'Lay guarded the small fire, dropping marijuana leaves into the flames, then inhaling the fumes as they spiraled up, the sweet odor hanging heavily in the air. Each member, other than Cow and Buckshot, dangled a joint from their lips.

"Help us, oh Lucifer," Buckshot intoned. "Help us in our quest for souls for you. Help us in our quest for good times. Help us in our quest for money to buy the pleasures we all want."

A drop of spittle fell from his mouth as

he looked at Cow, lying on the makeshift altar. Her breasts rose and fell in an even tempo contrasting with his own breathless way of speaking as he intoned the words of their satanic rite. A fine gold chain linked together the rings piercing her nipples. A cage at her feet wiggled as the four rats inside scurried back and forth, searching for some way out of the wire trap.

Buckshot picked up the long, thin blade that rested on Cow's stomach, its point directed at her pubic hair. "Accept the blood sacrifice we make to you, oh Master of the Dark and all that is evil."

He motioned to Mary Queen of Sots, who served as his acolyte, to bring the cage closer. When it sat next to Cow's hip, he opened the door and gingerly reached in and grasped one of the large rodents. As big as a housecat, he held it up over his head by the scruff of the neck.

"For you, Mighty Lucifer," he cried and brought the squirming animal down to his eye level. He deftly slit the rat's throat and held the bleeding wound over a small cup. When the life of the rat had drained into it, he moved the cup to one side before flinging the carcass into the darkness surrounding the coterie. Repeating the act with each of the other three trapped animals, Buckshot filled the cup with blood.

He slipped out of his T-shirt and

dropped his jeans. Naked, he held the cup over his head, then slowly brought it in an arc toward the floor where he lingered for several minutes.

"It is good," he whispered. "Lucifer accepts our offering." Standing erect, he held the cup over Cow's throat, tipping it enough to allow some of the gore to dribble onto her naked skin. No one made a sound. The gang's breathing wheezed through the quiet, as Buckshot continued making his sanguinary trail down Cow's chest, around her breasts, pouring a small amount on each nipple before continuing toward her navel where he poured more, filling the depression. Trailing the cup down each leg until a thin blood mark lined each one, he returned to her hairy triangle where he emptied the cup.

Aroused by the eroticism of the act he was performing, Buckshot cried out, "Strip your clothes off for Lucifer. Fuck each other for Lucifer. Pray to Lucifer for guidance and prosperity. We are yours, oh Mighty Lucifer."

The sound of zippers being opened and people undressing filled the air for the next half minute, and when the gang stood naked, Buckshot, dropping his head, stared at the floor. "Come be with us, Mighty One."

Crawling up onto the altar, Buckshot stood over Cow. She opened her eyes, smiling sensually at him. When she spread her legs, Buckshot dropped to his knees and plunged his erection into her. Pumping furiously, he shuddered and Cow pushed him away.

She peered into the semidarkness. Writhing bodies lay in a circle surrounding the table, locked in sexual embraces as they continued their ritual offering to the lord of darkness. "He came already. Somebody else get up here. We don't want to lose the momentum of the rite."

Gordo, who had no wife, left the mama on whom he had been lying and moved quickly to the table where Buckshot was getting off. He eyed their new leader, who looked away, shamed by his lack of staying power. After Gordo managed to get on the table, he mounted Cow. A rush of breath escaped her as the huge man lay upon her, entering her. The ritual continued.

The next morning, Buckshot called everyone together. "This is going to mark the beginning of a new era of prosperity for the Light Bearer's Chosen. I'm going to find a few jobs and make some contacts. Mule, you come with me. The rest of you, hang loose.

He kicked his motorcycle's engine to life and roared toward the building's door. Blaster opened it and Buckshot sped into the bright day followed by Mule.

6

Judd rubbed a tired hand over his tired face. How long had it been? Two days? Two weeks? Two months? When he thought about it, he concluded that two weeks had passed since the search party had found the bodies of Cindy and Tami. Whenever he thought of their lifeless, naked bodies lying close together, he would shudder, fighting the urge to vomit. The sight had been awful. The funeral had been a long, nightmarish experience. Much worse than when he and Cindy had buried their parents. Then they had had each other. At least their parents' deaths were understandable although not acceptable at the time. How could anyone ever rationally explain or justify the girls' deaths?

He had reached the point in his

muddled mourning where he could envision the murder site without focusing his mind's eye on the throats of Cindy and Tami. When that gaping, smiling wound blasted through his thin veneer of protection, his middle would heave and whatever he still held in his stomach would be vomited out.

Picking up the telephone, he dialed from memory the telephone number of the sheriff's department. He asked for Sheriff Kane and waited.

"Sheriff Kane."

"Anything yet, Sheriff?" Judd didn't bother identifying himself. The daily call had become a ritual. Call the sheriff's office. Ask if there had been any developments. If none, why not? Listen to the sheriff's rhetoric about other cases, how busy he and his deputies were, and then they'd say good-bye, with Judd reminding him to call if anything were uncovered.

"Good morning, Judd."

Judd half smiled. At first it had been Mr. Wellington, but now the Sheriff felt familiar enough to call him by his first name. He wondered if he should try doing the same with the lawman. "Well, is there?"

"I wish I could say there was something. But there isn't."

"What's being done?"

"Everything. Every law office within

three hundred miles has been contacted. The—"

"Have you heard anything yet from the lab where you sent the cast of that tire track?"

"Late yesterday. It—"

"And?"

"Be a nickel's worth of patient, Judd, and I'll tell you. Okay?"

"All right, Sheriff."

"The one track was a Goodyear tire. Fairly good tread on it. We don't know what sort of vehicle made it."

Judd paused, waiting to see if Kane would continue. When he didn't, he said, "What does that mean?"

"It might have been that of a motor-cycle. We're not positive. Out in the meadow, we couldn't find any other tracks in the vicinity that would have matched up as making it a four-wheel vehicle."

"So?"

"So, in all likelihood, it was a bike. There were indications in other parts of the meadow that at least one motorcycle had done a lot of riding around. On the other hand, it could have been a group of bikes that went through just once. At this point in time, we can't really tell for certain."

"Didn't the highway patrolman say something about bike gangs being around Rushton that weekend?"

"Yeah. He did. And we had reports on them as well. One was a bunch of fifty- and sixty-year-old married couples from Dumont. I doubted if they'd know any-thing. When they were asked, they didn't. One gang, a really big one, was going through to the West Coast and just passed through the area on Saturday."

"Are you positive they just passed through?"

"It would be pretty hard for close to a hundred bikes to return and not be seen. Besides, we checked west of here and found out that they passed through Boulder, Colorado, on Monday. Pretty hard to do that and be here at the same time."

"What's left, Sheriff?"

"Not much. One gang that centers its operations out of the state capital, the Light Bearer's Chosen, swears that they were busy selecting a new leader when their old one copped out and scrammed."

"You believe them?"

"The capital police checked their tires. None of them matched the casting. Besides, they've got some forty or fifty people to swear to each other's where-abouts. Without any hard evidence, we can't touch them."

"What else?"

"That's about it. Besides, where that tire track is concerned, we have no idea as to when it was made. It could have been made before, during, or after the time in question."

Judd wondered why he didn't say "murders."

"We did find a metal cross. I think one of my deputies said it was a Maltese cross. It has a skull scratched onto the surface of it."

"Where did you find that?" Judd wrote the fact down on a pad.

"Close to the—the bodies."

"Any leads on that?"

"Not at this time. But, like the tire track, we don't know when the cross was dropped. It could have been before, during, or after."

Judd mulled it over for a moment. "I'll check back with you, Sheriff."

"I'm sure you will, Judd."

They both hung up.

Judd picked up the note pad where he had scribbled, "Maltese Cross." What did that have to do with the murders? He tore off the sheet and gasped. Written on the next page were the words "Help me! Come to me! Help me!"

Judd hated the nighttime most. When it was dark. When he had to sleep to recharge his exhausted body. He wasn't working. He had turned the store's operation over to Mickey Higgins, his clerk. He stopped in at least twice a day, checking the register and taking care of the books. But when that was finished, he returned home, sitting next to the telephone waiting for it to ring, for the information that the killer had been caught, for the bastard's name.

He rolled and tossed, throwing back the covers. Clouds swept by his sleeping mind, caressing it in a soft embrace, gently shaking him. Where was he? What was going on? The call. The call was coming again. What were the words? He listened intently, straining to make out the tiny sound.

"Louder," he mumbled. "Can't hear you."

The plaintive cry came again, still unintelligible.

"Please," Judd cried out into the dark. "Louder."

And he awoke, sitting up in bed. The dream. He had had the dream again. What was it? What did it mean—if anything? The tiny sound, almost fragile in its makeup, spun through his mind. Not unlike a call. But what type of call, if indeed it was a call? Why did he feel compelled to call out? To answer? What was the call saying? Was it saying anything? Or was it some cruel joke his own subconscious mind was playing on him? Lying back, he closed his eyes, and tried to force the thoughts from his mind.

"You look awful, Judd," Peggy said, peering at him over her cup of coffee.

"Thanks a whole lot. Do I ever say nice things like that about you?"

"You look tired. Are you getting enough sleep?"

"I do when you're not staying over or when you invite me to your place. Why?"

"Because I think you're changing— and not necessarily for the good."

"What does that mean?"

"I think you're mourning too much for Cindy. I think you're not taking care of business. I think you're developing a real obsession about Cindy's death."

"Murder," he said correcting her. Every time she said death, he changed it to murder.

"See what I mean? Accept it, darling. Cindy is dead. She *was* murdered. There's nothing you can do about it. I feel as bad as you do about it, but I feel even worse that you're letting it affect you like it is."

Judd stood, moving away from Peggy's kitchenette table. She had insisted he come over for dinner and stay the night. She had been working both her jobs almost on a full-time basis and had not had much time to devote to him. An unusual number of new residents had entered the rest homes where she did bookkeeping part time, and Allen

Edwards, the attorney for whom she worked full time, had had a sudden influx of new cases that had required her to stay well into the night, typing depositions and contracts.

"It's not affecting me," Judd said. "Maybe you're working too hard and you're imagining things."

She stood and crossed the few feet to him. Circling her arms around his neck, she said, "I'm so sorry about Cindy. She's gone, but there's nothing you or I or anyone else can do to bring her back. You have to get on with your life. I'm waiting for you, you know."

He pulled her close and stuck his face into her neck, weeping softly without saying anything. After several minutes, he stepped back. "I know you're right. But it was such an awful way to die. Raped. Beaten. Throat cut." He shuddered.

Peggy took his face in her hands. "I'm patient. You know that. In time, the hurt will fade. I'm not saying it will go away, but it will fade. Just remember that I'm here, waiting for you."

He looked into her eyes that stared back into his in her usual direct, shrewd, no-nonsense way. Running one finger along her rosy cheek, he traced the outline of her V-shaped face. "I love you, Peggy. Don't ever forget that."

"And I love you, Judd."

They kissed, softly, gently, until both felt a sense of desire born within them. Taking his hand, Peggy led him toward the bedroom. Once they had undressed, they embraced, their nakedness finishing the job of awakening the desire that Judd had kept suppressed since Cindy's funeral.

Lying on the bed, Peggy gently made love to him, kissing away the fatigue of loss and crying. Her lips, barely touching his hairy chest, skimmed along the tangle of hair, stopping at his navel.

He reached out, fondling her breasts, his desire for her completely manifested. Urging her back onto the bed, he arose and positioned himself between her outstretched legs.

An unhurried breeze ruffled the curtains in Peggy's bedroom, but neither she nor Judd moved. The night was warm and they lay on the bed, naked, uncovered.

Somewhere off in the distance, Judd heard the sound. The call. It was coming again. Without warning, he sat upright in bed. "What?" he said loudly.

Startled, Peggy sat up next to him. "What is it, darling?"

Judd motioned for her to be silent, turning his head to hear better.

After several long moments passed during which his face contorted, Peggy slid off the bed, pulling her thin robe around her shoulders. "What is it, Judd?"

"You didn't hear it?"

"Hear it? Hear what?"

"This time, I was able to make out one word. 'Help.' That's all I could understand. 'Help.' "

"What are you talking about?"

"I've been having a dream for the last few nights. I hear someone—at least I think it's someone—calling. From a long way off. But I can't make out what the words are. Tonight, I distinctly heard the word 'help.' "

"What does that mean?"

"I don't know."

"I don't understand," she said, moving back onto the bed, sitting close to Judd.

"Neither do I," he said simply. His face brightened for a moment.

"What is it?"

"I—I just thought of something. The other day, day before yesterday, to be accurate, I was talking with the sheriff when he told me that there still wasn't a clue—remember me telling you about that?"

She nodded.

"Well, I wrote it down on the notepad by the telephone. When I tore off the sheet, I found the words 'Help me! Come to me! Help me!' written on the next sheet."

"Why had you written that?"

"That's just it. It wasn't my handwriting."

"Well, I didn't do it."

"I know that. Nor was it Cindy's. I have no idea who wrote it or when it was written. But it must have something to do with my dreams, because I heard the word 'help' tonight."

"What do you suppose the dream means? For that matter, what does the message you found mean?"

Judd slowly shrugged his shoulders. "I have no idea."

"I think it might be your own grief manifesting itself in a strange way."

"What?" he asked incredulously.

"Grief can do strange things. Look, Judd, Cindy was just nineteen. She was your whole family. She died a horrible death. You have to come to grips with it somehow. Maybe your subconscious is making you dream about Cindy calling to you for help so that you understand that her last thoughts were about you."

"That's pretty farfetched, Doctor Dixon."

"Don't call me that. And I don't think it's farfetched at all. The human body can do strange things. Think of what happens when someone has a limb amputated. For months—even years—that person can feel the sensation of wanting to scratch the

daughter. In a lot of ways, his and his wife's loss is worse than yours—now, don't get angry until you hear me out. I personally feel that it is much worse to bury one's offspring than it is to bury one's brother or sister. It's awful when parents, who are supposed to precede their children in death, don't, and have to bury them. Do you understand what it is I'm saying?"

Judd reflected on what Kane had said. After several seconds, he said, "Yeah, I guess I know where you're coming from, Sheriff. But, dammit, Cindy was all the family I had left. You understand *that*, don't you?"

"Of course I do. But the thing you have to do is get on with *your* life. Life is for the living. I hope you realize that and get your own priorities in line."

"Yeah, I will, Sheriff. You don't mind if I continue calling you from time to time, do you?"

"Just don't make it a daily ritual like you have since the funeral."

"Okay, Sheriff." He hung up.

He had left Peggy's apartment in a hurry that morning and felt that a shower and shave would perhaps get him looking at the world in a different way. The sheriff was right. He knew that. Peggy was right. And he knew it as well. He'd just have to reapply himself and get on with it.

The clouds of steam roiled and

billowed up to the ceiling only to be forced down outside the shower stall. The hot water felt good. Perhaps he was coming out of his funk. At least it seemed as if he wanted to be more active than he had been for the last fourteen days or so.

Turning off the water, he toweled himself off in the damp fog that quickly dissipated once he stepped out into the bathroom. When he finished, the mirror caught his attention. Written into the droplets of water deposited there by the steam were the words: "Help me! Come to me! Help me!"

Judd viciously wiped the words away, smearing them into oblivion. What did it mean? Who had written them? He rushed through the house but found nothing out of place. The kitchen was neat, clean and in order. The formal dining room was just as tidy, while the living room with its plush furniture and throw pillows looked like something out of a magazine adver-tisement. There had been no one there. Then, who had written the words? Had he done it? Could Peggy be that right about him? Was he trying to assuage his grief by writing messages that were purportedly from Cindy? But if that were the case, why wasn't the handwriting like his—or even an imitation of Cindy's? It was completely different from both of theirs.

While he shaved, he ran the sheriff's words through his mind again. Other cases. Sure, there had to be others. Perhaps he should go out to the woods himself and poke around. There might be something there that everyone who had searched had overlooked. Why not go himself? Mickey had been running the store, and there was no reason why he couldn't do it for one more day. He'd get dressed, go to the woods, and search for—? Whatever he might find.

Judd backed the Toyota out of the garage and rushed toward the street. Just as he was about to enter it, he slammed on the brakes. He'd need a shovel. Throwing the truck into low, he dashed back to the garage, stopping short of the yawning entrance. Jumping out of the cab, he hurried inside, picked up a spade, and returned to the truck. Once he was on the street heading for the highway that led to Morrison's Creek, he pondered his actions. Why had he gone back for a shovel? What made him think he'd need a shovel?

When he reached the bridge, he crossed it and pulled off the road, close to the spot where Tami had parked her car. Hesitantly getting out of the truck, he crossed the fence and entered the woods.

Foreboding thoughts of that awful night crushed in on him. A lump formed in his throat and he coughed at the uncomfortable feeling as the soreness renewed its attack on him. His eyes burned until tears formed to smother that particular feeling, but his grief continued flowing. Here and there, he ran into bits and pieces of the yellow police barrier that had been put up to keep the prurient thrill seekers out while the sheriff's men conducted their investigation.

Overhead, clouds gathered, blotting out the sunlight. A gloom fell over the woods when the birds, which had been singing, stopped, in anticipation of a thunderstorm.

The tears continued unabated when he entered the small clearing where Cindy and Tami had died. His head bent down, his watery eyes searching the ground, Judd made spiraling, concentric circles in the clearing until he had covered every square inch. Nothing. There was nothing here. Only the hideous memory of that terrible scene that would not leave him.

Then, for no reason, he turned, walking directly away from the clearing and the direction from which he had come. Moving forward through the thick undergrowth, he dodged trees here and there keeping in as straight a line as possible. His tears dried. And when the words formed in his head, *"Help me! Come to me! Help me!"* he didn't falter and continued walking unperturbed, directly to another clearing several hundred yards away. A clearing that had a small hill in its center. A hill with a mound of freshly turned earth on top.

7

Judd looked searchingly around the clearing. Dense brush seemed to seal it off from the outside world, creating a little pocket all to itself. The trees ringing the glade formed a leafy roof except for the small opening overhead. The clouds that had been building since he entered the woods roiled about, changing shades of black and gray intermittently as the wind grew stronger. For the time being, the trees and brush would give him some degree of protection from the elements. The wind moaned through the trees, rising and falling in volume as it satisfied its fickle whims.

The mound. What was the significance of the mound? What had brought him here? The voice came again.

"Help me! Come to me! Help me!"

Judd threw his hands over his ears. What did it mean? Who was calling to him? Now that he stood here in this clearing, he could hear the strange cry with no effort. But what did it mean? Who needed help? Who wanted him to come to—? Where? Who?

Without moving, he studied the mound more closely. The top, which was about six feet high, appeared to have been disturbed—as if someone had been digging in it. Freshly turned earth covered the entire hillock. He thought for a moment. There were a few Indian burial mounds around Rushton. Although he was interested to some degree in the past, the lore of Indians and their practices had never held much intrigue for him. This might be or might not be a burial place for aborigines. How could he tell? Even if it was such a site, someone could have been digging here, searching for artifacts of some sort.

"Help me! Come to me! Help me!" The words came again, even louder and clearer than they had before.

Not unlike a frightened animal that had been cornered, Judd flashed his eyes from one side to the other. "Who are you?" he cried out. "Where are you? Why can't I see you? Come forward. I'll help you if I can."

"Help me! Come to me! Help me!"

There was nothing more—other than the wind whining through the upper branches of the trees.

Judd turned slowly, making a full circle. When had he last seen a bit of the yellow paper ribbon that the sheriff's department had used to enclose the murder site? When he reflected on it, he thought that it had been quite some distance from where he stood at the edge of this clearing. If that were the case, had the police or sheriff's deputies even come this far or searched this particular area? Had they deemed that the area they had cordoned off was sufficient in which to search for clues to learn the identity of his sister's murderer? Would they have heard this strange voice if they had come here?

When he finished his circle, Judd refocused his attention on the mound. Could it in some way have bearing on the double murder? Slowly approaching the small hillock, he stopped when the words slammed into his head again.

"Help me! Come to me! Help me!"

This time the words were fairly shouted at him.

"Where are you?" he screamed desperately. If someone were nearby, someone who truly needed help, he had to have more to go on. Why did the voice keep repeating the same seven words over and over? "Where are you?" he shouted again, but a roll of thunder from overhead drowned him out.

Scrambling to the top of the hill, Judd kicked at the soft dirt. Someone *had* been digging here. But if it were an Indian burial mound, what would Judd find of interest here? Still, an overpowering sense of urgency swept away his logic, stripping him of any reasoning power he might have wanted to use at that instant.

"Help me! Come to me! Help me!"

The words fairly exploded around him as if they had been amplified. His eyes widened, while staring at the ground. *The voice was coming from within the hill.* Someone was buried there. Someone who might be alive needed his help and needed it right now.

Turning, he dashed from the hill, breaking through the dense wall of vegetation. Thunder crashed again, accompanied this time by the flashing of a ragged fork of lightning. Then the rain came, sweeping over the trees, filtering through the dense foliage, slowly drenching the floor and the man running through the trees.

The shovel. He had to get the shovel. He stopped short. The shovel? Why had he gone back for it in the first place? What had prompted him to return to the garage to get such an unlikely tool to take with him? Rain water ran down the neck of his jacket and shirt, chilling him, and he resumed his flight.

When he reached the road, he was fifty yards away from the truck. To his right, he saw a little-used service road that wound back through the trees toward the southern edge of the picnic area to which Cindy and Tami had been walking when they had— He choked back the urge to scream. He would drive back in. He'd be a little closer to the hillock that he wanted to dig around in and wouldn't have to get soaked going to or coming back from that place.

Reaching the truck, he climbed into the cab, thankful for the brief respite from the rain. He turned over the motor and drove along the shoulder of the highway until he reached the side road.

"Help me! Come to me! Help me!"

He was more vaguely aware of the words this time, rather than consciously hearing them as he had when he had stood near the hillock and then on top of it. Strange. No, more than strange. Scary. But he felt he had to return there. He had no control. Something—some unseen thing or force or power was drawing him inexorably back to the little clearing with the small hill in the center.

The Toyota bounced slowly along the rough road. Judd slipped the transmission into four-wheel drive to make certain he wouldn't get stuck. When he thought he had gone far enough, he stopped, peering into the rain-soaked woods, trying to get his bearings. If his mental calculations were correct, the hillock should be to his right, no more than fifty or a hundred feet away. The dense undergrowth blotted out any sign of the clearing from this side, and it was only when he broke through the wall of brush by swinging the shovel back and forth that he realized that he had found it once more.

"Help me! Come to me! Help me!"

It was much louder now that he had returned to the clearing. Without hesitating, he climbed back to the top of the mound and, after deliberating a second or two, plunged the shovel into the earth. Heaving the spadeful of mud to one side, he thrust the shovel in again, and again, and again, each time throwing the dirt to the same side. Each load brought a small avalanche of mud sliding down the opposite side of the hill. The rain filtering through the leaves and branches overhead drenched him, soaking his shirt and pants until he felt as if he might be drier if he took his clothes off.

Then he struck something. Something that clanked, and he stopped.

"Come to me! Come to me!" The words repeated over and over.

Judd didn't wait or think or try to reason out what the meaning of the words could be—he obediently continued digging, but more carefully. For some reason he could not figure out, he knew he must go slowly for fear of damaging something—the something that was buried there in the mound.

Hog!

The word formed in his mind. Why did he want to think of an animal now.

Hog!

Doing his best to ignore the thought, he carefully continued his excavating. Every once in a while, he struck the metallic thing and backed off, taking his time. He had time. He knew that, now that he had found the source of the calling. Who or what or why remained unanswered questions at this time, and he knew that he would learn the answers soon enough.

Then his spade struck something that didn't resound, that instead yielded to the sharp edge of the shovel. He stopped. What could that be? The blade of the tool in his hands swept away the last dirt concealing the top of the curved pipelike thing, and he stopped. It appeared to be a set of motorcycle handlebars. But what would they be doing out here in the middle of Morrison's Woods? He moved more dirt away and sucked in his breath when he uncovered a large hand, a man's hand, gripping the throttle. His own hands trembling, he stopped. Could he bear the trauma of looking at another dead person—another victim of some type of crime? It had to be a crime. There was no reason to bury a motorcycle and a rider out here in the middle of these trees unless someone was trying to conceal a crime—a crime of murder.

"Help me! Now! Help me! Come to me! Help me!" the voice pleaded.

"Who are you? Are you all right? Where are you?" Judd called out over the hiss of the falling rain. A roll of thunder overhead momentarily blotted out any response that might have been made, but Judd realized that there would be no answer that would sound in his ears anyway. It would only sound in his head, as it had been doing since he first became aware of the calling.

The thought suddenly struck him that in some way the grave he had accidentally uncovered might have something to do with the murders of Cindy and Tami. His mind raced as he stared at the hole he had dug. Without thinking, he launched his digging again, renewing his efforts in a dizzying way. The dirt and mud flew in all directions now that he had a reason to uncover the dead man and the motorcycle. To hell with being careful. Why worry about hurting the machine?

"Hog!" The word came to his mind, but he ignored it.

Unmindful that he might be destroying clues to the cause of the man's death and to the killer, should it be established that he had been murdered, Judd worked feverishly until he had cleared the earth away from the huge man and machine. Judd climbed slowly out of the hole.

The thunder rumbled again and lightning flashed as Judd stood at the lip of the grave, staring down. The man had been large, long hair, beard, no shirt, but a leather vest partially covered his dirt-caked upper torso. Hanging from either side of the vest, two metal crosses stuck to the surface, glued there by mud. His blue jeans, brown with dirt, slowly turned to muddy sienna which, as the rain continued, washed away, exposing the symbols sewn to the material. The goat's head, an inverted star, the number "666" embroidered above the right knee. When Judd moved a bit, he could see the same configurations on the left leg as well.

Didn't some of these things have to do with devil worship? Hadn't he seen a documentary on TV or someplace about that very thing? The number "666" was, as he remembered from a sermon in church once, the mark or the number of the "Beast"—Lucifer. Why would a motorcyclist be wearing things like that on his jeans unless—unless he were a devil worshiper of some sort.

Judd felt he had to drag the body out of the grave. Should he? Perhaps he would be destroying evidence. *"To hell with the fucking evidence!"* the voice rang in his head. Jumping back into the hole, Judd threw his body's strength into moving the man off the saddle. Little by little, he moved the hulk of the man up and away from the bike. Even though the man must have weighed well over two hundred and fifty pounds and was a dead weight, Judd managed to get him half standing, half leaning against the wall of the hole. Then, jumping from the grave, Judd grabbed the dead man's hands and pulled, inching him up and out of the earth.

When the feet cleared the lip, Judd stopped and turned him over. His scream mixed with the next roll of thunder when he saw the gaping wound in the dead man's neck. Partially clotted, filled with mud and dirt, the neck looked as if it had a second mouth, full of earth and grinning broadly at Judd.

Recovering from the shock, Judd dropped back into the hole next to the motorcycle. It too was caked with dirt turned to mud because of the rain, but the mud was washing off in the steady downpour. He ran a hand over the tank and found a design painted on it. Patiently waiting until more rain had fallen on it, he ran his hand over it again and gasped. A Maltese cross with a skull painted in the center of the symbol held his attention as if someone had hypnotized him. The Maltese cross and the skull swam in his vision. What had the sheriff said? Someone, one of the deputies, had found a metal Maltese cross with a skull scratched into the center of it. Here was the same symbol—exactly the same—painted on the tank of a motorcycle that had been buried in the earth.

The rain continued without lessening its attack on the woods. Judd's thick brown hair slowly plastered to his skull, while wet tendrils snaked along his forehead. He had to be patient. He had to be logical. He could not afford to run off half crazy with the information that indicated a third murder had been committed in the same woods. When had the man died? The body showed some signs of decay, but how long had he been buried here in the woods? Two weeks? How much damage would the earth do to human flesh—dead human flesh—in the span of time? A forensics doctor could tell, he was certain. But there wasn't one here right now, and he wanted to get the answer if at all possible—right now.

The logic of Sheriff Kane suddenly pierced his barrier of reasoning. What had the lawman said? There was no way of telling when the track in the meadow had been made—before, during, or after Cindy's and Tami's murder. He also said the same thing applied to the metal Maltese cross found near the girls' bodies. Judd imagined that the same principle would apply here. How could they prove that the dead man and motorcycle had been dispatched before, during, or after Cindy's and Tami's deaths? Had the man died here or was he brought here?

For an instant, Judd wondered who the dead man might have been. Crawling out of the grave, he slowly approached the corpse. He felt around the man's pockets but discovered nothing except change and a ring of keys. No billfold. Nothing that would indicate who the man might have been. The police might be able to trace him through his fingerprints, if he had been fingerprinted at one time or another. Judd studied the round, full face. In death or sleep the man appeared to be nonthreatening. But what would he have been like alive? Dangerous? Judd sensed an aura of evil about the dead man. Certainly, the symbols on his jeans would attest to his having been unconventional in certain ways.

Something caught Judd's eye—something at the end of one finger on the dead man's right hand. Crouching, Judd looked closely. The nail on the man's little finger had been allowed to grow to a length of an inch and a half. Much longer than any of the other nails. The reason dawned quickly on Judd. He had read about it and seen it on TV. Some people who snorted cocaine cultivated one fingernail that was used for spooning the powder together and bringing it to the nostrils. So the only things Judd had figured out so far were that the man used drugs and was into some sort of weird religious beliefs.

A thunderclap crashed loudly over him and Judd instinctively huddled down. He was not in a good place. The storm was centering right over him now, and at any second the woods could be struck by lightning. He could be killed or severely injured. He had to get out of there as quickly as possible.

The bombardment of thunder ·continued its rolling sound but moved away in a huge circle. It would be several minutes before a charge built sufficiently strong enough to strike the earth.

"Stay here!"

The words shrieked in his skull. And at the same instant he felt the little shock of what seemed to be electricity playing in his head. He looked about, but nothing was happening. There was no lightning striking a tree. But the sensation in his head spread, down his neck, to his shoulders, branching out into his arms and body. Tingling, almost tickling him, the feeling rose and fell in uneven pulsations. What was happening to him? He tried to move but could not.

Then, making a supreme effort to walk away, he slowly keeled over where he stood, falling across the body of the dead biker.

8

Raindrops continued dripping from leaves and branches through the trees long after the downpour had ended. Thick, slimy mud lined the open pit, which had caved outward on one side. The motorcycle lay in the grave, held firmly in place by the muck while its former rider lay on the far slope of the hill, away from the exposed flank of the grave.

Judd sprawled partially across the dead man. Overhead, birds began their songs now that the rain had stopped and the fury of the storm had passed. The continuous dripping of water tapped Judd on the forehead before running down the sides of his face. His eyes opened, blinking uncomprehendingly at his surroundings.

Where was he? What had happened? What was he doing on the ground? Without moving, he looked from side to side. Trees. Brush. A face. *A face?*

Sitting up, he turned to look at the dead man lying beside him. Where had he come from?

Then the memory smashed back into his mind. Finding the freshly turned earth . . . digging . . . finding the motorcycle and rider . . . all of it came back.

Bull.

The one word dominated his thoughts for a long moment of time. What did that mean? "Bull"?

James Sterling.

Who was James Sterling? Why was Judd thinking of someone named James Sterling? He knew of no one by that name. Still, the two words ricocheted through his mind. *James Sterling.* Then, *bull,* coupled with the name, bounced back and forth in his thoughts.

Judd struggled to his feet, his shirt and jeans damply clinging to him. He felt so uncomfortable that he wanted to strip them off to wring them as dry as possible.

Accountant! Accountancy! CPA! Numbers! Figures! Balance! Red! Black! Deficit! Profit! Money! Fuck it! Ride! Bull! Lead! Bull! Bull! Bull! Bull!

Judd's eyes widened, his breath coming in short, almost painful gasps. What was happening to him? Was he going crazy? Why was he thinking all these weird things? What did *"bull"* have to do with anything? And that name. James Sterling. What could that mean? Had he ever known anyone by the name of James Sterling? He desperately tried to recall, but the more he tried, the more bewildered he became.

"Get organized!" crashed through his muddled thoughts. *"Concentrate!"*

Get organized? Concentrate? On what? Judd's eyes rolled back in his head, his mind swirling, his body rigidly standing next to the cavader and the yawning pit.

James Sterling—accountant—dropped out—gave up normal lifestyle—rode a hog—gang—leader—Bull—murdered—buried here.

The words repeated over and over until Judd opened his eyes and the words stopped. James Sterling was the dead man lying at his feet. He had been murdered. But by whom? When? Why?

"Buckshot slit my throat!" the voice said, again sounding in his head.

Judd looked about the clearing. "Hello?" Turning in a full circle, he shouted, "Where are you? I can hear you but I can't see you. I don't know where you're at? Show yourself."

"Buckshot slit my throat on Labor Day."

Judd's muscles tensed until they pained him. The same day that Cindy had been murdered. But who was saying the things he was hearing? Was he actually hearing them? Or imagining them? Was he going insane?

"Shut up and listen!" the voice growled in his head. *"I don't know what the hell is happening any more than you do. Walk off this hill."*

Without hesitating, Judd turned and half ran, half walked down the hill. When he stood at the bottom, he shuddered. He had not wanted to move. Still, he had walked off the hill as if he had had no control over his actions. What was going on?

"Okay. I can control you to a certain extent. That's good."

"I don't understand," Judd said softly, his eyes darting from one side to the other. Holding his head in both hands, Judd concentrated. What had been going on before he had passed out? Had he actually passed out? He recalled the thunder and lightning directly overhead. Had he been struck by lightning? A quick perusal of the trees surrounding him, as well as their branches overhead, showed no scarring or torn trunks. But hadn't he felt something—something like a shock right before—right before whatever happened, happened? He was positive he had. If it wasn't lighting, then what was it?

"Good question."

"Who are you?" Judd asked again, softly this time.

"James Sterling. But I've been called Bull ever since I joined the gang."

"But isn't James Sterling dead? Isn't that is body lying on top of that mound," Judd said.

"That's my body, all right. But for some strange, fucking reason, I'm still around. Still functioning. What do you think of that?"

"But if you are, why can't I see you?" Again, Judd turned in a full circle, half expecting someone to step into the clearing with a silly grin on his face.

"I—I think I'm inside you."

"Inside me?"

"Crazy, huh?"

"Yeah, I think I'm just that. Crazy!" Judd tried to understand. Things like this just didn't happen. When people died, they died. If someone could come back, why couldn't it be Cindy? Or Tami? Why this stranger? A man he never knew? Why?

"Who's Cindy and Tami?"

"My sister and her girlfriend. They were killed not too far away from here," Judd said aloud. "What the hell is wrong with me? I'm sitting here carrying on a one-sided conversation with someone I can't see and who claims he's inside me. Jesus Christ, I'm going nuts!"

Judd leaped to his feet, dashing for the wall of brush. Plunging through it, he ran headlong through the woods, away from the clearing. He had to get away.

Cindy's death had proven to be too much. He had to get away. Get away from here. Get away from Rushton. Go someplace. Rest. Maybe he'd take Peggy with him.

"Stop!"

Judd ground to a halt.

"Not bad!"

"Let me alone. Go away, whoever you are—whatever you are. I don't want anything to do with you."

"Sorry. You're stuck with me. At least for the time being. I'm not sure how any of this is supposed to work. One thing I do know. I can control your body pretty goddamn good."

"So what are you going to do?" Judd asked, fearful of what the answer would be.

"I don't know yet. One thing I do know is I'd like to get even with that sonofabitch, Buckshot."

"Who?"

"The bastard who did me in."

"Oh," was the only word Judd managed before his mind was inundated with thoughts of fighting and of swinging something. What? Concentrating, he came to the conclusion that it was a chain of some sort. He felt a pain in his leg as his adversary's weapon struck him around the calf. Lashing out, he felt his own chain connect with something and thought he heard a scream of pain. Then his wrist ballooned with a sharp feeling—as if it had been sliced by a knife or some such weapon. His eyes bugged out when he looked at his wrist. Nothing. No mark of any sort. But the pain was unbearable. When he rubbed his wrist, the feeling came back quickly, but he thought he no longer held the chain.

Suddenly he felt his arms around something, squeezing. His head spun as if he were losing his balance and falling. The sensation of rolling about spiraled through his head, upsetting his sense of equilibrium. Although he had not moved from the spot where he had stood when the voice had ordered him to stop, he felt as if he were actually in a fight.

Then he felt the same soreness in his throat that he had felt several different times before—the thin line of pain across his windpipe.

All sensations drained out of him and his shoulders slumped.

"That's the way it was. Exactly the way I remember it," the voice said.

"But I've felt that pain before now. How do you explain that?"

"How the fuck should I know?"

"Were you calling me?"

"I don't know if I was calling you in particular. But, yeah, I think I was calling to somebody. Why? D'you hear me?"

"Yeah," Judd said slowly. Apparently the entity or spirit, or whatever it was with whom he was conversing, couldn't see into his mind, even though he could control his physical movements.

"*Wrong,*" the voice said. "*I can if I make the effort. Don't try to get cute with me. Understand?*"

Judd's thoughts spun and were suddenly dominated by the words *cow, ratface, blaster,* and strange names—*Mary Queen of Sots, Sweet Rosie O'Lay, Priscilla Puss, Gordo, Mule, Snake,* and other strange words and combinations that made no sense to him. What did they mean?

"*Gang members. Members of the Light Bearer's Chosen—my gang.*"

Judd turned, as if commanded by someone, to walk back to the clearing wherein the body of Bull lay. What would happen to him? He had to do something.

"*You don't gotta do nothin',*" the voice growled in his head. "*I ain't any fucking happier about this than you are. But we're stuck together, and that's that as far as I'm concerned. I ain't got no idea as to how long this'll last but don't fight me' cause I'll win every time.*"

"What—what are you going to do?" Judd asked, his voice trembling. What would happen to him? What would happen to his relationship with Peggy?

"*Don't worry about none of that shit,*" the voice said. "*I'll behave whenever you're around somebody else. But, you know, I'm hatching an idea.*"

"An idea?" Judd wondered if he really wanted to know what it might be.

"*Yeah. I'd like another crack at that asshole, Buckshot, but I'm dead. Right?*"

Judd said nothing, concentrating on Bull's thoughts instead.

"*You got a body. And I can control it. So I'll use your body to get back at that sonofabitch.*"

"What? Are you crazy?" Judd couldn't believe what the spirit was suggesting.

"*Sure. Why not?*"

"Because, you'll get me killed as well. That's about the dumbest thing I've ever heard."

"*I thought you felt bad about your sister getting herself killed.*"

"I do. But what has that got to do with it?"

"*Do you have any idea as to who did her and the other chick in?*"

"No. Do you?"

"*I think I might have. It would be just like Buckshot to do something that stupid.*"

"Stupid? What would you have done with them?"

"*That part of it's coming back to me. See, I was the one who caught Cindy Little-Tits and Tami. All I wanted to do was fuck 'em. Young stuff like that is good for a change when you're used to having older women. Cow, my woman, is about thirty or so. Nice tits and she's still pretty tight.*"

You know what I mean? But the thrill of fucking her is—er—was gone. A young one like your sister does wonders for the ego and the constitution."

Judd's vision blacked out. A rage like nothing he had ever experienced before in his life filled his every pore, flowing through him like molten lava from an erupting volcano. The sonofabitch. The dirty bastard. This Bull—this James Sterling—this fucking dropout from society, had planned on raping his sister and Tami. How could he get even?

He pushed his way through the brush surrounding the clearing. The first thing he saw was Bull's body. Mutilate it? Cut it to pieces? The dirty bastard's carcass didn't deserve to exist in one piece.

"Hey, hold it."

"Hold it? You tell me you were only going to rape my sister and not hurt her. Do you expect me to accept that and not be angry? I care more than that, you asshole."

"I didn't mean to tell you that. In fact, I don't think I did tell you that."

"If you didn't, then who did? I don't see anybody else around here. In fact, I don't see you either. I'm starting to wonder if you exist or aren't maybe just a figment of my imagination."

"You know what I think happened? You were able to tap into my mind."

"You said it."

"I didn't say anything. Don't you see? I merely think, and you know what it is. You don't have to talk to me, either. I can 'hear' in a way, whatever it is you think."

Judd didn't know if he could accept the wild theory. Or anything else that had happened since he had awakened. Were such things possible? A spirit invading someone's body and the two being able to converse as if it were the most ordinary of situations? Could that actually happen?

"It has." The words formed in his mind.

What was the next step? What would they do next? They? He and James Sterling who liked to be called Bull by the members of his bike gang.

"Look," the thoughts formed in Judd's mind, *"you'd like to see your sister's killer taken care of, wouldn't you?"*

"If you mean brought to justice, of course I would," Judd said aloud.

"And I want revenge as well. Right?"

"I suppose so."

"I think Buckshot killed your sister. How'd she die?"

Judd felt tears forming until they spilled over onto his cheeks. "She—she—her—her throat was cut. So was Tami's."

"Same way I was cashed in. Buckshot was always threatening somebody with his switchblade. I don't think he ever killed anyone before, but he sure made up for lost time. I guess he killed me because he

knew I'd eventually get him if he didn't.''

"So what are you saying?"

"Nothing. But I'm thinking a whole lot. Buckshot and the gang think I'm dead. Apparently my body is, but I'm not. They don't know you, and you could walk right up to Buckshot and cut the bastard's balls off and hand 'em to him.''

"And I wind up going to jail or getting a lethal shot of something to pay for 'my' crime against society. Thanks but no thanks.''

"I don't think so. First of all, you ain't got a choice. If I say we do it—we do it. But the gang is beyond the law. They wouldn't report it. They'd just bury Buckshot, like they did me, and let it go at that. If you wanted to be the new leader, you could. I'll tell you this, between the two of us we'd show 'em who the boss was.''

Judd thought of the plan, its consequences, the end result as outlined by Bull. "I'll help you find him, but then we call the cops. All right?"

There was a long pause. Then, "If you say so.''

Judd wanted to leave but found himself unable to move.

"I want my clothes.''

"Wh—what?''

"I want my hog too.''

"Your hog?''

"My wheels. My bike. My Harley. Get it out of the hole.''

"I can't lift that by myself."

"You don't have to lift it. The side's washed out. Push it out."

Judd turned, studying the bike. It would be no problem pushing it out of the three-sided grave, now that the one wall had fallen outward. "The clothes, too?"

"You got it." The words ground into Judd's consciousness.

When he stood next to the motorcycle, Judd felt a twinge of familiarity course through him—as if he had found an old friend or discovered something he had lost a long time before. The front fork turned easily enough, and he wheeled the bike out of the hole. After he had parked it next to a tree, he returned to the body of James Sterling. The vest proved no problem and slipped off. For an instant, Judd studied the metal Maltese crosses dangling from each side. He shuddered when he thought of Cindy and the fact that one of the same sort of medals had been found between her and Tami.

"Get on with it."

Judd loosened the wide belt and unbuttoned the jeans. Grabbing the pants legs at the bottom, he pulled, stripping the body that lay naked except for the boots. He examined the esoteric symbols more closely now that he held the pants in his hands.

"Six-six-six," he mumbled.

"The mark of the devil—the beast. We

worship him."

Judd said nothing, as if waiting for more explanation.

"Cow was the one who got me and the gang interested. She was raised as a worshiper of Satan and Lucifer. We've performed rites, and once even we managed to conjure up something. I don't know what the fuck it was, but it sure convinced the ones who were hanging back. After that our luck changed and everything seemed to come our way. According to Cow, we were supposed to perform this rite of blood and worship every so often. I don't remember everything. I sorta let her take care of that stuff."

Judd rolled the pants and vest together, cramming them into the saddlebags on the back of the motorcycle.

"Get on."

"I—I've never ridden one before."

"Don't worry. I'll take care of everything."

Judd threw one leg over the bike and wiggled about, looking for a comfortable position. When he found it, he sighed involuntarily. Why did he feel so relaxed and right sitting on the bike? He turned the ignition key and kicked the starter pedal. The machine coughed once. He kicked the pedal again, turning the accelerator handle at the same time. The engine caught, roaring to life.

Without hesitating, Judd pushed off

and the bike careened through the clearing, toward the spot where he had left the truck. Crashing through the undergrowth wall, he blasted through the trees, dodging them as expertly as if he had been riding a bike for a long time. But when he thought of it, he had been, in a way.

When he reached the truck, he stopped, turning off the motor. Ater he got off, he dropped the tail gate of the truck bed and, without hesitating, lifted the front end of the bike. Once the front wheel was on the truck bed, he walked around to the back of the bike, lifted the rear, and pushed the bike onto the truck. After it was lying on one side, he closed the gate.

Then he returned to the mound and tugged the dead man into the grave. While he reburied the large body, he pondered his feat of strength. How had he been able to lift that motorcycle? He wasn't capable of doing something like that. When he finished, he returned to the truck. He dug the little finger of his right hand into his ear, satisfying an urge to scratch. Withdrawing it, he flicked away the wax that clung to it and moved to the driver's side of the cab.

Easing his way along the tree-lined muddy road, Judd smiled grimly. To hell with law. To hell with the sheriff. He had a way to extract his pound of flesh for Cindy's loss. He *would* have his revenqe.

PART 3

The Light Bearer's Chosen

9

Judd swung the truck around, backing it up to the double door of the storage room behind the hardware store. He wanted to unload the motorcycle and keep it at the store where he would have access to a full array of tools. It seemed to him the machine would have to be overhauled to make certain that the time it spent in the ground had not harmed it any more than having made it dirty. There hadn't been much of an argument or discussion over the idea. Bull had simply taken over, planting the idea firmly in Judd's mind, and that seemed to be it.

While driving into town, Judd had reasoned that he knew nothing about motors or engines and that motorcycles at best were a mystery to him. Bull had quickly countered with the fact that it would be Bull's intellect, experience, and knowledge that would actually do the work, using Judd's hands as extensions of his own.

The door opened. Mickey Higgins stood in the entrance to the storeroom, his jaw dropping when he saw the Harley-Davidson. Judd had inherited Mickey along with the store when he assumed control. Mickey, a tall, thin, gangly man in his forties, was as honest and loyal an employee as Judd could ever have hoped for. In addition, he had found Mickey's qualifications and abilities to be most effectual when he had taken off so much time following Cindy's brutal death.

Judd satisfied his employee's perfunctory questions of where and how and why and what with thiny veiled lies. When Judd told Mickey to back off when he unloaded the machine, the man's angular face twisted in astonishment.

"You can't unload that thing by yourself, Judd," Mickey insisted. "Hellsfire! It must weigh seven, eight hundred pounds."

Judd grunted derisively and opened the tailgate of the Toyota.

"You're gonna rupture yourself or have the damned thing fall on you and bust you all up. Neither one is very nice."

Judd jumped into the truck and lifted

the machine to its wheels.

"Don't say I didn't warn you." Mickey stepped back, shaking his head.

Judd slowly lowered the back end of the bike to the floor of the garagelike storeroom. Leaping from the truck bed, he brought the front end down, letting it bounce several times.

"You look like you know exactly what you're doing, you know that, Judd?"

"Exactly, Mickey." The words were terse, almost unfriendly in the tone Judd used.

"But when in the hell did you learn about motorcycles and such? I never ever once saw you on one and—"

"Look, Mickey," Judd said patiently, "I don't want you hanging around, asking all sorts of fool questions and getting in my way. I want you to run the store while I get this hog back into shape. I'm going to totally rebuild the engine, clean and repaint the frame, and in general make a new bike of it. Understand? You're going to be in the store. Not out here, bugging me." Judd stared at him, waiting for an answer.

"Sure, Judd. Christ, I didn't mean to sound like a little kid, asking questions and bothering you 'n all. It's just that it's a little out of the ordinary to see a guy who's never expressed much interest in something—God, all of a sudden showing the know-how about unloading a motorcycle it should take at least two men to unload and making big statements about mechanical work like you know all about it."

"I do." Judd stared at him until Mickey turned away, hoping the discussion had come to an end.

Mickey dropped his eyes and turned toward the door that led to the store. "Okay, Boss. I'll run the store and you play mechanic. Who knows, maybe we'll wind up opening a motorcycle equipment and repair shop. Right?"

"Right, Mickey." Judd grinned magnanimously.

Mickey bounced up the two steps to the rear entrance and was gone.

Judd closed the double doors and stepped back to admire the bike.

Mickey ran a hand over his long, thin face. How could a guy as average in build as Judd Wellington have unloaded that bike by himself? Sure, he had not had to do much lifting, but the machine had to weigh a hell of a lot more than it appeared. At least seven or eight hundred pounds. And Judd had lowered it to the ground in a slow, deliberate way that indicated a lot of muscle power was handling the bike. Maybe he was imagining things.

The door opened and his face broke

into a wide grin. "Hi, Peggy. How you doing?"

"Hello, Mickey. Is Judd around?"

"He's in the back. He just got here."

"Thank you." Her heels clicking on the terrazzo floor, she walked to the back of the store. Just as she reached for the knob, the door opened and Judd stepped into the store. Startled, she jumped back before he ran into her.

"Hi, Peggy," he said, brushing by her.

"Well!" she managed in a surprised way. "Don't let me get in your way."

"Huh? Oh, I'm sorry. I—"

"You going to be around for a while, Judd?" Mickey coughed after asking the question, wondering if he had spoken at the wrong time.

"Why?" Judd turned to face his employee.

"I've got a few stops to make before I go home and I thought if you were going to be here, I could take off and get my running around done."

"Sure, go ahead, Mickey."

"Thanks." He turned, striding toward the front of the store. "See you tomorrow."

The door closed behind him and he made his way down the street. There was something a little different about Judd, but what it might have been, Mickey had no idea. It seemed to be more of an attitude than anything he could put his finger on in a physical way. And yet, he seemed to appear a little different as well.

Hurrying along the sidewalk, Mickey turned off Main Street four blocks from the hardware store and walked another block to a service station on the corner of Locust and Eleventh Street.

"Hey, Ed? You here?" he called when he stood in the entrance to one of the two repair bays.

"Sure. Oh, hi, Mickey. What's up?"

"How much does a Harley-Davidson motorcycle weigh?"

"What model?"

"An eighty, I think. Big sucker."

"That's the biggest one they build. I'd say between eight seventy-five and nine hundred pounds. Why?"

Mickey's face went slack. How could Judd have handled that much weight without so much as showing a strain on his face? He turned and walked away, lost in his confused thoughts.

Peggy studied Judd, who sat behind the desk in the open office, which was centered in the store. Why did he look different? She had sensed, more than perceived, whatever the change was when she had first seen him, exploding through the back door, almost knocking her down. Then, after Mickey had left, she thought she actually saw some little change in him. But what? She thought it was more like trying to see something in darkness. Staring straight at the object she wanted to see rendered nothing but more shadows. By looking to one side, her peripheral vision would take over and she could make out more of the thing she wanted to see. She tried that now, looking to one side of Judd hunching over a catalog from some hardware supply company. What was different about him?

His hair. That was it. What was wrong with it? Something. The waves! His straight black hair had suddenly developed waves. A smile crossed her mouth. Just as she was about to ask him about his hair, he brought his little finger up to his right ear and dug viciously.

When he flicked away the wax he had extracted, she said, "Oh, yuck!"

The word carried an air of wonderment as he looked up, a startled expression on his face as though he had forgotten she was there. "What did you say, Peggy?"

"If you've got that much wax in your ear, you'd best go see a doctor and have him flush it out. Don't go jabbing things into your—" She stopped. His fingernail. When had he allowed it to grow that long? From her position without moving closer to him, she examined the rest of his nails. They all seemed the same length except for the little fingernail on his right hand, and that appeared to be almost an inch and a half in length. Why would he let one fingernail grow so long? To dig in his ear for bothersome wax?

"What are you talking about? My ears are fine. I don't have any wax problem. What made you say something like that?"

She shook her head. "What about your fingernail? Why have you let it grow so long?"

"What the hell are you talking about?" He brought both hands to his front, holding them in half-clenched fists, to look at his nails.

The look on his face told Peggy something was wrong. It was as if he hadn't known that one nail was considerably longer than the rest. "Well?"

"I—I—I've decided to let one grow," he stammered. "That's all. My one ear is driving me crazy."

"But I thought you said your ears were fine."

"They have been. But lately, one is really bothering me." When he looked at her, he continued. "There's nothing wrong about that, is there?" He turned his hand to different angles as if admiring the extra-long nail.

"There's nothing wrong about it at all. I'm just surprised. I've never noticed it before now. 'S funny how something like that can escape one's attention, isn't it?"

He nodded.

"What about your hair?"

Judd stood, crossed the few feet separating them, and looked closely at Peggy, his dark eyes flashing in the neon light from the fixtures overhead. "What's wrong with my hair?"

"It's wavy."

"It's what?"

"Wavy." Her voice sounded tiny, fractured, actually frightened.

Judd laughed. "Of course it is. I was caught in the rainstorm this afternoon. Got soaked. My hair'll be fine. What's your trouble this afternoon?"

"Trouble?"

"Well, you've complained about my nail. Now, my hair. What's going to be next?"

His voice sounded forced to Peggy. It seemed he was trying to be lighthearted. "I—I'm sorry, Judd. I found it strange that I hadn't noticed the length of your fingernail and your hair—well, I've never seen it that wavy before. Forgive me?"

"For what?"

"For being strange." She looked up into his face, smiling, her own complexion more rosy than it usually appeared.

Bending, he kissed her lightly on the mouth. "Don't worry about it. No problem. How much time do you have before you have to be at the retirement home?"

Glancing at her watch, she said, "About half an hour. I'll have to get moving pretty soon. Why?"

"I want to show you something." He took her hand, leading her to the back of the store. After opening the door, he turned on the light and made a sweeping gesture with one hand. "Ta-da! What do you think of that?"

Peggy stepped around him, her eyes widening when she saw the motorcycle, caked with drying mud, standing in the center of the open floor. "What's that?"

"A motorcycle. Or as that one guy on the radio says, 'a *motorsickle.*' A bike. A—a—a hog!"

"A *hog*?"

"That's what some bikers call their Harley-Davidsons. A hog. What do you think?"

Peggy stared. What did he mean, what did she think? "I—I don't understand."

"It's mine. I found it."

"Found it? Where?" She looked suspiciously at him.

"In the woods."

"What woods?"

"Out by Morrison's Creek."

"Out by Morr—" Peggy stopped. What had Judd been doing out there? She voiced her question.

"I—I don't know, really," he began, his face clouding as he turned away. "It seemed as though something made me go out there. I guess I wanted to look around."

"Look around? Isn't that a bit on the morbid side?"

"I wanted to see if the sheriff's department had missed anything when they searched the area."

"And you found a motorcycle?"

"Not there. Not where—where—"

Peggy reached out, laying one hand on his. "You don't have to explain, Judd." She pulled back. His hand felt icy cold.

"I must. I feel I've got to explain everything to you, Peggy. Something seemed to draw me away from the place where—where—. Anyway, I found another clearing, quite a distance away, and there was this little mound in the center of it. The top of it looked like it had been dug up recently. I went back to the truck to get a shovel, and started digging. I found this." He motioned toward the bike.

"You'd better tell the police."

"Uh-uh! It's mine. I found it. If somebody took the time to bury it, they didn't want it very badly. So its mine."

"What are you going to do with it?"

"Restore it. Ride it."

Peggy laughed. A forced, sardonic laugh. "You don't know anything about motorcycles. Do you?"

When Judd didn't answer, she turned away, a shiver of fright running down her back. His face told her he knew everything about motorcycles, but when had he learned? She had known him for seven, almost eight years. Not once in that time had he ever mentioned the fact. Still, she realized that Judd Wellington suddenly knew everything there was to know about motorcycles.

Peggy stepped down to the floor of the storeroom, moving closer to the machine.

"Gee, you'd better get going, Peggy," Judd said evenly, his words dispassionately separated. "You'll be late for work."

"I just want to look at it more closely."

"Another time. It's really getting late." A sense of urgency clung to each word.

Peggy looked up at Judd. His face was calm, but the voice told her differently. He wanted her to leave. He didn't want her close to the bike. Why? Why, for heaven's sake?

"Come on, Peggy. Do you want me to drop you off? The store will be closing in another few minutes. Since I'm the boss, I can close it a little early."

"I'd rather walk. The exercise'll do me good." She climbed the two steps and stood next to him. "Kiss me."

He took her in his arms, kissing her gently before ramming his tongue into her mouth.

When they broke, she stepped back and entered the store. It was Judd's kiss, and yet it seemed to be somehow different. What could be wrong? Could his actions be a delayed reaction to Cindy's death? A shudder ran through her.

Reaching the front door of the store, she turned. "See you later, Judd."

" 'Bye, Peg-o-my-heart," he said lightly.

Peggy stepped through the door into the late fall afternoon. It was Judd saying good-bye, of that she had no doubt. She only hoped she would always be his heart's Peg.

During the next ten days, Judd immersed himself in dismantling, repairing, rebuilding, and reassembling the Harley-Davidson. On occasion, Mickey would come into the storeroom on the pretense of getting stock or some other excuse and would stand around until Judd asked him to leave and get back to the store. When he did stand around, he would praise Judd for his knowledge and question him as to why he had kept such abilities hidden. Judd would insist there was nothing to it and would continue working.

Judd, finished with the engine, turned his attention to the frame and tank. With paint remover he obtained from his store, he stripped the motorcycle to the bare metal and repainted it a lustrous black—the same color it had been. Three days after it was dry, he began painting the silver Maltese cross that had graced the original. When he finished, he stood back and admired his artwork. After finishing the skull in a bone-white, he went back to the black paint and finished the details of eye sockets, teeth, high-lights, and cheekbones. Once the cross and skull were complete, he went into the store and got an even finer brush than he had used for the black details. Carefully painting with black, he added the number "666" to each arm of the cross.

A puzzled expression crossed Judd's face, and he fished in his pocket for the crosses that had been pinned to the leather vest he had taken from the body of James Sterling. Tiny numbers, which he had overlooked before, were on each arm. He trembled like someone afflicted with a high fever when he thought of the dead man. When he had told Peggy how he found the bike, he had conveniently left out the part about finding a dead man astride the machine. That omission had been Bull's doing, he was certain. But Bull had been spending his own energies on the bike, and the conversations between host and guest had been sparse at best. Judd had found it peculiar to watch his hands working at something that was completely foreign to him. Still, he had marveled at the ease with which the machine was torn down and rebuilt until it sat in the middle of the storeroom, gleaming like some untamed wild stallion.

"*Hog!*" The word slammed into his consciousness.

"Hog!" he muttered half aloud.

"*Goddammit, call it by the right name, Judd!*"

"Right. How did I do? Is it all right?"

"*How did YOU do? Jesus Christ! You asshole! Do you think you did all of this? Without me running the show and controlling your hands, you'd have fucked it up royally.*"

"*I* wouldn't have done it at all."

"*Don't get feisty on me!*"

Judd wondered about his own temperament. How could he talk to this spirit—this strange entity—in this way? If Bull was alive, Judd would be intimidated to the point of being totally ineffectual.

"*You're right. But I need you, Judd. So, I let you get away with a couple of snotty, smart-ass remarks and thoughts now and then. Just don't get in the fuckin' habit.*"

"I'll do and say what I want to," Judd said aloud, picking up the canvas he used to cover the bike when he wasn't working on it. Flaring it out, he let it settle over the bike.

"What did you say?" The voice came from behind him.

Judd whirled around to face Peggy who stood in the open doorway. "I didn't hear you come in. How are you?"

"I'm fine. The important question is, how are *you*? I haven't heard from you in the last week and a half. Ever since you came home with that motorcycle." She nodded toward the shrouded bike.

"Hey, come on. It's all finished except for a wax job, and that'll be taken care of in the next day or two."

"Are you going to start paying attention to me a little bit then?"

Judd stepped away from the bike toward the steps. He looked up at her. "I'm sorry. I really am. I've treated you like—I don't know what the last few days. I'm sorry. But now it's finished and things will get back to normal. I hope."

"You hope?"

Judd turned away. He shouldn't have qualified the statement. Not with an element of doubt. He couldn't allow Peggy to wonder about their future together. All he had to do was finish with Bull and the spirit would leave him and things would be normal once more.

"What do you mean, Judd?"

Ignoring her question, he reached out, taking her hand. "Come on, let me show you my masterpiece." In his head, he heard a digusted, *"Hah!"*

Peggy came down the two steps and followed him to the covered motorcycle.

Judd pulled the canvas off with a flourish and stepped back. "Well?"

Peggy's eyes widened at the sinister beauty of the bike, and then she gasped when she saw the Maltese cross on the tank. Pointing to it, she whispered, "Why? Why that, Judd?"

"Why what?"

"Why the symbol of the medal found next to Cindy and Tami? Are you crazy? Insane? That's the most sick, perverted thing I've ever seen. How could you?" She felt tears forming but forced them back to oblivion.

"Hey, wait a minute. How did you find out about the medal?"

"If you weren't so busy playing mechanic and took time to read the newspaper once in a while, you'd realize that the sheriff told about it in an interview that was in the paper and on TV." Her eyes widened. "If you didn't hear about it or read about it, how did you know?" She stared at Judd, waiting for his answer.

"The sheriff told me a couple of weeks ago but made me promise not to tell anyone. Besides, the symbol was on the tank and—"

"What? Judd, you're concealing evidence. You know that, don't you? If that cross was on the tank and a medal like it was found next to Cindy and Tami, there has to be a connection of some sort. You can't hold that back from the sheriff." She reached out, touching Judd's hand. It was cold. What was wrong with him? Was he going out of his mind? He couldn't expect to keep something like the motorcycle a secret very long if he ever rode it around and someone saw it. Especially the decoration on the tank.

"Are you going to tell him, Peggy?"

Pursing her lips, she said, "No. I love you too much to see you wind up being arrested for being an accessory before or after the fact."

"You sound like a lawyer."

"I work for one, remember!"

He smiled and she relaxed a bit.

"What are you going to do, Judd?"

He reached into his jeans' pocket and pulled out the two crosses. "Here." He thrust them into her hand.

Dropping her attention to her palm, she felt light-headed when she realized what she was holding. "Where—where did you get these?"

Judd studied her for a long minute before answering. "He was wearing them," he managed.

"He? Who's he?"

"The dead guy who was on the bike—er—hog!"

She let the change in terminology slip by. "What dead guy? What are you talking about?"

He told her about the grave and how he found the body, holding back the information as to his identity and the strange occurrence that took place during the rainstorm.

"Judd, you're crazy if you think you can get away without reporting this to the police or the sheriff. What are you thinking? That since they killed Cindy it's all right for you to keep the motorcycle? You have to report this!"

"I don't gotta do nothin'," Judd growled.

Peggy fell back, startled by the tone of voice he had used and his sudden use of poor grammar.

"Are you promoting the very devils who apparently raped and killed your own sister?"

Judd felt the tension of Bull's presence leaving and he relaxed. He wouldn't be able to tell Peggy about Bull without her wanting to commit him to the state institution at Fort Lee. But he would have to tell her something. Why not some of the truth?

"What I'm planning on doing is

drawing out the killers. The cops and the sheriff's department haven't done anything to speak of as far as solving the murders."

"And you think you can?"

"Let's face it, I've got a better chance of attracting some attention with this motorcycle—er—hog—than the cops with their channels and regulations."

"Why do you keep referring to the bike as a 'hog'?"

"No reason. I think people who ride Harley-Davidsons call them that."

"I don't like any of this, Judd. You're not capable of taking care of yourself if someone would confront you, wanting to know what the reason is you're riding that thing—and with that Maltese cross on it. I'm really frightened for your safety." She watched him closely, wondering what he was thinking.

"Don't worry about me. I'll be all right. I've got something going for me that you don't know about."

"What?"

"Forget it. I won't tell you now. I will someday. But not now."

Peggy swallowed, forcing the lump she felt forming back to wherever it had come from. "If you're going to start playing guessing games and keeping secrets like a little school kid, you can do it without me."

She turned on her heel, storming toward the store door. Opening it, she slammed it hard and marched through the hardware displays.

Mickey, sitting at the desk, looked up. "Hey, wait a minute, Peggy. What's eating you?"

She stopped and turned, staring belligerently at the clerk. Mickey smiled kindly in his understanding way, and she lost her facade of anger. Why take it out on Mickey? She wasn't even angry with Judd. Just upset.

Mickey stepped out of the desk area and approached her. "Want to tell me about it?"

"Not really. It's just his fascination with that damnable bike."

"I know," he said softly. "Judd's sorta changed ever since his sister was done in the way she was. And that motorcycle hasn't helped any either, has it?"

Peggy shook her head.

"You should have seen him when he brought it in that day. Wow. I never once suspected that Judd was that strong."

"Strong? How do you mean?" Peggy looked up into Mickey's angular face, waiting for an explanation.

"He unloaded that damned thing by himself. He did. Just like he knew how to handle it and like it was nothing."

Peggy stared at him but remained

silent. Something was wrong someplace. Judd handled that heavy bike as if it weighed nothing, according to Mickey. His hair suddenly turned wavy. Sure, he had said, it was caused by being caught in the rain. But that was ten days ago and the waves were still there. And that fingernail on his right hand. What did that mean? Did it have to mean anything? It seemed it should, since he had never worn his nails much over the tips of his fingers. Then, all of a sudden, his little fingernail shot out to an inch and a half and he claimed that it'd been like that for some time. Something was wrong—something was crazy—but what?

If Judd was undergoing some changes, she wanted an explanation. There had been the subtle changes in his appearance, and he was acting differently from anything he'd ever done in the past. She also thought he was gaining weight. But with clothing on she couldn't really tell. And she hadn't seen him without clothes since he found the motorcycle. It always seemed to come back to that damned machine. Did the motorcycle have something to do with the way Judd was changing and acting? That seemed silly.

Worrying about it would solve nothing. She didn't want to develop a habit of procrastinating, which seemed the next logical step after worry. She smiled at Mickey. "Thanks, Mickey. I think I'd better go back in and make up with him. I'm glad you stopped me. If you hadn't, I probably would have done something about our relationship that would have made both Judd and me very unhappy."

She turned around to go back to the storeroom. She found Judd crouched alongside the motorcycle.

"Hi," she said softly.

He looked up.

"I have to work until seven tonight at the home, once I leave Allan's office. I'll make a casserole. Something quick. And we can have a relaxing time together. You're finished with the bike. You need the time off."

Judd stood. Bull was back. He glowered at Peggy. "I'm going to go for a ride on my hog! If I get hungry, I'll stop someplace and eat. Look, I know what you got in mind, Peggy. After I test out the hog to my satisfaction, I'll come over and fuck your brains out. Fair enough?"

Peggy stared at him. He had never— ever—used such language in her presence. What was wrong with him? She felt tears forming and could do nothing about it. They ran down her cheeks, but she didn't cry or sob. The shock was too great to allow such a mundane reaction.

She'd do that later. Once she got over her initial hurt.

Judd opened the doors of the alley and mounted the Harley-Davidson. He kicked the starter and the engine bellowed to life. Revving it up once or twice, he turned to look at her, a smile twisting his lips.

"You don't know how to ride," she screamed over the din of the bike's throaty roar.

Judd didn't say anything but continued smiling.

"Don't go, Judd. I think it's important that you stay. We've got to talk."

Without a word, he pushed off and the motorcycle swept around the corner of the door, into the alley and away from the building. He was gone.

Peggy, tears streaming down her face, stared at the yawning emptiness of the alley through the double doors. Something was wrong with Judd. Something dreadful.

10

Judd blasted out of the alley onto the side street that would take him to the highway. A Subaru slammed on its brakes to avoid broadsiding the motorcycle and rider. The driver shook his fist, screaming at Judd. Judd raised a fist, his middle finger pointing to the skies in response, and, laughing, roared down the street.

"God damn you any way He can, Bull," Judd said, forcing the words through the rush of air washing over him.

"What the fuck did I do?"

"You didn't have to say what you said to Peggy. That was awful. I never have spoken to her like that."

"You have now."

Judd bit his tongue. He didn't want to hurt Peggy. He loved her. He'd better go back and apologize. Trying to slow the bike, he tried to turn the handlebars. Nothing. No response. No response to his brain's orders. He was positive the machine would have obeyed if he had been able to control his own body. But he suddenly found he couldn't do anything. Bull was in charge.

"You bet your sweet ass I am, Judd!"

"I want to go back and apologize to her for what you said, Bull."

"Uh-uh. We're going for a shakedown ride. Make sure this baby is running smooth and right. Got it?"

"I *have* to apologize to her. She'll never speak to me again."

"Yes, she will. Christ, don't you know anything about women? Shit! They like to be talked to like that. Dirty words turn them on. You do fuck her, don't you?"

Judd didn't answer. It was none of Bull's business.

"Of course, I know you do. Don't forget, I can go right into your mind and find out just about anything I want to know."

"Then," Judd said aloud, "I guess I'd better not go around Peggy any more—at least until you decide to leave."

"She'll come around to you, Judd. Shit. She's horny for you. You haven't been performing lately, have you?"

"You know what I've been doing,"

Judd said, applying the brakes slightly to turn onto the highway without stopping at the stop sign. He twisted the accelerator and the motorcycle flashed ahead in a burst of speed.

"Tell you what," Bull's voice said confidentially, *"we'll go for a ride in the country and then go over to Peggy's. Fucking her brains out might not be such a bad idea. I haven't blown my nuts for a long time."*

"Forget it, Bull," Judd snapped. "Peggy's off limits to you. Do you understand?"

"Yeah, yeah. Besides, gaining revenge on that motherfucker Buckshot is more important than fucking some twat."

"Peggy's no *twat*," Judd said, mouthing the word that was strangely foreign to his mouth.

"What is she then, all mouth?" Bull's laughter ground into Judd's mind.

"Forget it, goddammit."

"Temper, temper. Sit back and enjoy the ride. You've never experienced anything until you've ridden a bike at a hundred. Relax."

Without an effort on the part of his conscious mind, Judd's hand opened the accelerator farther. He stared at the speedometer. Eighty. His face reacted to the increase in air stingingly washing over it. But it felt exhilarating.

Eighty-five. Judd's eyes widened as he watched the gravel shoulder of the road zip past his peripheral vision in a blur, like an unbroken sienna walkway. It was too fast. Surely Bull didn't want to push the machine to a hundred miles an hour.

Ninety. Judd tried to open his mouth to yell but found he couldn't because of the slipstream blasting into his face.

Ninety-five. He'd be killed. Judd would be killed and Bull's spirit released from him. But that would be counterproductive. If he were killed, everything would be lost. But at least he'd be rid of Bull. Or would he? Would the two of them be doomed to roam the earth bound together forever? That, he didn't even want to think about. The idea that Bull would quit Judd's body and spirit once he gained his revenge was the only thing that kept Judd's mental balance in place. There was hope that Bull would one day be gone and Judd's life would be normal once more.

One hundred miles an hour. The bike seemed to fly over the tar expansion joints in the concrete road. Judd could barely feel the quick staccato of bumps as the motorcycle sped down the road, practically airborne.

The one thing Judd could not deny was the sense of freedom—of elation—of sheer joy that pumped through his body like an overreaction to adrenaline. God! It was fantastic. He smiled and forced his mouth open to voice a cry of wild ecstasy. He felt as if he were drunk—absolutely intoxicated but with a feeling of sweeping independence—a sensation he had never before experienced.

"Ain't that fucking great?"

Judd couldn't speak, the air pushed the words back into his throat, but he mentally agreed. Even though the bike might sail out of control any second because of some slight error in judgment or some unseen rock or obstacle on the roadway—ignoring the fact that if such a thing did happen, it would take quite a while to pick up the remains of Judd Wellington—Judd recognized the high rush of excitement and savored it.

Then Peggy's face surfaced in his mind and he blinked. She was still crying. Why? Was he imagining her reaction if something did happen to him? Or— She had been crying when he left the store room. Because of what Bull had said. Did Bull treat his own woman like that?

"Fucking-A right!"

"Why? Don't you love them or her? Wait a minute," Judd said, picking up Bull's thoughts. There was a woman. He envisioned an attractive woman who had large breasts whose nipples were pierced with gold rings and who wore no top—only a vest like the one he had taken from Bull's body. When he concentrated on the woman—Cow—Marcie Enright—that was her correct name—he saw a beautiful woman but one who had been raised in—in—a witch's coven? Cow was a witch. And she had taught Bull and the others about witchcraft and had introduced devil worship as well. Judd sensed that the two did not go together and that Cow was careful to avoid mixing the two for fear of the consequences. They worshiped the devil more than they practiced witchcraft because of the more devious results that the former gained for them. And Bull really loved this woman—even though he treated her like a chattel—a piece of property—like his bike.

"Hog! I like my hog better than I ever liked Cow."

"That's not the way I see it in your mind, Bull," Judd said as the motorcycle slowed to sixty miles per hour."

"Fuck you! Stay out of my mind!"

"Deal! You stay out of mine, too!"

The emotions aroused by his intruding perusal of Bull's mind brought the vision of Cow back to Judd. It intermixed with that of Peggy, and the feelings for Cow from Bull and his own love of Peggy wove together into a tapestry of lust and love, disdain and affection, manipulation and enjoyment. Judd swallowed.

Such an intermingling of emotions would, if he allowed them to, envelop him and devour his own personality until he would be more the way he imagined Bull had been in life than he would be like himself. And that, he didn't want. Somehow, he would have to get rid of Bull or pay an awful price—the price of his own personality and existence as Judd Wellington. What would he become if he didn't get rid of Bull? A shudder ran through him when he pictured a husk of himself, sitting in a chair, staring into space—unable to move—incapable of communicating—simply existing as—as—nothing.

Still, a certain degree of compassion overrode the sense of fear that he felt for his own well-being. A feeling of sorrow for Bull and the manner in which he had looked at life swept through him. The man had been successful and, for no reason other than boredom with his own profession as an accountant, had turned his back on society and had become a renegade—a throwback to a long-forgotten and dark age when men were more like beasts.

"Ain't that the fucking truth?" Bull's presence asked rhetorically.

"Why, then?"

"Let's not worry about me, Judd boy! Don't feel so smug in your sanctimonious way of looking at life and somebody like

*me. I made the choice. I made the effort. I
lived with it. I enjoyed it. Fuck society.
Who the fuck needs it?"*

Judd said nothing and the bike roared
ahead.

The sun hung in the western sky, well
above the trees bordering both sides of
the road. Judd looked at his watch, dis-
covering that bike was just as easy to
control with one hand as two. It was
almost two-thirty. He would go a bit
farther and then head back to town. He
still wanted to see Peggy and apologize to
her.

After twenty minutes passed during
which Judd enjoyed the ride and the quiet
that Bull had imposed on himself, the
voice slammed back into his mind.

*"We're going to go to the state
capital."*

"Why?" Judd wondered what would be
in the state capital that would make Bull
want to go there.

*"That's where the gang—the Light
Bearer's Chosen—hangs out. I'm surprised
that you didn't learn that by sticking your
nose in my mind."*

"I guess I could have but I haven't
really gotten all that used to snooping. I
suppose I'm more content to let this thing
happen and get it over with so you can
leave."

"Snoop all you want," the voice said,

"I can't stop you."

Judd concentrated. A warehouse. The gang hung out—no—lived in a warehouse. A large room. Different areas set aside for each gang member. Almost like campsites.

"So what are we going to do there?" he asked.

"Find Buckshot and kill the sonofabitch!"

"Won't that be a little dangerous? I mean, suppose the gang catches on to who I am and that you're with me. Won't that set them off?"

"Set them off?"

"You know, they'll come after me?"

"Hey, don't worry about it. I'll take good care of you."

"Remember one thing, Bull. It was Buckshot who killed you in the first place. He cut your throat and you couldn't do anything about it. Remember? I don't want my throat cut. Do you hear me?"

The buzzing in Judd's mind took him off guard. It wasn't really a buzzing when he focused his thoughts onto it. It was—words! Words coming so fast that they seemed like an endless procession of sounds—like bees protecting their hive from an intruder. The indistinct meaning of the words ricocheted through his brain, leaving an imprint here and a thought pattern there, but the messages—their significance—their substance meant nothing.

Unable to control his bodily reactions, Judd felt his hands clamping on the brakes, the back end of the motorcycle skidding first to one side, then the other as it fish-tailed down the road. The speedometer needle dove toward the zero, and when the bike stopped completely, Judd dropped both feet to the ground, maintaining his balance. Without thinking, he leaped from the Harley-Davidson, letting it fall to one side, bouncing on the verge of the road.

Judd dashed headlong into the gutter that paralleled the road, up the far side, scrambling through the barbed-wire fence that enclosed the stand of timber next to the highway. He made no effort to protect his face from the low-hanging branches, and twigs and leaves brushed against him, tearing at his unshielded face, ripping open small gashes on his cheeks and forehead.

"Goddammit!" The word roared from Judd's mouth in Bull's voice, grinding it out until the hatred dripping from the words seemed to take on a semblance of tangibility.

Without stopping his flight, Judd reached up, tearing off a branch whenever he could reach one, throwing it as far as he could.

"The dirty rotten sonofabitching no-good motherfucking bastard!" Bull's voice screamed. *"I'll kill him. I'll tear him apart with my bare hands. He had no right to kill me! He had no right. I should have killed him, but I didn't know he would kill me."* Judd stopped at the edge of the woods, facing an open pasture. Throwing his head back, he screamed loudly and long as Bull vented his anger.

When he stopped, he looked around, his eyes wild, until he spotted a branch, one he had thrown ahead of himself just before he ran to the edge of the trees. Running to it, he picked it up and beat at his legs and body, continuing the self-flagellation over his shoulders, onto his back. When the branch broke from the force of the blows he had rained on himself, he stopped, throwing away the small piece of wood he still held.

Panting like a maddened animal of prey, Judd stood, his head hanging and arms dangling at his side. Spent, weary, exhausted, he dropped to his knees, falling forward on his stomach. Bitter tears erupted as Judd wailed the anguish Bull felt. Pounding his fists on the ground, he wept uncontrollably.

Peggy watched Judd turn and disappear around the edge of the door opening, the building across the alley wavering in her watery view. The only thing she could think of was how frustrated she felt. It hadn't been Judd—her Judd—who had spoken to her like that and simply rode away. Something was bothering him—something that was causing him to act unnaturally—completely unlike himself. But what? She wasn't even sure if she would like Judd Wellington if she were to meet him for the first time, considering the manner in which he was acting.

Turning, she decided she had to force herself to think of other things. Going to work. Doing her job—first at Allan Edwards's law office and then hurrying to the retirement home where she would help in the office until seven that night. Without so much as a sidelong glance at Mickey Higgins, who was waiting on a customer at the plumbing section of the store, she walked deliberately through the hardware store to the street entrance. She could feel Mickey's eyes on her as she opened the door and stepped through. She didn't want him feeling sorry for her. Anything but that. Any problem or situation that had occurred between her and Judd, she would handle in her own way.

The shops and stores lining Rushton's Main Street blurred into a collage of colors and shapes as Peggy walked toward the office building housing Edwards's law offices. She suddenly found herself questioning her ambition. Working two jobs. Why? To save money for her and Judd? So they could marry? Someday. When? Before, it had been when Cindy finished her college education. Now, when would it be? If Judd hadn't started acting so differently—so strangely, they might have broached the subject soon. As soon as an acceptable time period of mourning had passed.

But now she wasn't even certain if she wanted to be with Judd anymore. He had changed. And not for the good. He was using strong language—filthy language in her estimation—and had become totally immersed in the restoration of the motor-cycle. The thing that frightened her most, however, was his reasoning for wanting the bike in the first place. To flush out the killers of his sister. That had to be some sort of insanity in itself. What did he know about motorcycle gangs? Why not leave that sort of thing to the police? She didn't want Judd becoming involved in something that would jeopardize him and his safety.

Was that her problem? She wanted a certain amount of *status quo* in her life. She must want it for Judd as well—especially once they married. But would they marry now? Did she want Judd? Did Judd want her anymore?

After she entered the building and

stepped in the elevator, she waited patiently for the door to close. It was slow. It had to be the slowest elevator in town—even slower than the ones at the courthouse and the post office. At least, as Allan Edwards reasoned, it gave people an opportunity to relax the few minutes it took to reach the top floors. When the elevator bumped to a stop and the doors slid open, she stepped off.

She had taken a late lunch break and, after looking at her watch, knew she wasn't too late. She had spent more time at the hardware store than she had intended. But then, she had not planned on arguing with Judd.

When she entered the office, Allan Edwards turned and looked around. He was just about to enter his private office when the door had opened.

"Hi, Peggy," he said, adjusting the glasses on his thin nose. Allan, a mid-sixties widower, had slowed his practice somewhat in the last years since his wife's death from cancer. He had been planning on taking in a junior partner but decided that it would be better to accept the work he wanted and refer that which didn't appeal to him. His regular clientele kept him as busy as he wanted to be, as long as it didn't interfere too much with his hunting and fishing.

Peggy didn't answer right away, wishing he had been in his office, which would have given her an opportunity to fix her face. Her eyes had to be red and her cheeks flushed from crying. "Hi, Allan," she managed, without looking directly at him. Hurrying to the closet, she hung her handbag on a hook and glanced in the mirror on the inside of the door. Her eyes weren't that red and she didn't look too bad. Maybe he wouldn't notice.

Closing the door, she crossed the room to her desk and sat down.

"All right, what's bothering you?" he asked, stepping around to the front of her desk.

Looking up, she forced a smile. "Bothering me? Nothing. Why?"

"Come on, Peggy. I know you well enough that when you walk in and only say, 'Hi, Allan,' that something's on your mind. Want to talk about it?"

"Not really. Yes."

He grinned. "I thought so. Come on into my office. Teddy Papin called in and canceled his appointment. I'm free the rest of the afternoon."

"I thought you were never free but always reasonable." She forced a grin of her own, following him into his private quarters.

"I'm always free wherever you're concerned, Peggy. You know that. Now tell me what's bothering you."

She sat down in the chair she usually used for taking dictation and, crossing her legs, looked directly at her employer. "It's Judd."

"Now that comes as a bit of a surprise. I thought the two of you were thicker'n thieves."

"We were—we are. But he's changed."

"Changed? How?"

"The last couple of weeks. Ever since he came home with a stupid motorcycle."

"I remember you telling me something about it. What's the matter, is he spending too much time with it?"

"Every waking hour. I don't think he's spent an hour or two in the store since he brought it to the shop." Why did she avoid telling Allan the truth? Judd had claimed he had dug it up in the woods—not far from where Cindy and Tami had been found. He had just told her that he also found a body with it. Maybe she felt that the bike and dead man wouldn't pose such a permanent problem and she would avoid trouble if she didn't tell Allan everything. After all, he was an officer of the court and as such would have to inform the authorities if she told him something that might have a bearing on the solution of the double murders.

"That doesn't sound like Judd. He's always been so conscientious about the business. Maybe he's just trying to forget Cindy's awful death. You know, sometimes people will change for a while after the death of a loved one. Sometimes it's for the good and sometimes it's for the bad. But I'm not sure I'd worry too much about it at this point. After all, it's barely a month since the girls were killed."

"That's not the only thing that's bothering me." She might as well tell him almost everything that had her concerned where Judd was involved. Everything except the partculars about the motorcycle. She would hold that in abeyance until the time was right or she knew what the consequences would be.

"His hair is wavy. And he's grown one long fingernail. And I think he's gaining weight. He—"

Allan held up one hand. "Wait a minute, Peggy. Are you saying that Judd has changed because his hair is wavy and he has one long fingernail?" He covered his mouth with one well-manicured hand, stifling the laugh he felt rising.

"Don't laugh, Allan. Hear me out."

"Okay. Go ahead."

"The day he brought the motorcycle home—or I should say to the hardware store—he said he had been caught out in the open during the rainstorm. At least, then it was believable. His hair had deep waves in it. But the waves were there the next day and the next and they're still there now. He's never had wavy hair. You know that. It's as straight as mine is curly." Peggy lifted one lock of her own dark brown curly hair for emphasis, then let it spring back into place.

"I'm not certain but that could happen, couldn't it? I went to school with a guy who had real straight hair and when he started going bald, his hair that was left started developing the most deeply pressed waves. It was unbelievable."

"But Judd's not going bald. He's gaining weight."

"Why should that bother you? He has a long way to go before he'll be fat."

"True. But he hasn't been eating that much or that regularly. It's the damned motorcycle that's been keeping him busy. I've invited him over for dinner lots of times in the last two weeks and he says he'll have to take a rain-check and grab a bite at a restaurant. But, even if he's doing that, he wouldn't be showing that much of a gain in two weeks."

"How much has he gained?"

Peggy shrugged. "I don't know if he has. But his face is getting a little fuller—more fleshy, if you know what I mean."

Allan frowned. "I knew both of his parents and both sets of his grandparents. There wasn't an overweight one in the crowd. In fact, if anything, one would have to say that the family's trademark would have been their lean, hungry look. That *is* strange. What else?"

"The fingernail really bugs me."

"Fingernail?"

"The one on his little finger, right hand. It's about an inch and a half long."

"So?"

"The day before he found the motorcycle, his nails were all the same length. When I saw him the day he brought the bike in, his one nail had grown tremendously."

Allan said nothing, puckering his lips in thought. After a few minutes, he coughed. "Is that it?"

"He's acting strangely, too."

"Strangely? How?"

"At times he's gruff and really short-tempered. Other times, he won't speak when someone says something to him. I'm really worried about him, Allan."

"Well, as I said before, it could be a delayed reaction to his sister's death. But if you're really concerned, why don't you talk with a psychiatrist or psychologist?"

"If there were any in town, I would."

"There is."

"Since when?" she asked, feeling a ray of hope for the first time since leaving the hardware store.

"At the school. He comes into town on Thursday and stays over, working here all day Friday. Name's Montgomery, I think. I read about him in the paper."

Peggy turned away for a moment. It was one thing to tell someone like Allan, a friend and employer, things that were secret, innermost thoughts and impressions. But how could she possibly tell a stranger about Judd and the strange things she'd noticed lately? He'd probably laugh her out of his office. "Besides," she said, suddenly voicing her own thoughts, "he's probably trained to work with children and students. He might not know how to handle an adult."

"You're being silly, you know that, don't you?"

She looked at Allan. Of course he was right. She knew that. It just didn't seem right to talk about the man she loved behind his back to some total stranger and tell him all her weird thoughts and ideas where Judd was concerned. "What did you say his name is?"

"Montgomery. I don't recall the first name, other than that it was unusual. If you call the school office, I'm sure they'll give you his name and how to reach him."

Peggy jotted the name down on a slip of paper she took from the memo box on Allan's desk. "If I don't see any changes, I just might give Mr. Montgomery a call."

She stood, thanked Allan for his time, and left his office. When she sat down at her own desk in the waiting room, she quickly busied herself with typing. The next two hours seemed to fly by, and Peggy gratefully locked the office an hour after Allan left at three thirty. She had thirty minutes to reach the retirement home by five o'clock. Then, after two hours of book work there, she'd head home and—. A whimsical expression crossed her face. She wished Judd were coming to dinner. It would make the next two hours fly by and she'd hurry home to prepare a quick meal and they could spend the evening and maybe the night together. But in his present state of mind, he'd probably tell her to jump off a cliff or stuff her dinner someplace where the sun wouldn't shine on it anymore.

Blinking back the tears she felt forming, she lowered her head and continued walking toward the retirement home.

Judd rolled over, staring at the cumulus clouds overhead. He saw them but he didn't see them. What had he been doing? Why did his body and arms and legs hurt so much? What *had* he been doing? In fact, where was he? Someplace in the country, but where exactly? How had he gotten here?

"You rode my hog here, Judd!"

Then the wild ride, Bull's sudden fit of madness, running through the trees, beating at his own body all came back to Judd. No wonder he ached.

"I'm sorry about what I did to you, pal."

"Yeah, sure. In the meantime, I'm hurting like hell and you feel as if you've gained a good release on your pent-up frustrations. Right?"

"No. I'm really sorry. I seldom said that when I was alive and heading up the Chosen. Look, Judd, all we got is each other. I've—we've got a job to do. Once that's finished, I'm gone. I don't relish having you look into my mind any more than you do having me look in yours."

"You forget, Bull, that I can't control you the way you do me. You're making me do and say things I'd never do. You made me hurt Peggy this afternoon with your foul mouth."

"Look, Judd. That's the way it is. I didn't plan this. Neither did you. We're stuck together for the time being. Let's make the most of it and get our pound of flesh. What do you say?"

Judd knew he had no choice in the matter. "Will you behave when Peggy's around?"

"Promise!"

"Once Buckshot is turned over to the cops and taken care of, you'll leave?"

"Promise!"

"All right, then."

"It's the smartest thing you've ever done, Judd. Believe me."

"I have to believe you. I don't have any other choice, do I?"

"None that I can think of."

Judd stood, each ache and pain caused by the blows Bull had rendered on him screaming its location and presence.

Slowly making his way through the trees, Judd hobbled down into the gutter after crossing the barbed-wire fence and up the other side to the motorcycle where it still lay on its side.

Bending, he tried to lift it, but the injuries hurt him too much and he didn't think he'd be able to manage it alone.

"Try it again. I wasn't paying any attention."

At the sound of Bull's voice in his head, Judd obeyed and lifted the Harley-Davidson without a struggle. Could Bull make him superstrong as well? He recalled some of the things he had done while rebuilding the bike. At the time he had not thought too much of them, but now in retrospect, he realized that Bull had done all of the work.

He kicked the engine to life and whipped around in a circle, heading back toward Rushton.

When he reached the city limits, he caught the time of seven-thirty on a gas station clock and turned at the next intersection to go to Peggy's apartment. Standing at her door, he knocked gently.

In several seconds, he heard her coming toward the door. She opened it, and when she realized it was Judd, threw herself into his outstretched arms. They kissed. Picking her up in his arms, he walked into the apartment. She shoved the door closed behind them.

"I was worried about you," she said softly into his ear. "I didn't know if I'd ever see you again. At least in one piece."

"Hey, I was perfectly fine. Nothing to worry about. Will you forgive me for this afternoon?"

"Of course not. That's why I'm fighting like crazy to make you put me down." She hugged him around his neck.

"I really don't know what came over me. If I get that crude again, just hit me with something, will you? I'm really sorry."

"Let's not talk about it any more. It's ancient history. Never happened. All right?"

"It couldn't be more perfect."

He lowered her to her feet and for the first time noticed how she was dressed. A white satin robe, slit up both sides but not the front, exposed her legs all the way to the top of the thigh. Her tanned skin contrasted sharply with the whiteness of the gown. Her breasts were not exposed by the high neckline which made them seem to stand out even more, begging for attention—to be seen in all their naked beauty.

Judd felt his penis jerk. He wanted Peggy. He wanted her here and now. But he hesitated. Who was sexually aroused? Judd Wellington? Or a motorcycle gang leader named Bull?

11

Judd sat at the kitchen table in Peggy's apartment while she grilled hamburgers, seeing her and yet not seeing her. For the moment, he felt at ease. He had suppressed the sexual desire he had felt when they entered her home only because he felt he might lose control, that it might be Bull's sexuality rising to the surface. Not sure if he could contain it, he had forced the lust he had felt for Peggy from his being. How long he could restrain the craving he had no idea.

Peggy glanced up to find him staring at her and quickly turned her attention back to the hamburgers on the stove.

Judd smiled. In some ways they resembled each other. Both had triangular-shaped faces, both had dark hair—he with a rather high, curving forehead line while hers was more of a straight line across. Her hair was wavy and shoulder-length while his was straight. Well, not exactly straight. He had noticed some waving taking place recently. How could that happen? Straight hair suddenly turn wavy? Was something like that even possible? No one in his family, not even Cindy, had had wavy hair. She, too, had had the high Wellington forehead and no waves.

Peggy bent down to retrieve something from the floor, and Judd admired the flair of her hips. Peggy had a lovely body. Nicely proportioned—her breasts were not too large nor too small. He recalled how Cindy would often bemoan the fact that her bust wasn't larger. Cindy. He forced the thought of his dead sister from his mind. The last thing he wanted to do was become upset and ruin his and Peggy's evening together.

He looked down at his clothes—greasy jeans, a blue denim shirt, equally oil-stained and dirty. He felt filthy. He should have stopped at his home first to clean up. How could he expect Peggy to want to be near him dressed like this? Even undressed, he'd need a shower and shave.

When she turned to put their sandwiches on the table, he said, "After we eat, and while you wash dishes, I think

I'll run home and clean up. I'm filthy."

Peggy sat down on Judd's right side. "You *could* use a quick run through a dip of some kind." Reaching out, she stroked his cheek. "Better shave, too."

Judd picked up his hamburger after dripping some catsup and mustard on it. "I intended to."

She smiled and bit into her sandwich.

"You should have been with me this afternoon, Peggy. It was simply fantastic. Practically flying through the countryside. Really, it was quite an experience." He took another bite.

She sobered. "Is it that easy to ride a motorcycle? I mean, you've never driven one before, have you?"

"It's nothing," he said, his mouth full.

"Don't talk with food in your mouth," she said, frowning good-naturedly.

He swallowed and took a sip of milk. "I know I've never been on one before, and I can't—well, I can't explain it to you, but I simply can ride the hell out of one of them."

Shaking her head, she refocused her attention on her food. That seemed a little on the wild side. How did one just get on a bike and, to use Judd's words, "ride the hell out of one"?

"I'm too dirty now, but later, maybe tonight or tomorrow, I'll take you for a ride. Want to?"

This time Peggy frowned for real. Would she be safe? Would *they* be safe? Would he be able to take her as a passenger and have the same degree of control and confidence that he had found when he was alone? "I don't know, Judd. I might wait until you have more time on it. After all, you did just start today."

"I know that. But I feel as if I've been riding one all my life. The feeling is fantastic. I've never felt so free or independent before. You'll love it." He grinned, shaking his head in an unbelieving way when he recalled the experience.

Peggy wondered if perhaps Judd wasn't feigning the lighthearted attitude he was displaying. When he popped the last bit of sandwich into his mouth, she caught sight of the long nail. A shudder rippled down her body. A fingernail that long on a woman would be out of the ordinary. But on a man, it was practically revolting. What purpose could it serve?

Swallowing the last of his milk, Judd set the glass down and rammed his long-nailed finger into his right ear. Wiggling it back and forth, he stared into space.

Peggy wondered how he didn't slash the inside of his ear canal to shreds. The nail was certainly long enough and it looked sharp enough to do just that.

When he finished, Judd flicked the

nail, freeing it of any wax or dirt he might have dislodged. Peggy turned away. Disgusting. Revolting. What was happening to Judd? Would she want to marry someone who acted like this? Would she be willing to spend the rest of her life with a man who at one time had been gentle and well-mannered but suddenly became a social boor? A slob? At least he had suggested that he go home to clean up. That seemed like the Judd she knew. But this man who cleaned his ear with an abnormally long fingernail and then flicked any residue about the room, was not in the least like her Judd.

She looked closely at him, over the top of her own glass. He was even gaining weight. At least his jowls were fleshier than they had been. His arms, what she could see of them, jutting from the rolled-up shirtsleeves seemed larger, too.

"Are you gaining weight, Judd?" Her voice seemed too loud, almost shouting. She waited for him to answer.

"Me? No. Why?"

"You look heavier."

"I do? I don't think I have."

"Your arms look bigger. And so do your cheeks." She reached out to pat his face, withdrawing her hand at once when she felt the loose, flabby consistency of his cool flesh. Instead of showing her reaction, she dropped her hand to his arm, marveling at the hardness and tightness of the muscle beneath the skin.

He winked. "Maybe it's the work I've been doing on the motorcycle. I've been lifting a lot lately. Maybe I'm developing into a muscleman."

Peggy searched his eyes. "Are you all right, Judd?"

Judd looked away. She knew. She knew something. How had she found out?

"Don't panic. She's only worried about you, Judd."

The sound of Bull's voice in his head brought him to his feet, where he stood rooted to the spot. He looked about, his head jerking in this direction, then that.

"Easy. I'm here, but don't let on."

"What is it, Judd?"

"Huh? Oh, nothing. Nothing. I think I'd better get going. I'll clean up and be back. All right?"

Peggy looked up at him, before standing. "Fine. I'll wash the dishes and you hurry back."

"I got some ideas about what we'll do when I get back." He wiggled his eyebrows and grinned wickedly.

At first Peggy reacted, thinking that this, too, wasn't like Judd to make innuendoes about their lovemaking. Still, she wanted him and she wanted him tonight. It had been too long since—"Such as?" she found herself asking.

"You'll find out. But you better wear earmuffs."

"Earmuffs?"

"Right. I don't really want to fuck your brains out." He laughed and spun on his heel, walking toward the door.

Before she could react, he was gone. She wanted to cry. She wanted to scream. But what good would it do? He had made a joke. A vulgar joke. And it was in line with the one he had sprung on her earlier that afternoon. The one that had upset her so. Now that she thought back to the incident in the storeroom, she decided she had overreacted. She didn't want to do the same thing now. She didn't want him to come back here and find her crying over something so stupid as his poor choice of words and jokes. She'd do the dishes and get ready for bed. If he came back, fine. If he didn't, she'd have to worry about that when the time came.

Judd stepped from the shower, toweling his body before slipping into his jockey shorts. When he stood in front of his closet, something caught his attention —something resting on the chair next to the bureau. The jeans and leather vest that he had taken from the body of Bull. He had laundered the jeans and cleaned up the vest. Hesitating a moment, he decided and pulled on the pants. They were a little big around the middle but he wouldn't lose them. Donning the vest, he stepped to the mirror on the inside of his closet door. The metal Maltese crosses dangled on either side of the vest. Judd smiled broadly.

He parked the bike and ran up the steps to Peggy's apartment. She opened the door without looking at him in the half-light of the hallway.

Judd grinned, running his tongue over his lips when he saw the gown Peggy wore. It had been his gift to her for her birthday last year and she had remarked at the time that it made her feel positively wicked and decadent when she wore it. He could see her breasts, her nipples, her pubic hair through the transparent material.

Turning, Peggy stifled the scream she felt rise in her throat. "Where—where on earth did you get that?" She pointed a shaky finger at the vest, her eyes widening when she saw the esoteric patches and symbols embroidered onto the legs of the jeans.

"Not where *on* earth but where *in* earth. I dug them up." He laughed, throwing his head back.

"I—I don't understand." Peggy backed away at the sound of Judd's peculiar laugh. It didn't sound like him. It didn't sound like his laugh at all.

He caught the look of trepidation on Peggy's face and sobered. "Hey, I'm sorry. It's just a joke."

His jokes quickly were becoming something she wished he'd forget. They weren't funny. "I—I'm sorry, Judd."

"Look, let's both stop being so sorry. If I upset you, I'll try not to do it again." Judd swallowed hard. He'd have to placate Peggy somehow or she'd be through with him before he had an opportunity to help Bull gain his revenge, his own vengeance, and be rid of the invading entity. The last thing in the world he wanted to do was lose Peggy. He loved her. She loved him. It was that simple. Neither Bull nor his revenge could interfere with that. Nor could Judd's own sense of justice. If he could get rid of Bull, he would, and if he had to forget about finding Cindy's murderer, he would. He would not pay the price of losing Peggy to gain any of those things.

He held out his arms to Peggy, who slowly, reluctantly came toward him. "I think I might be going through some sort of phase. All I can ask you to do is to be patient with me, Peggy. I love you. I really do."

Peggy nestled into his embrace. His hug felt good. He seemed more solid now than he ever had before. But was that good? Did that mean Judd was merely going through a physical change of some sort that would result in a firmer body—more muscle? She could live with that as long as he didn't change as a person. She nuzzled the leather vest. It carried a smell, one peculiar to leather. Opening her eyes, she cried out. The crosses. She hadn't noticed them before. Picking one up, she exclaimed it closely. It was like the one he had painted on the motorcycle's tank. One like the newspaper described. Then, stepping back, her eyes widening in horror, Peggy could see the other one. Judd Wellington, the man she loved, was wearing two of the symbols. Had Judd had something to do with the murders? That was preposterous. She stared at him.

"What's the matter?" He held his arms out to her, startled when she backed away, shaking her head. "What's wrong?"

Pointing to the Maltese crosses, she tried to speak but found herself unable to do so.

"These?" He fingered the medals. "I found these at the place where I found the bike. Remember? I showed them to you before."

She shook her head. "What are you trying to prove, Judd? My God! You find a dead body and don't report it! You start riding a bike! You dress like this! You're acting like a motorcycle gang member without a gang. What do you hope to accomplish by wearing those things?"

"Same thing as by riding the bike. I hope to draw whoever had anything to do with Cindy's and Tami's deaths out into the open. When that happens, I call the cops and they're arrested. Then I can live with myself because I'll know that I had something to do with the apprehension of the murderer."

She stared at him, her lips moving slightly as if she were about to speak, but said nothing.

His eyes widened. "You don't think that I—" He couldn't finish the statement.

Peggy rushed to him, throwing her arms around his neck. "Of course not. That idea's ridiculous." She kissed him. "You have to admit that it looks a little suspicious, but I know how much you loved Cindy. Anyone who knows you or knew her is aware of that. I wish you wouldn't try this, though. It sounds dangerous."

"It could be, but I won't be hurt. I promise."

"How can you promise something like that?"

"I—I can't tell you now. But when I find them and they're behind bars, I'll tell you everything."

She pulled away from him. "I don't like secrets like that. Maybe it's dangerous and you're overlooking something."

"I'm not overlooking anything. The plan is set."

Turning, she looked at him. "What about your fingernail? Why that? What's its purpose?"

"You mean this?" He held up his right hand, flashing the long nail in a swordlike fashion. "No real purpose. I just grew it. If I ever want to snort some coke, I've got my own built-in spoon." He laughed, but it was hollow, mirthless.

Peggy turned away. Judd seldom drank. An occasional beer. Every once in a while, he'd have a mixed drink, but liquor simply didn't play an important role in Judd's life. Now he was thinking about using cocaine. Was he serious?

"Hey, I'm only kidding," he said, throwing his head back and giving in to a short, harsh laugh.

"You'd better be. I've seen enough change about you to last me a lifetime." She moved back to him.

Tipping her chin, he kissed her on the mouth, a tender buss that promised nothing, yet everything. Peggy thrilled at the touch of his lips. That was Judd's kiss.

Suddenly, without warning, he roughly grabbed her upper arms and continued kissing her, hard, savagely jabbing his tongue into her mouth. Taken off guard, she couldn't fight. She could bite, but that was dangerous. Perhaps he wanted her as badly as she wanted him. His tongue explored the inside of her mouth as far as it would reach, skimming over the top of her teeth, slicking along the inside of her cheeks, down to the softness beneath her own tongue. Unable to resist, she returned the kiss, touching his tongue with hers, welcoming it to the secret places within her own mouth. A sharp tingle ran down her spine, careening through her legs, back up to her body where it worked its strange effect on her, arousing her sexually to the point of making her want to scream.

When he pulled away, holding her at arm's length, he grinned.

She was breathless. The kiss actually had taken her breath away. It wasn't the way Judd usually kissed her, but she liked it. She had enjoyed it to its fullest.

Suddenly Allan Edwards's words flashed through her mind. *"Judd's maybe trying to forget Cindy's awful death. Sometimes people change for a while following the death of a loved one. It could be a delayed reaction to his sister's death."*

A minute tremble raced through her. If that really were true, she had to go along with Judd. She had to help him and do everything within her power to see him through this problem. If she turned her back on him, he would want nothing to do with her once he came through the situation on his own. That, she didn't want. Relaxing in his grip, she allowed him to pull her back to his chest. "I love you," she said softly.

"I love you, too. Look, Peggy, I know you think I'm acting strangely and doing some dumb things. All I'm asking you to do is humor me. I'm not going crazy. I've got something to do and I wish I could tell you all about it, but I think it's better if you stay out of it for the time being. Okay?"

She slowly nodded. Something else Allan had said came back to her. The name of the new school psychologist, Mr. Montgomery, blasted into her consciousness. If Judd didn't want to share his plan with her, she wouldn't share hers with him. She'd call on this man and explain the circumstances and see what a professional thought about Judd's strange behavior. The next day was Thursday. She'd do it.

She coughed. "I guess you know what you're doing. I'll go along with you—for now. But please hurry. I'm getting anxious about the two of us."

"Maybe I can help relieve some of your anxiety," he said, swooping her up into his arms. The back panel of her gown fell away and he felt her nakedness against his arm.

Entering the bedroom, he lowered her to her feet. She reached along her side, fumbling for the tie, and pulled it. Slipping her arms from the sleeves, she stepped out of the gossamer gown. Her breasts jutted out, the nipples hard, erect, still throbbing their desire from the brutal kiss Judd had given her. Pulling back the covers, she sat down on the edge of the bed.

Judd took off the vest, turning to hang it over the back of the chair next to the wall.

Peggy screamed. "My God! What happened to your back?" Her eyes widened at the sight of the dark welts and bruises that had risen. She leaped off the bed, hurrying to Judd's side.

Judd bit his tongue. He had forgotten about the whipping Bull had inflicted on him. "I—I fell." It was a lie, but he couldn't tell her what actually had happened. She'd have him locked up once and for all.

"On the motorcycle? You fell on the motorcycle and you want me to ride with you? I told you you'd hurt yourself."

"It wasn't on the bike. I stopped along the way today and went for a walk through so trees. I lost my footing and fell down an embankment. I hit some rocks when I landed on my back."

She eyed him, suspicion etched on her troubled face. "Are you telling me the truth?"

"I wouldn't lie about something like that. It really happened that way. Believe me."

"I want to."

"Then, do." He opened his pants and stopped. His legs were bruised as well as his back. Both the front and back of his legs. She'd never buy the story if she saw them. "If you don't want to look at the marks, turn the light out. In fact, I wish you would. Out of sight, out of mind.

Right? We want to enjoy this tonight, don't we?"

Peggy turned, walking back to the side of the bed. "I guess so." She turned off the nightstand light, plunging the room into darkness.

Judd slipped the jeans off and hurriedly got into the bed. He had to get her mind off his bruises and onto more exciting things. Reaching out for her in the inky blackness, he found her shoulder and placed one hand on a breast. Gently massaging it, he rolled the nipple between his thumb and forefinger, sensing her state of arousal despite her show of concern just a few seconds before.

Peggy's hand snaked out toward him, brushing against his side. It traveled down until she was even with his penis, before moving toward it. It jerked to life, quickly growing to its fullest proportions as she held it. When Judd pinched her nipple too hard, she bit her tongue rather than cry out. Instead, she wriggled away, searching for a more comfortable position.

Judd reached out for her face and, finding it, moved closer until he could kiss her. Tiny shocks of electricity flowed outward from his groin as she rubbed him. Jamming his tongue into her mouth, he rolled on top of her and positioned himself over her.

Peggy tried to comprehend what Judd's action would result in next, only to find that she was having a difficult time breathing, his mouth so completely enveloped her own as well as most of her nostrils. She fought, desperately trying to free her mouth. When she did, she found herself excited to a feverish pitch, wanting more of his brutish attentions. This wasn't like Judd at all. She felt as if she were in bed with another man. Someone she wouldn't care for very much. Still, she wanted Judd to have his way with her. It would satisfy her as well. She found herself hoping for more roughness in his treatment of her. In seconds, when he rammed his penis into her body, she found her desires fulfilled.

Judd's hips thrashed back and forth, thrusting his penis in and out. He continued holding his mouth on hers, their tongues in rhythm with their lower bodies. After several minutes, she felt her own climax building, mounting to a peak of sensation she had never before experienced. What was happening? What was prompting Judd to be so animalistic? It was the only way she could describe his movements, his actions. And yet, despite herself, she found it to be enthralling. She could not contain herself as the waves of her orgasm built, spilling over the cup of her very being. When it finished, she spiraled down, unmindful and uncaring that Judd continued hammering at her. Then, when his climax erupted, she felt a new twinge of gratification as his semen flowed into her.

Judd's movements diminished little by little until he lay full upon her, exhausted. She waited. She could feel him withering inside her, shriveling up, spent. True, it had been several weeks since they had made love. She had to attribute his almost ferocious lovemaking to neglect on both their parts. They had, without speaking of it, mutually agreed to abstain following the funeral of Cindy. Other than the one night they had spent together, there had been no opportunities for them to renew their physical relationship. Then he found the motorcycle and that had accounted for his time since.

Judd rolled off her and lay on his back.

She wanted to say something. But what? *That was terrific? Don't throw that particular script away. I liked it.* She had to say something. "Judd?"

A soft snore came in answer.

"Are you sleeping?"

A louder snore bubbled through the dark bedroom.

Propping himself up on one elbow, she stared at his shadowed shape. Another uncharacteristic thing. He seldom went to sleep after they made love. At least not immediately. They would lie there and talk—talk about their feelings for each other—their plans for the future and almost anything else that involved the two of them. And snoring? That was another thing she had never heard Judd do.

Picturing him in her mind's eye, she reached out to touch him. He felt normal except for the clammy coolness of his skin. What could be troubling him, if anything? Why was he acting so strangely?

"Be all right, Judd. For me. For us. Be all right. Please?" she whispered in the dark.

In the middle of a loud snore, she thought she heard something. A voice. A rough, gravelly voice. One that said, *"You're not bad, baby!"*

Peggy sat up in bed, a cold, chilled feeling sweeping through her. She peered int the sable night. Now she was hearing voices. It had to have been her imagination. Judd was snoring when she thought she heard it. What had it said? Something about not being bad. And she had heard the word *baby* as well. Was she losing her mind? Was she the one who had a problem? Maybe it was she and not Judd who was changing, and she was merely trying to cover her own situation by calling attention to Judd, fabricating things about him.

That was too illogical. Judd *had* changed. There were things about him that Peggy couldn't understand or comprehend. Now he was snoring like an old man who couldn't breathe properly. He never snored.

Lying back, she stared at the darkened ceiling. What would this Mr.

Montgomery be like? Would he be willing to talk to her or would his job with the school not allow him to visit her—much less help her?

She closed her eyes forming a simple prayer in her mind. *Please, God, let this man talk to me. Let him help me—us—Judd. Let everything work out all right for Judd and me. Please.*

Her eyes opened involuntarily and she stared into the black for a long while before falling asleep.

Buckshot lay on his back, snores rippling through his nose and open mouth. Cow, cuddled next to him, had one arm thrown over his chest. Sounds of heavy breathing, snoring, and attendant night noises filtered through the warehouse.

Buckshot walked through closely set trees, searching for something. What it might be that he was looking for escaped him. It was—whatever it was—something he needed, needed desperately. Whenever he looked directly at a tree, all he saw was the trunk and its branches. But out of the corner of his eye, he could see faces etched into the wood. Faces that he felt he should have recognized but seemed incapable of doing so. Whose faces were watching him, then conveniently disappearing when he turned to identify them? The gang? Different members of the gang? People with whom he associated, but who didn't want to follow his leadership? That could be, but if that were the case, why didn't they simply step forward and challenge him? That he could understand. This thing of walking night after night through a forest that he dreamt about did nothing to relieve his feelings of inadequacy.

Then, as always, he came to a clearing, an open space that seemed somehow familiar. In the center, a mound caught his attention. Usually he would awaken at that moment, but tonight he stood there at the edge of the trees surrounding the hillock and waited. He knew something was about to happen.

When he heard the throaty roar of a motorcycle engine being kicked over, he turned halfway around, expecting to see one of the gang behind him. But he was alone. Redirecting his attention to the clearing, he screamed when the mound exploded and a biker on his hog erupted from the earth.

Buckshot sat up, screaming, throwing Cow's arm off. "Bull's coming! Bull's coming! Bull's coming!"

Cow, along with the others, sat up wondering what had disturbed their sleep. She placed one arm around Buckshot when she realized he had been dreaming, a worried look crossing her face when she recalled what Buckshot had yelled.

12

Judd opened his eyes and stared at the ceiling, trying to recall where he was and what he had been doing. The rush of the previous evening slammed into his consciousness and he sat up, turning to look at Peggy, who slept nude next to him. What had—? The whole experience of making love to her ran through his mind like a slow-motion movie. But it wasn't he who was making love to Peggy. It was someone else. Someone who—*Bull!*

"I helped, that's all."

The voice wove through Judd's head. By what right—Who had given him— "You had no right to do that."

"Hey. Relax. She's only a fucking woman, for Chrissakes! You fucked her and I helped. Look, Judd, it's been quite a

while since I rammed a fucking twat. Have a heart."

Judd shook his head, leaping from bed. The whole situation had gotten totally out of hand. If the spirit of Bull could take over his body and—and—make love—

"I didn't make love to her, goddammit! I fucked her. She's yours. I simply used her for a while, that's all. There is a difference, you know."

When he reached the bathroom, Judd dropped to his knees next to the stool. He wanted to vomit. He felt sick. Why couldn't he heave his guts out and be rid of the thing in him that called itself "Bull"?

"It doesn't work that way. Look, Judd, we've got an agreement. Today we'll ride into the capital, look up my 'friend' Buckshot and have a go at him. Then, we're done, you 'n me."

"Why can't I believe you anymore, Bull? I don't think I can trust you. Not after what happened last night." Judd slowly got to his feet and splashed cold water in his face. Maybe all of it would go away. Maybe all he had done was dream—that was it—he had dreamt the whole thing. Cindy's death, finding the motorcycle, thinking that a dead man, one called Bull, had invaded his soul, taking command of his thoughts and bodily actions. All it was was a bad dream. Maybe—

"If you believe that all of this is a dream, Judd ol' boy, you've got one piss-whistler of an imagination."

"Shut up. Go away. Get out of my life."

"Don't I wish I could. Although, after last night that might prove to be a bad idea. Peggy likes a little roughness. Did you notice that? Slamming ol' George into her like I did seemed to turn her on. Ain't you ever done that before, Judd? Oh, I know you fucked her—er—'made love to her' before, but get a little rough with 'em. They love it."

Throwing his hands over his ears in a futile attempt to shut out the voice of the spirit, Judd wanted to scream. But that would only bring Peggy running to find out what was wrong and he wouldn't be able to tell her. Not without running the risk of having her think he had totally lost his mind. Maybe that was it. Of course! He had gone insane. Completely gone crazy since Cindy's body had been found. He had been living in a dream world—a world of fantasy he had created just for himself.

"Don't you wish I was a figment of your imagination? You know better. This is all real. We're a partnership, you 'n me!"

"You betrayed me last night, Bull. It's all over. I quit. I won't help you anymore. You can go to hell as far as I'm concerned."

Ignoring the spirit's presence, Judd tiptoed into the bedroom. At least Peggy was still sleeping. He picked up the jeans and the vest. Bull's jeans. Bull's vest. Why had he worn them? Now he had to wear them to get home and get a decent change of clothing.

"I probably will wind up going to hell. For me that's a reward. I've prayed to Satan enough. If I wound up going to heaven, I'd figure there wasn't any fucking justice anyplace. Other than that, let me remind you, Judd, that I control you. You don't have that much to say about me and what I do. Understand?"

Judd didn't respond while pulling on the jeans and slipping into the vest. He'd go home, change clothes and go to work, despite what Bull wanted of him.

"We're going to the capital and that's that!"

The words boomed in Judd's head. He'd see about that. He'd do everything in his power to do what he wanted. Bull could go to hell. "Maybe."

Judd closed the door to Peggy's apartment with a soft click and hurried down the steps. Maybe he'd abandon the bike—just leave it parked where it was. There weren't that many people who would associate him with it.

Unable to control his own steps or the direction he wanted to take, Judd crossed the parking lot to the Harley-Davidson, climbed on and kicked the engine to life. A thin smile worked its way onto his lips.

Revving the engine, he pushed off and roared out of the lot, toward the highway and the state capital.

The sun had climbed quickly from the horizon where it had clung, appearing almost hesitant to leave, when Judd had first awoke. Now, as he glided down the two-lane highway in the warming sunlight, he felt the same sense of freedom he had experienced the day before, washing over him again, filling every pore in his body with a sense of exuberance. Anyone who didn't ride a motorcycle should give it a chance at least once, he thought—give it the opportunity to convert the stodgiest of people to a new sense of life, of fun, of thrills.

Overhead a few cottony puffs of clouds floated lazily, meandering in the gentle morning breeze. Judd found hardly any traffic at all and confidently rode down the middle of his lane. On either side of the highway, fields of grain had been harvested and the stubble of stalks, like the earth's beard, outlined the rolling contours of the hilly terrain. The leaves of trees had not yet begun to change color, but within a month there would be a wild splash of reds, yellows, and rich browns heralding the approach of winter.

By that time, Judd hoped he would be rid of the thing harboring within him.

What did a spirit look like? A wispy shape of smoke? Or was it something solid? Something one could touch and see and feel?

"Will you be gone soon, Bull?" he asked in a whisper, fearful of the answer. What if the entity simply said he liked the situation the way it was? What would happen to Judd Wellington's spirit then? Was it possible for two beings to exist within the same framework of one body? Judd looked to one side of the road, ignoring the highway, letting the machine move by itself without giving it any of his intelligence. But what was Bull doing at that precise moment? Wasn't Bull the brains behind driving the motorcycle? What was Judd's function if Bull was running the show?

"I don't know. I hope so. You pose some tough questions that seem to buzz around my mind something awful. Let me put it to you this way, Judd. If we take care of Buckshot and I can leave, I will. I don't know what lies ahead of me beyond that. All I do know is that the idea of revenge and killing Buckshot is almost overriding any other thought I might conceive."

Kill? Kill Buckshot? Judd trembled. When Bull had broached the idea initially in the woods, Judd had merely thought of it as an idle, passing thought. A threat. But now? Now they—they?—he—Judd

Wellington—was on a motorcycle, driving down the highway toward the state capital, with the purposeful idea of killing someone. Was he capable of doing such a thing? If the act were actually committed, would it be Judd who would be responsible, or held responsible if he were apprehended?

"I don't think we should do this, Bull."

"And why not?"

"Be reasonable. I want the killer or killers of Cindy and Tami found and punished. You want revenge. More than likely, if either one of us gets our way, the other will be satisfied. You seem to be absolutely certain that this Buckshot is responsible for the girls' deaths as well as your own. Right?"

"I want to see the bastard squirm. I want to see him suffer. I want to see him begging for his life."

"Won't you be just as satisfied if the law takes its course?"

"Are you fucking crazy? Of course not!"

"I—I don't understand."

"We've got our own set of laws. Our own set of standards. Our own set of morals."

Judd hesitated before he spoke or even thought again. What would happen to him if Bull killed Buckshot and the law intervened and he was arrested? He'd go to jail or be executed for something he didn't want to do—something that he actually abhorred. Sure, he had thought of what he would do to the person or persons responsible for Cindy's awful death, but at best that could be passed off as idle day-dreaming. This was real. He was doing something right now that he wasn't capable of doing—driving a motorcycle. How much will power did he have? Could he resist Bull and his sense of vengeance if this man Buckshot was in the immediate vicinity?

"Isn't there some other way, Bull?"

Bull didn't answer.

Judd searched for some thread of thought from the spirit. Nothing. He could detect absolutely nothing. Was the spirit gone? Or had he merely tuned Judd out?

Then the thoughts exploded in his mind. He could see a large, gray room. The same room he had seen before when Bull projected his thoughts into Judd. Motor-cycles were parked at irregular intervals around the walls near bedrolls spread out on the floor. A gathering of people stood in the center of the area, not unlike a herd of threatened cattle or buffalo. They seemed to be staring at him. The group shuffled about, and for the first time Judd noticed the peculiar garb they wore. Blue jeans with esoteric symbols sewn on—symbols like those he had found on the jeans in the grave—printed shirts, solid-color shirts, undershirts or no shirts at all. Some of them wore vests like the one on his own body. One woman who wore a vest but nothing else under it, her large breasts thrusting outward, stepped forward, dragging a man with her. The man wore a scraggly goatee and hid behind mirrored sunglasses. A cap was cocked on one side of his head, and the dirty white T-shirt under his vest looked as if it hadn't been washed or taken off for weeks.

Judd sensed himself approaching the crowd, and the man and woman stepped out to meet him. Why didn't he feel something? Anything? Fear? Exultation? Jubilation? Anger? Hate? He should feel something, but he sensed that he was experiencing nothing—as if he were witnessing a movie or TV show the outcome of which he didn't particularly care to witness. If he felt anything, it was an overwhelming sense of indifference.

He felt something in his hand, and before he knew what was happening, he saw his own left hand flash out, a long-bladed knife clenched in his fist and pointed directly at the man's throat. He could feel the warm blood spurting out over his hand and arm. He heard the woman, standing helplessly next to the murdered man, scream one word: *"Bull!"* Then the thoughts and images were gone.

"Well?"

The bike slowed to forty-five when he reached the city limits of the capital. *"Well, what?"*

"What did you think of that little scene? That's the way it's going to go down. Buckshot dies. It's that simple."

"And the others are just going to stand there and let you do it?"

"Not me. You. And yes, as long as you show a weapon, they know that Buckshot is being challenged for the leadership. The law is they stay out of it."

"I don't believe any of this!"

"Best you do 'cause we're going to be there in a few minutes."

"This is insane, Bull. Don't do it. I—I need more time to think about all of this."

"I—you—we may not do it this morning. But when it happens, that's the way it'll be."

Judd turned the motorcycle off the highway onto a service road and drove along it for several minutes. Then he turned onto a street lined with warehouses. Some of the buildings, out of use for a long time, stood forlornly along the street, trying to hide behind their dilapitated docks, fearful of being seen. Others, still in use, storing commodities and products, supplies and store stocks for businesses far removed from the area, crowded together.

Judd watched his hand reach down

and turn off the ignition key. The sudden quiet of the late morning pressed in on him as the motorcycle coasted to a stop. He leaned into it and turned off the street, gliding behind a wall where he came to a complete halt. Tipping the bike onto its kickstand, Judd got off and walked into the street.

Determined, with a goal in mind, Bull guided Judd toward a building a block away. Halfway there, a boy no more than eleven or twelve years old suddenly materialized from a doorway.

"Hey, Bull. How's it going?"

Judd stopped short. Why did the boy call him Bull?

"Hey, there, Little Nuts. What's the good word?" He heard his own voice speaking to the boy, apparently calling him by name. But why had the kid called him Bull? That made no sense. Maybe the clothing was distinctive enough that the boy made a mistake. Then he thought of the clothing he had seen in his thoughts— the thoughts put in his mind by Bull. All of the people he had envisioned there had been dressed in similar ways. It couldn't have been the clothes. If not that, then why?

He continued walking, feeling the boy's eyes on him. Something was wrong. Something terribly wrong was going on. But what? A feeling of apprehension filled him. He was in danger. Going into this place was foolhardy at best. He was committing suicide, as far as he could see. It would be like walking into a den of rattlesnakes without any protective clothing or weapons of any type. He was taking his life into his own hands. He fought to stop walking. He couldn't go through with this. It was insane. Yet, as hard as he tried to stop walking, his legs continued moving, carrying him closer to the entrance ahead.

"Don't fight it, Judd. I'll do everything. If it's any consolation, I probably won't do anything this time around. I want the sonofabitch to suffer a little, knowing I'm around."

"But—but how's he going to know? Are you going to tell him what happened? Do you expect him to believe something as wild as that?"

Judd stopped next to a dirt-encrusted window.

"Look," Bull's voice ordered.

Judd turned to the window, which reflected the street like a mirror and swallowed the scream he felt rising within him. Instead of his triangular-shaped face, framed with his straight dark hair, a fleshy round face, surrounded by long wavy black hair, stared back at him.

Unable to comprehend the image any longer, he turned away, his head swimming. What the hell was happening?

That wasn't his reflection. Then whose was it?

"It's mine," Bull announced proudly. *"But without my beard."*

"But what happened? What's going on? Where am I?"

"You're right here. I think it's only for a while. I felt the change coming on ever since we left Peggy's apartment."

No wonder the street kid had called him "Bull." He didn't look anything like himself. What did that mean? That Judd Wellington no longer existed? Bull had said he thought it would only be for a while. But would it happen again? Longer the next time? Longer until Judd simply no longer existed?

Judd stepped up to the door that had the name Holmes stenciled in fading letters on it and tentatively put his hand on the latch. The words *"Satan be with me"* surfaced in his mind and he wanted to choke. Before his hand touched the door, it opened suddenly and a tall, thin man froze in the entrance, staring at him.

"What the fuck? Who the hell—?" Then the man's eyes widened as recognition smothered his shock, only to be renewed when the full implication hit home. "Bull?"

Judd felt his face tighten into a smile. He heard the words, "Hey, Snake? How's it go? That asshole Buckshot around?"

"He's—hey, you ain't Bull. He's dead. Who the fuck are you?"

"You called it right, Snake. Take me to him."

Snake stepped back, still blocking the doorway, his cold glare drilling into Judd's face. Judd wanted to scream but felt as if he were watching from a detached viewpoint. He felt nothing. No power over his own body. No sense of ability to control his own senses.

Snake looked closely at the man. "Same clothes. But that don't mean nothin'. You could have copied them somehow. You look a little like Bull, but, Jesus Christ, I helped bury the poor bastard."

"Take me to Buckshot," Judd ordered.

"Christ, you even sound a little like him. But you ain't him."

"Stop using the name of Christ around me. You know better than that, you ass-hole."

"You're even pushy the way Bull was. Come on, you. I'm taking you to Buckshot. He's got to see this." Snake chuckled, a thin, sinister laugh that sent a trembling shudder down Judd's spine, and though he wanted to react to the whole situation by turning and running, he simply stepped across the threshold of the doorway and entered the warehouse.

Peggy lay back on the soft, lush meadow. A mild breeze wiped over her, sending the long-bladed grass into an impromptu, waving dance. A serene sky, dotted here and there with soaring birds, covered the landscape from horizon to horizon and she felt secure, warm, safe. She wished Judd would hurry back. Where had he gone? Someplace to get something, she recalled. But where? And what? She tried to sit up but couldn't, her own sense of well-being and comfort over-riding any desire to move out of the comfortable position in which she lay. A loud roar, a buzzing roar destroyed the calm. What was that? She turned on her side, reaching out for something—something to cover her head—to blot out that awful noise. But it was too late. The source of the sound, a motorcycle, suddenly flew over her—leaping from a small hill to the level floor of the meadowland on her far side. The bike swooped to a halt, turning a full half-circle until the headlight and the rider faced her. The biker looked familiar in a strange way. He looked like—like—

"Judd!" She sat up, calling out his name. Where was she? What had happened to the grass—and the sky—and the birds—and the motorcycle? She shuddered. She was beginning to dream about that damned thing. And Judd—Judd riding it. Why had her life and his taken such a bizarre turn? They would have overcome the trauma of Cindy's death in time. Then they would have married and settled down to raise a family. But Judd had had to find that motorcycle. And learn to ride it. Would it ultimately come between the two of them and drive them apart?

Peggy opened her eyes, reaching out for Judd at the same time. He was gone. When had he gotten up? Was he still in the apart— "Judd?" Slipping from the bed, she pulled a robe around her nakedness and ran lightly to the living room. "Judd?"

The kitchen yielded nothing, and she hurried to the window overlooking the parking lot. Except for a few cars, it was empty. The bike was gone and so was Judd. Where could he have gone? To work? Maybe, but for some reason she felt that he wouldn't be found at the hardware store. Not today.

For the first time since she had awakened and jumped out of bed, she felt the aches of her body. her lower abdomen and back hurt. The muscles were tender to her touch—as if she had been doing strenuous, unfamiliar exercises. What had—? Last night came rushing back. Judd and she making love. Judd more active than normal. Active? Hardly the right word. He had been almost animal-like in his drive to complete the sex act. Why did she suddenly think of their intimacy as an act of sex as opposed to one of love? Because Judd had not acted like Judd. He had behaved as if he had not been with her for a long, long time. Other than the one time before he found the motorcycle, they had not been intimate. He had even made some excuse about his roughness and boisterousness, saying that the two of them hadn't been together for so long that he was just plain horny for her. But she didn't, at the time or now, feel that that was the case. He had been spending an inordinate amount of time on the bike, day and night. And he had not come to her apartment for a long time—in fact, not since he had found the bike. When she went around to the store, he usually made her feel as if she were intruding on a stranger who was working on something very important. To her, Judd and the machine had become a source of irritation. Then, when he did come around, he behaved like an animal, passing it off as simply being horny for her. She didn't buy it. There had been occasions when they went relatively long periods of time without making love, simply enjoying one another's company. When they did get around to making love, it was always in a loving, caring way. But last night she had had at least six orgasms, and that was something new for her. At the most, she would climax once—maybe twice. But last night—no wonder her stomach muscles and back muscles hurt her so badly.

A hot shower would fill the bill and maybe alleviate some if not all of the pain. She glanced at the clock. She had about an hour before she wanted to arrive at the school. But should she go there unannounced? Maybe she should have an appointment. If this Mr. Montgomery would consent to see her, it would have to be on his terms. After all, he didn't have a practice as such. She would be intruding on his school time.

When she stepped out of the shower cubicle, she toweled off her body and, without dressing, went to the phone. After looking up the school telephone number, she dialed it and prayed he would be there already. The syrupy tones of the woman's voice answering asked her to hold, and she rang Mr. Montgomery's phone.

After several long rings, during which Peggy breathed a prayer for him to answer, the receiver was picked up and a deep voice said, "Maceo Montgomery."

"Mr. Montgomery," Peggy began and told him who she was and what it was she wanted.

"I do happen to have time this morning, Miss Dixon. Could you come in around nine-thirty? I'll have a free period then."

"Nine-thirty'll be fine, Mr. Montgomery." After she jotted down his office number and the directions how to find him, she hung up. She called Allan to tell him that she'd be late this morning. When she told him the reason, he readily agreed, adding that she would feel much better once she talked with the psychologist.

Peggy slowly reached for the knob and turned it without making a sound.

"Come in," the deep voice boomed from inside.

Without hesitating, she pushed the door in and stopped. Maceo Montgomery, tall, well-muscled, stood with his back to the door, closing a file drawer. Peggy didn't react when he turned, his even, white teeth gleaming from his black face.

"Come in, come in. You must be Peggy Dixon. Sit down. Normally, I don't have anything to do with cases outside of school. But there was something in your voice that told me you have a problem. Am I right?" He gestured for her to be seated.

"Since you're breaking your own rules, I sincerely hope so," she said, forcing a smile. "I wouldn't want you to be disappointed."

He grinned, taking his seat behind the desk when Peggy had sat down. "Now, what's on your mind?"

Peggy took him in in a glance. He was self-assured and confident. She could tell that in the way he moved and spoke. His almost square face was balanced perfectly with wide-set eyes, a finely chiseled nose, and broad jaw. When he smiled, his eyes twinkled good-naturedly as if he enjoyed a joke. Even if he couldn't or wouldn't help her, she felt she could like Maceo Montgomery as a person.

She told him everything that had been bothering her since Cindy's death.

"I can fully appreciate the pain and suffering Judd must have felt." He put the tips of his fingers together and waited for Peggy to continue.

She told him of the motorcycle, his sudden ability to ride it after he completely rebuilt the machine, displaying at the same time a remarkable aptitude for mechanics, something he had never shown before then.

"Everything you've told me is really most interesting. But couldn't the fingernail have been growing without your noticing it?" He stared at her, waiting for an answer. It seemed he wanted her to sell him on the veracity of her statements and observations.

"I don't think so. All during the funeral and services, we held hands. I would have felt it or at least have noticed it. It just suddenly seemed to be there. An inch and a half long."

"His weight might be explained away. Did it seem that he gained much?"

She shook her head. "Judd normally

weighs about one-seventy. I think he must weigh close to two hundred now or maybe more. At least he looks like it."

Maceo frowned. "You could be mistaken, though, couldn't you? Maybe the change in clothing made him appear heavier. If he always wore shirts and slacks before and suddenly showed up without a shirt and wearing only a vest, it might make him appear heavier, or even lighter."

Peggy swallowed. Last night, Judd had lain his full weight on her when they were making love. He was heavier. She knew that for a fact. But could she tell that to this man? This stranger? Granted, it was the job of a psychologist to deal in these matters, but did this Maceo Montgomery, who handled high school students' problems, understand? A wry smile crossed her full lips. The way students behaved today, she felt positive that Maceo Montgomery was eminently qualified.

"Last night," she began, "when we made love, I thought I was with a stranger."

"How do you mean?"

"Well, first of all, Judd felt much heavier. And he acted differently."

"Differently? How?"

"He was rough—rougher than he'd ever been. You'd have to know Judd to understand that, but he is a most gentle person. Tender. Caring. Loving. It always seemed as if he worried more about my personal gratification during our love-making sessions than about his own."

Maceo nodded. "He's a considerate man. That's all."

"Yes, he is that. And he's always been like that. But—" She hesitated.

"—not last night?" he finished for her, peering intently at her.

"Not last night." Her voice barely spoke the words.

"What happened?"

"I'm not sure I should tell you."

"I assure you, I'm most qualified. I do know I don't have any colleagues in town. I'm what you might say is the only show in town. You can tell me and let me try to help, or you can keep it inside and take it home with you. One way, you have a chance. The other will only lead to more misery for you." He waited.

"He was very rough last night. I have never reacted to him before like I did last night."

"And how was that?"

Peggy waited for a long minute before continuing, forming her answer. "I climaxed six times."

Maceo fought to control his smile. "You simply enjoyed it more than you normally do."

"But, Mr. Montgomery, there are other things. Last night he didn't try to keep his weight off me. That's why I feel he has definitely put on extra pounds. He was very heavy."

"But Miss Dixon, if he's never done it before, how do you know that he hasn't always weighed that much? You've just said he'd always kept his weight off you."

"I know that. But then he fell asleep right away. And he snored. Oh, Lord, how he snored. He's never done that."

Maceo looked away. "Perhaps *you're* overreacting to Cindy's death, looking for changes in Judd that maybe aren't there."

"What about his language?"

"His language?"

"He said something to me that he had never, ever mentioned before. He said something that was very insulting. And he knows how I feel about the language he used."

"Whoa. What are you talking about?"

"He said that he'd come over to my apartment and, to use his words, 'fuck my brains out' once he tried the motorcycle out."

"Maybe he was frustrated when he said that. We don't know, do we?"

"Maybe you don't, but I do. He growled the words. He sounded agitated, as if riding the motorcycle was the most important thing he could ever do. Anything beyond that would be relegated to second place or worse."

"Tell me what it is you're saying, Miss Dixon."

"I think Judd is a changed person. He's like—like—I don't know, someone else."

Maceo's eyebrows shot up. "Someone else? Do you mean that literally or figuratively?"

Peggy shrugged. "I don't know. One minute he's Judd and the next he's someone else."

"He might be undergoing some personality changes because of his sister's death. But on the other hand—" His voice trailed off.

Peggy waited. Then, when he seemed lost in thought, she said, "On the other hand, what?"

Ignoring her question for the time being, he posed one of his own. "You said, his face was puffed, ah—I think you used the word fleshier. Right?"

She nodded.

"You said that at times he looks and acts like an entirely different person. Right?"

Again Peggy nodded.

"Do you know anything about parapsychology?"

"Parapsychology? You mean the study of things that go bump in the night?"

He laughed. "Not entirely correct. It's studying phenomena that doesn't fall into set categories in the other sciences. I've always found it intriguing. There are certain things that simply defy explanation. Things that would have gotten people into trouble a long time ago if they had openly talked about them."

"I don't understand."

"Let me give you an example. It's only within recent years that psychiatry will address the incidence of multiple personalities. Today it's not that uncommon to read about someone with several personalities rooted within the same body, all fighting for dominance. Psychiatrists have been gaining a lot of success combating it. But one hundred years ago if someone had that happen, the individual would wind up in an asylum for the insane."

"Are you saying that that's what's wrong with Judd?" She frowned.

"No. Not at this time. There are many things that could be causing Judd to do what he does and act the way he does. I'm just pushing open a door a crack for you to peek through. To show you that there are other avenues open for exploration."

"What do you know about parapsychology, Mr. Montgomery?"

"I didn't formally study it. I've just had an interest in it. Sort of looking at alternative solutions to otherwise normal problems. Do you know what I personally believe?"

"What?"

"I think your Judd has been saddened greatly by the loss of his sister and that you're going to have to be very understanding with him."

"Do you mean humor him?"

"Not in so many words, but try to be understanding. From what you've told me, Judd is the last of his family. He's alone. Completely alone."

"But I'm there any time he wants me."

"I know that. And you know that. And I'm sure Judd knows that. But put yourself in his place. How would you feel if you had no living relatives. The idea is overwhelming if one concentrates on it long enough. Totally alone. One of a kind."

Peggy thought for a moment. If Judd truly needed someone like Maceo Montgomery to help him, how would she get him to go visit such a person? Would she have to trick him? What if Judd had developed a dual or multiple personality? What would happen to the Judd she knew and loved? What if it were something completely out of the ordinary? Something that dealt with parapsychology? What would she do then? Who could help Judd then? Maceo Montgomery? She aired her questions.

Maceo hesitated a moment before answering. "At this point, Miss Dixon, I don't think you or I should be making any snap diagnosis. Do you?"

She didn't react. She wanted to see what else he would say.

"This is probably a phase that will pass in time. It was probably brought on by his sister's death."

"Mr. Montgomery, don't say that. If I hear one more person say that Judd's actions are because of his sister's death, I'll scream. Judd is not the type of person to react to any trauma in the way he has. I know him. I love him. It has to be something else."

"What?"

She shrugged. "I don't know. I thought perhaps you could tell me. I don't know what I'll do now."

Maceo sat up. "Look, Peggy. May I call you Peggy?"

She nodded.

"Then you call me Maceo," he said, writing something down on a notepad. "I'm going to give you my home telephone number in Springville and the number of the motel I stay at here in Rushton whenever I stay over. I'm always here on Thursday nights. If, for any reason, you feel Judd might have need of me, call. Please? Will you?"

"Do you think there's reason I might have to?" Peggy eyed Maceo in a wary way.

"Nothing of the sort. But in the event that you become concerned because of something, I can perhaps help you over the moment. If Judd displays some aspect of his personality that might frighten you, call."

"Frighten me? I—I don't understand."

"I'm sorry, Peggy. I don't want to upset you. The way you've told me everything tells me that you are, in a way, frightened of Judd."

"I suppose that's true. But it's not really Judd I'm afraid of, it's the way he acts out of character. Do you know what I mean?"

"I think I do, Peggy."

A bell sounded in the hall and Maceo stood.

"Well, my morning break is over. I've got to get to work and take care of my problems here in the school." He moved around the desk, extending his hand.

Peggy stood and accepted his hand, feeling hers being encompassed by his large hand, which was warm and gentle.

"I'm sorry I took so much of your time."

"Just promise to call me if you think I might be able to help in any way."

"I will, Mr. Mont—Maceo."

She walked down the hall away from the small office, feeling Maceo Montgomery's eyes following her. He was a gentle man, a strong man. And intelligent. Perhaps she would find solace in calling him in the event she needed someone to talk with. She breathed a quiet prayer that she wouldn't need that remedy.

13

Judd allowed himself to be dragged into the warehouse. After Snake had reached for him, Judd's first instinct had been to run, but Bull intervened, hissing orders into his head.

"Don't run. Stay put. Let Snake take you in. How else we gonna get to Buck-shot? Remember, he's your sister's killer."

Snake grinned, showing the space where his four upper incisors were gone, his pointed canines prominently high-lighted by their absence. "Come on, you."

Judd had frozen, first at Bull's orders and secondly at the touch of Snake, which felt cold. He shuddered when he picked up the man's name from Bull's subconscious.

Snake pushed his captive ahead of him, once he had resecured the door to the warehouse. Judd looked about. It was pretty much the way Bull had envisioned it for him. After walking down a short runway, the two men entered the main storage area. Along both walls of the long, narrow room, people lay sleeping or sitting up and stretching as they awoke. Motorcycles parked at regular intervals seemed to mark off each gang member's private quarters. Charcoal grills, stationed between the bikes and the sleeping area, sequestered the cooking spot, if a man had a mama do his bidding. Otherwise, a loner would share with his neighbor on one side or the other.

Judd wrinkled his nose when he moved farther into the area. Engine exhaust hung heavily in the air, mixed with a subtle lacing of urine, garbage, and marijuana smoke. In one corner, apparently the dump for the gang, rats ran here and there, searching out the latest deposit for something edible. He turned away. How could this be called living?

Then he thought of the various impressions he had picked up from Bull. The more shocking their lifestyle appeared to regular society, the better a biker of this type liked it. Not that they went out of their way to find methods of attracting attention. It was just that other people seemed to frown on a person urinating on the sidewalk, in front of a dress shop or wherever the gang happened to have parked at the moment. Their manner of dress was another area of self-expression that seemed to escape outsiders' understanding. A name—Johnny Balls—popped into Judd's head. It was followed by a vision—a mental picture of a man with the area of his jeans covering his penis and scrotum cut out, exposing his genitals. A familiar face appeared when Johnny Balls disappeared. A woman. An attractive woman who wore no shirt or blouse—just a vest—a leather vest like the one Judd wore. Her large breasts fought to spread the two sides of the covering, succeeding whenever she took a step or turned one way or the other. Cow. Judd felt his face twist into a smile. Bull's smile. He would see Cow any moment. Wondering what her reaction would be at seeing Judd/Bull, Judd stopped when Snake reached out and grabbed his shoulder.

"We got company!" The sound of Snake's voice echoed around the high-ceilinged room, sailing through the dirt-encrusted metal beams overhead.

Those gang members who were awake turned languidly to stare at Snake and the intruder. Without hurrying, they stood, walking slowly toward them. After they formed a half-circle around Judd, peering at him intently, they stepped aside to allow a man and a woman enter the ring.

"Well, what have you got—" Buckshot stopped speaking when he saw Judd, his eyes widening in half recognition. His head bobbed up and down as he studied the newcomer. "Who the fuck are you?" He squinted at Judd, trying to identify him.

Judd wondered why they simply didn't call him by Bull's name. He didn't look like Judd anymore, that was for certain. But then, maybe he didn't look exactly like Bull either. Maybe he just resembled him in some way—a way that made the man confronting him think that he recognized him but couldn't quite place him. Judd found it interesting, until the name *Buckshot* filled his mind. Bull was identifying the man standing in front of Judd as Buckshot—the man who definitely killed Bull and more than likely was responsible for the deaths of Cindy and Tami. Judd quivered in his anxiety to reach out and strangle him. Bull held him back.

Buckshot turned to Snake. "What the fuck did you bring him in here for?"

"His clothes! Look at his fucking clothes. He's dressed like—like—Bull. Aren't those Bull's jeans and vest?"

Buckshot stepped closer to Judd, peering intently at the pants and their symbols and the Maltese crosses hanging on the sides. He nodded. "They sure look like it, don't they?"

Cow pushed past Snake and Buckshot. "I should know. I sewed the patches on his jeans."

Judd caught his breath. Despite picking up a definite odor of a body too long unattended with personal hygiene, he had to admit that Cow was a beautiful woman. She stepped closer and he held his breath.

Without looking at his face, Cow crouched, studying the symbols—the goat's head, the numbers "666," the inverted pentagram. Nodding, she stood and, when her face hovered mere inches from Judd's exposed chest, she looked up. She stifled her scream but, without fliching, reared back and slapped him across the face.

Judd felt tears forming in his eyes from the stinging blow. "What the hell did you do that for?" he asked, his own instincts for survival running immediately below the surface of the calm that Bull forced on him.

"Who are you?" she hissed.

"I'll ask the questions." Buckshot pulled her back and away from Judd. "Who the fuck are you, man?"

"Do you feel you should know me?" Judd was amazed at the calm in his voice. If it weren't for Bull's bravado pushing his own trepidation aside, Judd felt he would be whimpering like a baby. The looks of the motorcycle gang alone were sufficient to cause the staunchest of men some concern. But to be surrounded by them, some close enough to reach out and touch him or, worse, pull a knife, shot a wave of nausea and panic through Judd's body.

"Yeah. Yeah, you look sorta familiar." Buckshot strutted back and forth in front of their prisoner. "Yeah. You sure do. Just who the fuck are you?"

Cow stepped closer to Buckshot. "He looks enough like Bull to be a brother," she hissed. "Ask him that."

Buckshot turned to her for an instant, then refocused his attention on Judd. "You related to Bull?"

"Who?"

"Bull. A guy who used to ride with us."

Judd felt his shoulders shrug. Why was Bull playing with them like this? Why didn't he simply come out and state his reason for being here and get on with it? The sooner that happened, the sooner Bull would leave him.

"In case you didn't notice, Judd ol' boy, we're fucking surrounded. We can't lick 'em all—not at one time. I know what I'm doing. Don't worry."

Bull's voice crashed into his mind. Apparently the entity did know what he was doing. He had a plan, which would either divide the allegiance of the gang or get Buckshot alone for his and Bull's revenge.

"Right."

Judd relaxed just a bit.

Buckshot turned to Cow. "You remember my dream. I said Bull was coming. How do you explain this?"

She shrugged. "You just had a dream. This guy ain't Bull. Oh sure, he resembles him a little. But Bull was a lot bigger, heftier, more muscle." She stepped closer to Judd, her hand shooting out toward his crotch, grabbing his penis. "Yeah, and he had a lot more cock than this wimp. No, he ain't Bull. But he's wearing his clothes and he sorta looks like him. What's your story, man?"

"I'll ask the questions, goddammit! What's your story, man?" Buckshot parroted the question and glared at Judd after a warning glance at Cow. The woman submissively stepped back, behind her leader and lover.

"God, you people get bent out of shape awfully easy."

"No smart-ass comments. Tell us where you got the clothes." Buckshot stepped closer to Judd, a menacing grimace twisting his suet-colored face.

"Hey look, I'm about the same as you people are." Judd's eyes flashed from one face to the next before settling on Buckshot again.

"How do you mean?" Buckshot suspiciously narrowed his eyes.

"Well, you're all dropouts, aren't you?"

No response from the gang.

"I'm a dropout."

"Oh, yeah? What the fuck did you drop out of?"

"Come on, hear me out. I ran a hardware store and got fed up. I walked away one day and just quit."

"Big deal. So you're lazy. What else you got to say?"

"Hey, I don't pay taxes. I don't give a shit what other people think of me. I do what I want to, where I want to, and when I want to. I don't answer to anybody. Nobody."

"Okay, so you're a fucking rebel. So what? We're all like that," Buckshot said, sweeping the circle of people with one flabby arm.

"Well, then, I'm like you. Aren't I?"

" 'Aren't I? Aren't I'?" Buckshot mimicked. "No, you ain't!"

"Ask him about the clothes," Cow persisted from behind Buckshot.

"Yeah. Where'd you get the jeans and vest?"

A quiet fell over the warehouse before Judd spoke. It seemed to him that the gang was more interested in the clothes he wore and where he got them than who he was and how he resembled Bull.

"Okay. I'll tell you. I went out into the

country one day. After a while, I was near this woods, see? And I went into it. Just sort of walking along, enjoying the peace and quiet. No hassle from the establishment. No nothing. After I walked for maybe fifteen minutes or so, I came to this clearing, and you'll never guess what I found in it."

When Judd stopped, he realized how deathly still everything had become. The people surrounding him were barely breathing, waiting for his every word. Then Buckshot broke the silence.

"What? What the fuck did you find in it?"

"A mound."

Quick, concerned glances shot around the circle of faces surrounding Judd before redirecting their baleful glare on him.

"A—a mound?" Buckshot repeated.

"Right. And it looked like somebody had been digging on the top of it. So I went and got a shovel and started digging. Man, I thought I'd found a treasure or maybe an Indian burial mound with some artifacts in it or something. You know, I thought I'd found my meal ticket. Well, you'll never guess what I *did* find."

Buckshot grabbed Judd by the shoulder and shook him. "Stop playing around, motherfucker. Tell us now, or—" he brought up his hand, a clicking sound accompanying the movement, to reveal the four-inch blade of his knife, "—you've had it."

Judd stared back at him. He wanted to scream, but Bull squelched his attempt. Instead of reacting to the threat, Judd heard himself laughing. "Go ahead. Do me in. Then, you'll never now what I really do know about the Light Bearer's Chosen."

"So tell us and then I'll kill you," Buskshot growled.

"You'll never know if I told you everything. Maybe I've got a bunch of stuff written down someplace that'll go to the right person if something happens to me. You'll never know—till it's too late, Buckshot."

Buckshot paled. "How'd you know my name?"

Judd smiled, and he hoped, considering the way Buckshot and the others had reacted, that the smile appeared sinister. If they put high stock in wearing the cabalistic designs on their clothing, and in dreams, considering that Buckshot had said something about a dream, the Light Bearer's Chosen must surely be superstitious to a great degree.

"Right. That they are. You may have picked that up from me," Bull said to Judd. *"But I think you figured it out for the most part."*

"Tell me! Goddammit!" Buckshot

waved the knife back and forth under Judd's chin.

"All right! Don't get so goddamned hyper! I've been watching you and your gang for a little while. I know some of your names. That's all."

"Like who?" Buckshot stepped back, appearing to be convinced by Judd's explanation.

"Cow." Judd nodded toward the attractive woman. "Snake, here, who brought me in. There's Gordo. Mary Queen of Sots. Sweet Rosie O'Lay. Mule. Priscilla Puss."

"So you're sneaky. Big fucking deal. Now, tell us what you found in the mound."

Judd hesitated, more for effect than any other reason. He wanted to play with their superstitious minds. "I found—I found a bike. A—a hog!"

As one, the gang sucked in their breath and stared at the man they surrounded.

"Any—anything—anything else?" Buckshot asked.

"You know I did, Buckshot. I'm wearing what I found."

Fearful glances bounced around the circle of faces, from one to another. Then the gang, their eyes fixed on Buckshot, waited for him to say something.

"You dug up one of ours?" His voice cracked, his throat obviously dry.

Judd nodded. "But don't worry. I reburied the body."

"You defiled one of our graves," Buckshot growled. "You low bastard. You fucking grave robber. Ain't you got a sense of decency?"

Judd wanted to roar with laughter. This indecent scumbucket wanted to be treated in a decent manner. That was a laugh.

"I guess I'd want to be, too, if I were still alive." Bull's words shot to the surface of Judd's mind.

"I've heard of everything, now," Judd cried out, suddenly overriding Bull's control. "You bury a guy out in the middle of nowhere and you want him to be treated decently? Why don't you people join the human race?"

"What happened to your hatred for society, Boy Scout?" Buckshot asked, stepping forward to almost touch Judd when he faced him. Turning, he looked at the gang members. "One of our dead has been defiled, his grave desecrated. Bull's remains have been disturbed. This turkey comes waltzing in here with a cock and bull story and expects us to believe it. Sure, he might resemble Bull in a way, but he ain't Bull. He's too fucking little, according to Cow, here."

"What about the other two?" Mule asked suddenly, interrupting Buckshot.

Buckshot spun on his heel, darting to

Mule's side like a panther. Grabbing his lieutenant's arm, he pushed him away from the coterie until they stood twenty feet away. "What the fuck's the matter with you? Why'd you mention them?"

"What if he knows?" Mule whispered hoarsely.

"He don't know nothing. The cops was here. They checked us out and gave us a clean bill of health. That asshole over there don't know nothing."

Mule's long, thin face, whitened in fear, turned up to allow him to look at Buckshot. His close-set eyes didn't leave his leader's face. "I think he knows. He's been sent here to hassle us. By the cops, probably. I don't know. But I say we don't take no chances with him. If he knows we raped and killed those two girls, we'll all wind up in the jug."

Buckshot roughly shook Mule, enough to have his head bob back and forth. "Snap out of it, you jerk. He don't know nothing, I tell you."

"Yeah? Well, he knows about Bull and where he's buried. What if he gets outa here and goes and tells the cops? Then what? They can come back here, take us out there, dig up Bull's carcass and do some tests. They can find out that it was your knife that killed him as well as the two girls you did in. Then, we've all had it. What are you gonna do, Buckshot?"

Buckshot relaxed his grip on Mule. "I—I never thought of that. I guess you got a point." Buckshot turned toward Judd. Had the intruder heard Mule spilling his guts? If he had, there was no way he could be let go. He'd have to die. And damned soon, too. The longer he lived with the information that he surely possessed now, if he hadn't before, the more likely someone else might learn of it. That, Buckshot could not risk. This man would have to die.

Judd felt Buckshot's stare. He had the killers of Cindy and Tami. Or rather, they had him. How could he get away now? He had to summon the police.

"Forget the cops! You gotta be more concerned with getting outa here in one piece than squealing to the cops. That comes second—maybe. I still want a crack at Buckshot."

Suddenly Judd felt a wave of nausea sweep over him. He was in greater danger than he had been before Mule started confessing everything. In order for the gang to be safe, Judd would have to be shut up—permanently. Amazed at his degree of coolness, he looked over the heads of the gang and studied the room. There were doors that opened overhead, lining the back wall. Probably faced onto railroad tracks or a shipping dock of some sort. They looked as if they hadn't been opened in a long time. To either side, solid walls without windows paralleled each other. There were windows higher up closer to the ceiling, but they were of no use. Behind him, there were the double doors and the entrance through which Snake had brought him inside. It appeared to be his only avenue of escape. And it was cut off by a dozen people standing between him and it. He was trapped.

Buckshot entered the circle. "It seems that Mule has brought up a good point. Our visitor here knows too much and is a threat to the Light Bearer's Chosen. He's gotta be gotten rid of. And pretty damned quick. Any ideas?"

"I'll do it," Mule said, shouldering his way through the ring.

"Don't worry about him. We can take him." Bull's confident words did nothing to allay the feeling of apprehension and fear building inside Judd.

"I think we'd better pray first," Cow said to Buckshot while glaring at Mule. "He's too ready to further complicate the issue by killing this creep."

"What you got in mind, Cow?" Buckshot turned to the woman.

"I say put him on ice in the cellar, and tonight we'll hold a ritual and try to conjure up Bull's spirit. We'll ask him what this guy here knows. Then, depending on what we learn, we can do what we gotta do."

Buckshot slowly nodded. "That makes sense. Our prayers to Satan have paid off in a big way most of the time. Why shouldn't they now. Can you get through to Bull?"

"I know enough about necromancy to pull it off. Sure." She winked at Buckshot. "Besides, everyone here enjoys a good ritual. Right?" She turned to survey the others, who nodded collectively.

"Okay, then," Buckshot said. "Mule. You and Gordo take Mr. Smart-Ass here to the cellar and lock him up. There's no way out of that place. Tonight—tomorrow morning—Cow and I will fuck and get a hold of Bull's spirit."

Gordo and Mule each took one of Judd's arms and half dragged, half pushed him toward a door. Once they passed through it, they hurried down a flight of steps and stopped at a door on the far wall, opposite the staircase. Gordo, his beefy hands clamped around Judd's upper arms, waited for Mule to open the heavy, metal-lined door. It swung back soundlessly, and Gordo pushed Judd inside, through the black maw of the doorway.

Losing his balance, Judd fell to the floor and was not able to see his surroundings before the door slammed shut. The stygian gloom folded him into its embrace. He was trapped in a darkened room. Pulling himself into a sitting position, he circled his arms around his legs and said, "Thanks a bunch, Bull. You really got us in a fix."

"I didn't plan on this."

"So what do I do?" Judd looked about. Blackness everywhere. Not a touch of light anyplace. He couldn't recall ever seeing anything so dark as the place in which he found himself.

"The room you're in is an old storeroom. There's no windows or entrances other than the one you come in."

"So what do I—we—do? I can't just sit here and wait for them to come back and do whatever it is they're planning on." Judd wanted to scream. To curse. To do something besides just sit on the floor holding his own knees. He wished he could get up and move about.

"You can. Be careful that you don't run into the walls. There's nothing in here other than the walls to bump into."

Judd slowly got to his feet. At first he felt dizzy, as if he might fall over when he found nothing to fix his eyes on. It seemed as if he were trying to walk a tightrope, blindfolded. In seconds, the sensation passed and he had control of his equilibrium.

"What happens next, Bull?"

"Well, Cow said something about performing a rite. She also said something about necromancy. I don't know what she's planning there."

"What's that?"

"*Conjuring up the dead—*" Bull hesitated. "*Maybe, no, in fact she said something about conjuring up my spirit. That's what they're planning. They want to find out from me what's going on. That's pretty good.*"

"I don't understand. Is that possible? If they can, what good will it do them?" Judd wondered just where the predicament in which he found himself would lead. The only thing he had going for him was his communication with Bull.

"*Sure. It's possible. You gotta do the ceremony right, but it can be done. Cow's good at that sort of thing. That and fucking.*"

"But what will it accomplish?" If Judd didn't see the reason, it had to be obscure at best. He could think of no point to be gained by conjuring up Bull's spirit.

"*If they can converse with me, they'll know about you.*"

"Don't tell them."

"*If they're strong enough in their magic, I might not be able to resist. I don't intend on going. Because if I do, I have to obey them and answer their questions.*"

"I see but I don't see," Judd said, his mind whirling. "When will they do it? How much time do you—we—have before they try?"

"*They won't perform the rite until three tomorrow morning.*"

Judd felt his face scew up in a puzzled frown. "I thought that midnight was the hour for that sort of thing."

"A lot of people do. According to Cow, and she's the daughter of a witch like herself, when you want to invoke the black powers, you do it at three in the morning."

"But why three? Why not four-fifty-one or one-oh-one in the morning? Or nine at night?"

"Lotsa reasons, according to Cow. There are supposed to be three gods in one in the Christian religion. There were three nails in Christ when he was hung on the cross. And he died at three in the afternoon. There's other reasons but I don't remember them. Something about most people are sleeping then and can't focus their positive energy the way they normally do in the course of their waking hours. Something like that. It keeps the pathway to Satan open."

"Well, that gives us a lot of time to think of a plan of action," Judd said. It had been around eleven in the morning when Snake took him into the warehouse. It couldn't be much later than twelve or twelve-thirty now. That gave them—him and Bull—almost fifteen hours to think of something.

He sat back down, circling his knees with his arms again. He had to think. He and Bull had to think of something or Judd felt he would be killed soon after three o'clock the next morning.

"We've got to draw the double circle on the floor," Cow said to Buckshot as she fumbled in her bag of charms and devices. Finding a piece of chalk, she handed it to Buckshot. "Draw the circles big enough for the entire gang to be inside. If we succeed, we don't know how Bull will first appear. It might be as himself or as a wild animal. Whatever, all of us will be vulnerable while the spirit is here."

Buckshot turned away without commenting. Cow was the expert in these matters, and, like Bull, he felt it best to let her do her thing, and in that way the Chosen would prosper.

Cow went to the center of the warehouse, while Buckshot bent down making a huge circle with the chalk as he walked. "Listen, everybody. We've got to rest for the ritual. I want everyone to concentrate while you're awake on Bull. We're going to conjure up his spirit and find out if the asshole in the cellar is real or a cop or just what the fuck he is. Got it?"

Murmurs of agreement and heads nodding brought her the answers she wanted. With that much concentration and a good rite with Buckshot, she should succeed.

When Buckshot finished, she took the chalk from him and wrote the names of Astaroth and Asmodeus and drew the goat's head which sufficed for the inverted pentagram. She finished by inscribing the number of the devil at intervals around the border created by the double circle.

When she finished, she stepped out of the diagram and went to Buckshot's campsite. "I want you strong tonight. I want you to fuck me with all you've got, to give me the strength and ability to enforce the cone of power after I invoke it. Set the traps for rats. We'll need blood."

Buckshot turned to do her bidding. He didn't like being subservient to Cow, but her strength as a witch and practitioner of black arts had brought a period of prosperity to the gang as never before, after Bull brought her in as his wife.

When he finished, he returned to his camp to find Cow laying on her back, her vest off, her breasts thrusting straight up. He lay down next to her and bent over her nipples. His tongue flicked out, licking the brown aureoles before sucking on the gold rings imbedded in her flesh. She tasted salty. She always did. Cow reached out for him and pulled him on top of her. Buckshot grinned. He always enjoyed rehearsing for a ritual.

Judd lay on his back, sound asleep. He had dozed off several hours before, hovering in the clouds of slumber, unaware of his surroundings or where he was at. Off in the distance he could see a girl. As he approached her, he saw that it was a woman, and when he could make out her face, he began running toward her. Peggy. She looked good to him, but when he was close enough to see her better, he realized she was crying.

"What's wrong, Peggy?" he asked, stopping opposite her but afraid for some reason to touch her.

She didn't respond to his question. She didn't react to his standing a few feet away from her. It was as if he didn't exist—as if he were nothing more than a shadow.

"Peggy?" he cried out.

She still didn't react. Could she hear him? He reached out to touch her, but his hand passed through her arm. What was wrong? Then she opened her mouth and cried out.

"Bull?"

Why would she call Bull? She didn't even know of Bull's existence.

"Bull? Come to me!"

What in hell was going on? She shouldn't be calling Bull. She should be calling for him. Judd Wellington. Not the ghost of some dead biker. Some dropout who called himself Bull.

Then he became aware of words that made no sense to him at all. *"Exurgent mortui et acmo venuient!"* And the words seemed to be coming from Peggy.

She opened her mouth again. This time she spoke in English. "I require of you dead that you come to me."

One word suddenly bombarded his sleeping mind until he awoke. *"No!"*

Judd sat up. "What's going on, Bull? What's happening?"

"Exurgent mortui et acmo venuient! I require of you dead that you come to me." The words hammered in his skull along with the voice of Bull screaming, *"No! No! No!"*

"What is it, Bull?"

"It's Cow trying to conjure up my spirit. I won't go. I think I'm strong enough to fight her magic."

"But how can I hear her?"

"Bull! Come to me! We need you!"

"No! Never! Never!"

Judd waited while the pleading and the refusals continued. Then the voices fell silent. Nothing. He had to be going crazy. There simply was no other explanation.

After a few minutes, during which he felt Bull's exhaustion, Judd said, "How can I hear her? I'm not dead. Am I?"

"No, you're not dead, Judd. You heard her through me. It's over. She's failed."

"Now what happens?"

"I don't know. We'll have to wait and see."

Judd fell silent while Bull repaired his spent energies. The only sound in the room was his own quick, labored breathing as he tried to anticipate what would happen next.

Then he heard it. A slight noise at the door. Someone was there. He heard the lock turn and the door scrape open. Someone was coming in.

A little after two o'clock, the members of the Light Bearer's Chosen were awake and milling about, preparing to partake in the ritual that Cow would conduct.

Two large packing crates were shoved together in the center of the double circle Buckshot had drawn earlier. Once she made certain that each person was within the circle, Cow repeated her orders for them to concentrate on Bull even more than they had been and not to step outside the circles under any circumstances until the ritual was completed.

She stripped off her jeans and dropped the vest to the floor. Naked, she climbed up on the makeshift altar with the help of Mary Queen of Sots and Rosie O'Lay.

They handed her two black candles that she gripped tightly, one in each hand. She closed her eyes. Buckshot quickly undressed and picked up the bottle with the blood he had drained from the rodents caught in the trap. Trailing a thin line of the gore from Cow's throat to her pubic hair, he repeated the act, tracing a dark line from her right hand holding a candle, along her arm across her chest and the tops of her breasts, to the other arm.

Gordo helped him climb up on the altar. When Cow spread her legs, he entered her.

"Go slowly," she breathed. "You've got to make this last as long as possible to reap the full benefit."

Off in the distance, a clock in a church steeple tolled three times.

Buckshot pumped slowly and in a few minutes climaxed, and although Cow would have wanted more time, she gave up the candles to her attendants and pushed her lover off her body. Without speaking, she looked to Rosie, who laid down one candle and picked up a small bag, handing it to Cow.

Cow sat up and opened the bag, throwing its contents on the altar between her bare legs. Pieces of bone and several hanks of dark hair fell out along with a piece of flesh that had long since tanned into a buff-colored piece of hard, brittle leather.

Studying the talismans lying before her, she closed her eyes and peered skyward. *"Exurgent mortui et acmo venuient!* I require of you dead that you come to me!" she intoned. "Bull! Come to me! We need you!"

She waited. Nothing.

Again, she intoned the order. "Hear

me, oh, Astaroth! Hear me, oh, Asmodeus! Help my voice to cross that boundary that separates the living from the dead. Help it to reach the ears of him who was Bull here on earth. Let him hear my voice. *Exurgent mortui et acmo venuient.* I require of you dead that you come to me! Bull! Hear me! Bull! Come to me! Bull! Bull! Bull!"

She waited again. Nothing.

Cow's shoulders slumped forward.

Buckshot stepped forward. "What's wrong? Did you fuck it up?"

She shook her head. "I did everything correctly. If he's not coming, it means he either can't or won't for some reason. More than likely it's because he can't. Since that jerk in the cellar messed with his grave, poor Bull is probably all mixed up and doesn't know what happened to him."

"What do we do, then?" Buckshot stared at Cow, hoping she would have a solution to their problem.

"The man in the basement must die. Then, we'll be safe."

"I want to do it," Mule said, pushing through the crowd standing around the crates.

"You got it," Buckshot said, helping Cow off the crates. Turning to her when she stood next to him, pulling on her jeans, he said, "Is it safe to step outside the circles now?"

She nodded, slipping on her vest.

The gang accompanied Mule to the top of the steps and stopped, Buckshot produced a flashlight that he had grabbed before they left the camping area of the warehouse. With Mule leading the way, Buckshot followed him, flashing the light ahead for Mule's benefit. When they reached the bottom of the steps, Buckshot stopped, beaming the light toward the door through which Mule would have to pass.

"You got your knife?"

Mule held up the switchblade. "Wouldn't be without it."

"You're going to be as much at a disadvantage as he is in that room. There's no lights of any kind."

"I know that. If you want, you can come with me and shine your flashlight on him."

"No. You wanted to kill him. You do it in the dark and you do it now."

Mule swallowed and said, "Right."

He walked across the intervening space separating the stairway from the door and paused for a second while Buckshot played the beam of light on the doorbar. Mule reached out and lifted the latch, opening the door with a scraping sound.

Buckshot turned off the flashlight as Mule closed the door.

14

Judd held his breath. The entrance opened wider and he could see a back-lighted figure hesitate for a second before stepping forward through the doorway. Then the light, whatever it was, went out and all Judd could perceive was his own breathing until he heard the door being pulled shut.

"Where are you?" Mule's voice sounded hoarse, just the least bit tremulous.

"Try not to make a sound."

Bull's warning hissed in Judd's head, and for fear his breath might give him away, he held it. If only he could see something. Anything. A shadow. Or even a lighter or darker variance of the ebony shade surrounding him. Something that would lend a sense of reality to the utter black holding him, enveloping him, suffocating him. But he had to breathe and he exhaled as noiselessly as possible. The rush of air seemed to be amplified as it gushed through his nostrils, but at least he would be able to control it now. Perhaps he should move. Since he had let out his breath so loud, the man who had entered the room might have gotten a fix on his location and be closing in at that instant.

Carefully lifting one foot to avoid making any scraping sound on the concrete floor, Judd moved to his left about two feet. He brought the right next to it. Then, repeating the movements, he changed his location by ten feet or so after another four or five steps. Satisfied that he had been successful, he waited. Now what? What would happen?

A shuffling rasp of boot leather against the floor grated on the deathlike quiet holding the room.

"I think I know where you're at, asshole."

Mule's voice still quavered, but to Judd he sounded confident. Could the man see him? Could his adversary somehow see him? If that were the case, Judd would be vulnerable. He had no weapon. And according to what little he knew of the gang from his own experience and from what he had picked up from Bull, the man was more than likely armed. Another disadvantage. But could the man see him? Judd didn't see how he could. If Judd was hampered by the eternal night of the room, the other man had to be as equally disadvantaged.

"I can see him!"

Bull's words shot through Judd's skull. How? Was it possible? Could Bull really see him?

"I said I can. I'm really picking up something like vibrations from his thoughts. But I know exactly where he is. Just stay put. You're holding the high card now."

"But—" Judd froze. Why had he spoken aloud?

"So there you are. Just stay there and I'll come to you. We might as well get this over with in a hurry. Right?" Mule's voice had assumed an air of confidence after Judd's blunder.

"It's okay. He doesn't have an inkling where you are. He's moving in a direction that will let him pass about six feet away from you. But he's got his switchblade out. He's swinging it back and forth in front of him. Just don't breath too loud. Got it? And don't answer me."

Judd didn't think he'd ever speak in the dark again. This experience would remain in his memory, rooted there forever. Whenever he found himself in darkness, he would think of a man searching for him with the sole intent of cutting his throat. A quaking ran down his spine, but he fought to keep from breathing too loudly.

"I'm coming for you."

"Hey, Mule! You fuckhead!"

Judd almost screamed. Bull's voice. Speaking. Aloud. He had actually heard it. It wasn't in his head. He had heard it. And it was coming from across the room. How had he—? More importantly, *why* had he left and suddenly spoke?

"Who—who's there? Who are you? How do you know my name?" Mule's voice was constricted as if someone were choking him. "I—I can't see you. Where are you? Show yourself. How can you see me if I can't see you?"

Bull's laugh filled the ebony chamber, sending chills through Judd's body. It sounded so ghostlike. Haunting. Frightening. Threatening.

"Do you know who I am?" Bull asked.

"No—no. Who are you?" Mule whined.

"Who do I sound like?"

"I know who you sound like now. You didn't before when you were upstairs. You sorta looked like him but—you're not Bull. You sound like Bull now, but you're not. I don't know what you're trying to prove by acting like him. He's dead. Buckshot slit his throat. Just like he did the two girls all of us gang-banged. Who the fuck are you?"

"He's going to crack."

Bull was back inside Judd. But where was the man called Mule?

"He's got his back to you now. He's looking in the wrong direction. Don't move. Not yet. When it's time, I'll take over and Mule will be nothing but a pile of shit laying on the floor. Got it?"

Judd felt paralyzed. He didn't think he could move if he wanted to. All of this was like a dream. A bad dream.

"Hey, Mule. You're going to die. You know who says so?"

At first there was no answer. After several long seconds passed, Mule whispered, "Who?"

"Me! Bull! That's who. I've come back to take care of you and that sniveling piece of shit upstairs who thinks he can lead my gang."

Mule's scream rent the raven blackness, rising to a high pitch before plummeting to the depths of a blubbering whimper. While the man cried, Judd remained motionless, fascinated by the voice from within him and from the man he couldn't even see. Still, he pictured the terrified biker cowering on the floor, his eyes wide, horrified by the voice of his dead leader.

"I—I didn't have nothin' to do with killin' you, Bull. You gotta believe me. I didn't."

"I know that. But you were ready to

*jump to Buckshot's aid and be his right
hand man. Weren't you?"*

"Where are you, Bull? How come
you're back, Bull? Did Cow's ritual bring
you back, Bull?"

"You're going to die, Mule."

"No! No! It was Buckshot. It's Buckshot you want. Not me. Christ, Bull, you
gotta believe me."

*"You're his lieutenant. That means
you're gonna die, just like him."*

"But, Bull—" Mule's voice died away in
a simpering cry.

*"You haven't been true to my memory,
Mule. You should not have gone along
with Buckshot."*

"But it was a fair fight."

*"He had his knife out. I didn't. I
suppose it was a fair fight to a certain
degree. But that doesn't matter. You and
Buckshot are going to pay. Both of you!"*

Judd felt his legs moving. He tried to
resist but found himself powerless. He had
no control over his own body. It had been
just like that when he had been rebuilding
the bike. He had watched his hands do the
work, completely mystified at their
dexterity and apparent knowledge as to
what to do. But he didn't want to harm
Mule. At least he didn't want his own body
or hands or any other part of him to have
anything to do with hurting Mule. All he
wanted was to know who had killed his
sister. Then he'd report it to the police.

That's all he wanted. His legs continued moving, walking forward in the dark. Then he stopped. His arms lifted outward, his hands opened, reaching for something. He felt the man's throat in his hands, and, just as the fingers began closing, Mule wrenched away.

Judd heard him dash away, headlong toward whatever was on the far side of the room. Mule screamed at the top of his voice, babbling Bull's name and other incoherent words. Yelling, cursing, the terrified man raced away from Judd and ran full tilt into a concrete wall. The thud sounded as if he had fallen and struck the floor, but his voice continued, bubbling as he fell. The words stopped, replaced by a gurgling that seemed to pass for words.

Judd felt his cheeks tighten as his mouth spread into a grin.

Peggy rolled over, throwing the covers back. Clouds rolled in her sleeping mind, milling about in a roiling dance that troubled her. Why couldn't she see anything? Where was everyone? Where was—Judd?

She sat up. Reaching out to the empty side of the bed, she searched fruitlessly for him. Where was he?

Slowly, the night came back to her, playing in slow motion the awful sense of loneliness she had experienced last evening while she waited, hoping, praying that Judd would come back. By midnight, she had decided that he had probably gone home if he had returned at all. She felt he was slipping away from her. He was preoccupied with something that truly mystified her, something she wasn't certain she wanted to know anything about. Something that could cause a person to change the way Judd had changed had to be undesirable. And for that she felt like a traitor. She should be willing to stand by him and help him. But what could she do if he didn't want her help? She was realistic enough to know that if someone refused help or didn't want another's presence around, it was stupid and foolish to persist under those circumstances. And it appeared that Judd had reached that point. He didn't want her in his life anymore.

Even their lovemaking the previous night had been an experience she'd just as soon forget. He had been rough. Uncaring. Selfish in his lovemaking. Could she even categorize it as lovemaking, or had it been sex for sex's sake?

Lying back on the bed, she closed her eyes. Of course she had climaxed more than she ever had before with Judd, but the circumstances and the manner in which that end had been accomplished were a high price to pay for the pleasure she had experienced.

Turning her head, she focused her

eyes on the digital clock. Four. Four in the morning. Where was Judd? Had he gone home? Was he all right? Was he—? She sat up, reaching out for the telephone. The dial lighted up when she lifted the receiver and spun Judd's number. She didn't care if he was sleeping. She had to know if he was all right. She had to know. The connection completed, the buzzing ring crashed into her ear.

"Please, God. Please, let Judd answer," she said softly.

Another ring.

Peggy dropped her legs over the side of the bed.

Another ring.

Was he sleeping? Sleeping so soundly he didn't hear the phone?

Another ring.

Was he snoring? She recalled the way he had snored the previous night after they had—

Another ring.

She remembered her feeling of loss and chagrin when she had awakened to find him gone.

Another ring.

He wasn't there. She dropped the receiver back into the cradle. Where could he be? Who was he with? Was he safe? All right? She had to do something. But what? Call the police? That would be silly at best. They'd laugh at her. *"Hey, come on, lady. He's having a party someplace. He's okay.*

If you don't hear from him by tomorrow, call. We'd be interested then — maybe." And the police would laugh and laugh and laugh.

What could she do? Call somebody. But who? Who would understand? Allan? Not hardly. He wouldn't appreciate his secretary calling at four in the morning wanting to cry on his shoulder that she and her boyfriend had had a spat and she didn't know where he was at this hour. Then who?

She suddenly awakened fully. Maceo Montgomery. He had said to call if she needed help. Didn't she need help now? Of course she did. But would she incur his annoyance if she disturbed him at four in the morning? She looked at the clock again. It was almost four-thirty. Completely out of the question. She couldn't call now. Too early. But she would call as soon as she felt he might be awake. Perhaps she would force herself to wait until he got to school. After all, she didn't know for a fact that Judd was in any sort of difficulty.

Oh, God, what was happening to her life? A couple of months before, she and Judd seemed to have everything going their way. As soon as Cindy finished her college education they were to have been married. Then Cindy and Tami had been found, and all of their plans — hers and Judd's — had disappeared. At first it seemed as though they would only be delayed, as well they should have been, at least for a reasonable period of time following Cindy's funeral. But everything changed when Judd brought home that damned motorcycle. It had changed everything—even Judd—even Judd's appearance.

Peggy lay back on the bed, tears meandering down her cheeks and the sides of her face. She needed someone to whom she could talk—to pour out her feelings of frustration, of loss, and, yes, even of hatred—hatred for the motorcycle. Was it possible to hate an inanimate object such as a Harley-Davidson motorcycle?

Staring into the dark above her, she whispered, "Please, God, let Mr. Montgomery—Maceo—see me this morning. Let him understand what I'm going through. Let him help me. Please."

She covered her eyes with the backs of her hands, her fingers interlaced. She'd wait. She had no other options.

Buckshot grinned in the darkness at the foot of the steps when he heard the long, piercing scream. It was over. Turning, he shot the beam of light up the steps, exposing the faces of his gang peering down at him. "Did you hear that? It's over. The fucker's dead. Serves him right. Be sure to compliment Mule when he comes up."

The faces nodded in mute unison.

"Come on down here and let's give him a hero's welcome."

The gang filed down the steps in a slow way, fearful of falling in the half-light of the flashlight Buckshot held.

When everyone stood at the foot of the steps, they heard the latch on the door at the far end of the open basement lift, and then the scraping as the door opened. Buckshot flashed the beam of light in that direction. When the door was pushed open all the way, a hoarse cry of disbelief went up from the Light Bearer's Chosen.

Framed in the doorway, Judd held the limp body of Mule under one arm as though the man's inert form were a bed-sheet. He glared defiantly into the light, not seeing anything but still searching out the face of each person hiding in the bright aura. He didn't say a word, just stood there staring. Then he took a step toward the light—then another and another.

The gang fell back making room for the man to walk unimpeded through their ranks. They made no sound. What had happened to Mule? Who had screamed? Collectively they had thought that Mule had killed the intruder—the man who resembled Bull.

"Jesus! He carries Mule like he don't weigh nothing," a voice whispered from the dark. "Look at that. That's something Bull would have done."

At the mention of Bull's name, a broad grin crossed Judd's face as he continued walking. The smile brought a shudder to the gang and they fell back even farther.

Judd walked up the steps to the main floor. The grayness of dawn filtered through the dirt-encrusted windows along the top of the wall to his right, announcing the breaking of another day. At least up here, he would be able to see something. When he reached the crates that had served as the altar for the gang's ritual, he unceremoniously deposited Mule on the floor, letting him drop in a heap. Mule didn't move, his eyes staring fixedly at the floor close to his face. Spittle dribbled from his mouth, and although he breathed, he made no other noise.

Judd could hear the motorcycle gang coming up the steps behind him, and he turned to face them. When he did, they stopped, the last man poised with one foot on the floor and the other on the top step.

"I suppose you're going to tell us that you took care of Mule all by yourself?" Buckshot said, raising his voice in a false sense of bravado.

Judd grinned but said nothing.

"Mule outweighs you by forty pounds at least and he's a bit bigger than you," Buckshot persisted. "How'd you do it? Did you have a sap on you that we didn't find?"

Judd stared at him.

"Come on, goddammit! Talk. What happened in there?"

"Why don't you ask him?" Judd said softly.

"I don't believe you beat him in a fair fight." Buckshot took several menacing steps forward but stopped when Judd didn't move.

"What's your idea of a fair fight, Buckshot?" Judd glared defiantly at him. He could feel Bull's presence weighing heavily on him. But for some reason, Bull was using Judd's voice to speak. He wondered why.

"Hey, don't talk to me about fair. What the hell did you do to Mule?"

"You sent Mule in to kill me, didn't you? He had a knife. I didn't. You killed Bull in the same way. You pulled your knife and cut his throat without giving him a chance to defend himself. Is that your idea of fair? There's nothing wrong with Mule that a long rest in a nut house someplace won't take care of." Judd threw his head back and laughed. He could see the effect his brazen attitude had on the gang. They seemed confused, almost frightened.

"Gordo! You and Blaster search him. He's got to have something on him. G'wan! Do it, goddammit!"

Gordo and Blaster stepped out of the

ranks, walking tentatively toward Judd. As they approached they hesitated even more, slowing their pace until they were taking one deliberate step after the other, pausing between each for several seconds. The expressions of their faces looked as though they half expected Judd to either attack them, annihilating them on the spot, or disappear in a cloud of smoke.

When Judd didn't move, they came to his side, and while one patted him down on his legs, the other, without taking his eyes off Judd, lifted the vest.

"He's got nothing," Gordo said, and the two men half ran, half walked back to the safety of the group.

Assured that Judd was weaponless, Buckshot advanced toward him. The gang gathered behind him in a show of force.

"Hold it, Buckshot," Judd held up his hand.

The gang stopped. "What?" Buckshot glanced from side to side. It wasn't doing his image any good to be ordered around by this stranger.

"I want to talk to you—alone."

"Whatever you've got to say, you say it out loud for everyone to hear."

"This is for your ears—and eyes—alone."

Without taking his eyes off Judd, Buckshot leaned back and said, "Gordo. Blaster. Follow me."

"Have them keep their distance, Buckshot. At least ten, fifteen feet away. You got it?"

Buckshot hesitated for a second. "Yeah. I got it. Do what he says, boys."

When Buckshot stood five feet away from Judd and Gordo and Blaster were another ten feet behind that distance, Judd smiled.

"Well, Buckshot, it's nice to know I'm dealing with a chicken-shit, no-good sonofabitch!"

"Watch your mouth, asshole!" Although he tried to sound tough, Buckshot felt his knees quiver, and his voice seemed to echo his sense of fear.

"Hey, look. I'm willing to fight you to the death, right now—right here. But—" Judd let his voice drift off, letting the threat hang in the air between them.

Buckshot paled. "Who said anything about a fight to the death?"

"I did. If we fight, and I'm positive we will, you'll want to pull your switchblade and try to cut my throat like you did Bull's. Am I right?"

"Say, how do you know about that fight? Did you figure out what happened when you saw Bull's body? What did it look like?"

Judd shook his head at the prurient question. The man had a problem in his head, of that fact he was positive. "Do you really want to know how I know all about that fight, Buckshot?"

He nodded.

"Come a little closer, this is for your ears only." Judd motioned for him to come nearer.

Buckshot took one step, then another before he stopped again. Less than three feet away now, he glared at Judd, trying to figure out the man's intentions, his reasoning, his motivations. "Just who the fuck are you, man?"

Judd's jaw moved slowly and froze when the lips were an inch apart. Bull's voice whispered from the confines of Judd's mouth, "You're going to die, Buckshot. Not now. But soon. Real soon. I just wanted you to know, that's all. It's more warning than you gave me."

Buckshot's eyes rolled up, disappearing, leaving the whites blankly staring at Judd. "I—how—you—but—no— It can't be—who—," spilled from his lips, his mouth jerking spasmodically, sending his sparse goatee into a twitchy dance. The blood drained from his face, and as he stood for one long, agonizing moment without moving, Buckshot felt his strength draining from him. His knees buckled and he slowly collapsed to the floor, half sitting, half leaning forward, ready to fall, face down.

"Hey, what's happening?" Gordo boomed and took a menacing step toward Judd.

"Hold it right there, Gordo!" Judd said, surprised to hear his own voice again. "You, too, Blaster. All of you stay right where you are. Buckshot's all right. He's just fainted. That's all. The guy who's been leading you couldn't take what I just told him."

Judd stepped over Buckshot's body and around Mule, who lay in the same position that he had assumed when Judd had dumped him on the floor.

"I'm going now. I *will* be back. You can count on it. You can tell Buckshot for me that I will definitely be back. You got it?"

The heads of the members bobbed disjointedly.

"He didn't touch Buckshot," one voice said from the group. "I watched real close, too."

"Hey, I did too. You're right. Whatever he said to Buckshot is what scared the piss out of him to make him faint like that. Some fucking leader."

"Yeah, we better think about somebody else. That asshole Buckshot is worthless."

As one, the gang turned, watching Judd walk slowly, deliberately toward the exit. When he reached the door, he stopped and turned. "Boy, you guys are a bunch of sorry assholes," he said, Bull's voice booming out into the warehouse. "You follow a jerk like Buckshot and think you're tough. You're as tough as your leader, and he's a piece of shit. It sure would be a shame if your glorious leader wound up like Mule, there—a babbling idiot. I'll see you assholes around."

Judd threw open the door and stepped through, leaving the Light Bearer's Chosen behind in the gray light of predawn as it filtered through the windows overhead, their mouths hanging agape.

Several long seconds after the door banged shut, Gordo moved. The gang milled about for a moment, not knowing what they should do.

"Is Buckshot all right? What about Mule?" one asked.

Cow stepped out of the ranks and hurried to Buckshot's side. He opened his eyes and stared at her.

"Are you all right, Buckshot? What did he say that made you pass out like that?" She stared into his eyes, searching for some logical reason for a man like Buckshot to act the way he had done.

"That was Bull," he whispered hoarsely.

She shook her head. "It wasn't Bull. He sounded like Bull, but it wasn't him. He's dead. And buried, I might add. The guy was able to imitate him somehow, that's all. You let him get to you."

Buckshot struggled to his feet. "No, I tell you. That was Bull's voice. He said,

'You're going to die, Buckshot. Not now. But soon. Real soon. I just wanted you to know, that's all. It's more warning than you gave me.' That what he said. How did the guy—a stranger—know all about the way Bull died? There's no way.''

''Maybe he was hiding in the bushes and saw everything.''

''Naw. That's bullshit. He knows. Somehow he knows, and Bull is on his side. He's going to kill me.'' Buckshot looked about the warehouse, his eyes widening as he searched for something, but he had no idea as to what it might be.

''What are we going to do, Buckshot?'' Gordo moved in closer.

''Well, he's gone now. I'm glad he's gone. Maybe he won't come back.'' Buckshot looked from face to face searching for agreement. Instead he saw expressions of concern, of worry, of sadness. ''What's wrong with you people? He won't be back. I guarantee it.''

''The last thing he said before he left was 'You can tell Buckshot for me that I will definitely be back.' '' Gordo looked away when he saw Buckshot ready to turn to face him.

''I don't believe it.''

''Have it your way. I think he'll be back. And looking for you.'' Gordo's grim face turned back to confront Buckshot's.

''Hey, look, I'm not going to worry about some straight asshole who can imitate Bull's voice. That's what Cow says. He's imitating Bull's voice somehow. That stupid shit ain't got nothing going for him. He's weak."

"Yeah," Blaster said, "real weak, the way he carried Mule under one arm. He's just about the biggest cream puff to come along in a long time." Blaster laughed gruffly and turned away.

"If he comes back," Buckshot said, "we'll be ready. Right now, I want to fuck somebody. You, Mouth, come here." He reached out and pulled one of the women to him.

"Hey, that's my wife," Blaster said.

"Just what the fuck you gonna do about it?" Buckshot asked, flicking the blade of his knife open and swishing it in slow arcs in front of him.

Blaster fell back. The whole situation was quickly disintegrating. Now the leader was breaking one of their few laws where the members were concerned. No one— but no one—ever had anything to do with someone else's wife. The mamas were free game anytime. If a guy wanted to sell his wife's ass for a little money, that was no problem. She was his to do with as he wished. But no one did it without the man's permission.

Buckshot took Mouth to his camp area and ordered her to undress. Cow stood a few feet away, glowering. As Mouth undid her shirt, Buckshot pulled off his jeans.

When she stood naked, he lay down, pulling her after him.

The gang sullenly moved away to their individual campsites.

Blaster glanced at Cow. "Come on over till they're finished.

"Might as well," she said quietly. "The whole fucking night has been one big nothing. A failure. The rite didn't work. Buckshot's acting like an asshole. Want to fuck me, Blaster?"

He shrugged as he entered his area and took off his shirt. "Might as well."

Judd raced down the highway, the Harley-Davidson purring between his legs. The speedometer needle hovered between ninety and ninety-five. At this rate, he'd be back in Ruston within another hour's driving time. He felt exhausted but elated at the knowledge that he knew who the killers of Cindy and Tami were. He knew definitely. All he had to do was contact the sheriff in Rushton and let him take over.

"It worked, Bull. We got 'em, haven't we?"

He waited. Bull didn't respond.

"Bull?"

Nothing.

"Come on, Bull. Speak to me."

Still no response.

Where was he? Had he left? Did he feel that his job was completed now that Judd knew where the hideout was?

"Bull?"

Judd's face screwed up in a frown. He couldn't have left. How else would Judd be able to drive the motorcycle at ninety miles an hour plus without killing himself?

"Come on, Bull, I know you're still with me."

Still the spirit refused to answer, and Judd suddenly felt powerless to do anything about his own life, his own convictions, or his own future. His troubled sense delved further. Did he even have a future?

PART 4

Evil Is As Evil Does

15

By six-thirty, Judd had slowed the bike to forty-five miles an hour as he approached the city limits of Rushton. There was no sense in blasting through town and attracting the attention of the police. He turned off the highway after entering the town and drove down Maple Street. Pulling into his driveway, he decided to put the motorcycle in the garage, behind the Toyota truck. After he turned off the engine, he closed the overhead doors and hurried inside.

Before he did anything else, he picked up the telephone and dialed Peggy's number. While he let her phone ring, he dumped several scoops of coffee into the basket and poured water into the reservoir. Just as he emptied the carafe, the connection was completed when Peggy answered.

"Hello?"

Her voice sounded good to him, but he detected a note of weariness in it, coupled with an edge of tension. Both qualities were strangers to Peggy, but she possessed them now. He wondered for a second why, and then blanched, feeling a thin film of moisture form on his forehead. Was he the cause?

"Hi," he said simply.

"Judd? Where are you? Are you all right? Where have you been? You're not in trouble or hurt, are you? Where are you?"

"Hey, wait a minute. I'm here at the house. I'm fine. If you're interested in a cup of coffee and maybe a quick breakfast, why don't you come over?"

"I was awake almost all night. I kept waking up. I dreamt about you—that you were in all kinds of trouble. I've got to take a shower and then I'll be right over. You will be there, won't you? You won't take off again, will you?"

"Geez, you're making me sound like an irresponsible kid, Peggy. Of course I'll be here. Hurry. I've got something really important to tell you."

"What?"

"It'll hold until you get here."

"What's it about? Give me a hint."

"It's no light matter. In fact, it's pretty darn heavy. And, I won't play games with it. I'll tell you when you get here."

She didn't answer right away, and Judd pictured her on the other end, her dark eyes flashing back and forth before settling on the mouthpiece of the phone, trying to visualize him, a slight pout forming on her lips.

"Okay?" he asked.

"Okay. I'll hurry. Have the coffee made by the time I get there."

"It is already."

"See you in a few," and she was gone.

Judd hurried to the bathroom, stripping out of the jeans and vest. He ran his hand over his face. His beard was at least two or three days old. He had never cared for the unkempt look started by the cops-and-robbers TV show about the Miami police department and decided he'd shave. He wanted to be at his best for Peggy. Now that he had found the murderers of his sister, he felt his life would soon be back to normal.

Normal? The picture of his own reflection in the warehouse window crashed into his mind. He didn't even look like himself. Or had he imagined that? Had it been some trick that Bull had played to confuse the gang? He hadn't looked in the mirror yet, and now he felt almost afraid to do so. What if he still looked like he had in the capital? How would he explain it to Peggy? She was on her way over to see him, and she expected to see Judd Wellington—not some beefy-faced, wavy-haired guy—not some stranger she didn't know.

He stepped in front of the mirror and relaxed. He looked like himself. He looked closely. Yes. It was he. His cheeks seemed to be puffed a bit—a little fleshier than normal, but he looked like himself. Perhaps his face was swollen because of his lack of sleep. He had dozed for a few minutes in the black room but had been awakened when he heard that eerie voice calling Bull. He shuddered and turned on the hot water.

While he shaved, his thoughts went back to the ride that morning from the state capital to Rushton. What had happened to Bull? Where was he? Had he left, knowing that Judd would call the police and have the Light Bearer's Chosen arrested? It didn't seem likely that the entity would simply leave him and not say anything. But what did Judd expect when that would happen? An emotional good-bye?

He ran a hand over his smooth face, inspecting for any wayward whiskers that might have escaped the razor. Satisfied, he pulled the plug out of the bowl and turned on the shower. In seconds, he felt hot water gushing over his body, washing away his fatigue for the moment. The bruises, although still visible, didn't hurt him as much, and it was only when he had been shaving that he had noticed them in the mirror. The thought of the marks brought the memory of Bull back again. It seemed strange that, as talkative as the spirit was, he would simply vanish. Of course, Judd had no idea if that was the way the situation was supposed to work. Did anyone? He felt that what he had been through was most extraordinary, and he wondered just how much he should tell Peggy. Should he tell her anything? Would she believe him? Would she believe any of it? What would her reaction be? Accept it? Believe it and then, with Judd, try to forget it? Maybe it would be better to invent a story—one that had more credibility—one that almost any person would believe—and tell it. That way there would be no chance for her to misinterpret his motives, his story, or him. The last thing he wanted was Peggy thinking that he'd lost his mind and that she should do something about it for his own good.

Turning off the shower, he stepped out and toweled his body dry. Without hesitating, without a thought about it, he picked up the jeans, stepping into them in one fluid motion. Donning the vest, he pulled on the boots and went to the kitchen.

Ten minutes later, Peggy arrived.

At first they simply stood opposite each other. She looked so good, so whole-some, so clean to him, especially when he thought back to the warehouse and the women of the gang. He wanted to hug her and smell her cleanliness. He held out his arms, and she closed the space between them and was lost in his embrace.

She smelled like flowers. Clean, deliciously scented flowers. "It's so good to hold you, darling," he whispered in her ear.

She squeezed him around the neck and they kissed. A gentle, loving kiss that barely allowed their lips to touch. But the fire of love, the feeling of desire, the sense of want—all were present, encompassed in the delicate contact.

"You look all right. Are you?" Peggy stepped back to scrutinize him from head to toe.

Judd turned slowly, in a full circle, a silly grin on his face. It felt good, normal, to be foolish for a moment. "You'd better check all of me. I might be hiding something." When he faced her, he made a move to open his jeans but, wiggling his eyebrows, stopped.

"You're a little on the giddy side, but you look fine. Now tell me everything."

"Everything?"

"You heard me. I want to know where you were, what you did, and if you found anything."

"What do you mean by anything?"

"I assumed you were doing your investigating thing. Weren't you?"

He nodded. "I found them."

"What?"

"I found the killers."

Peggy sat down on one of the kitchen chairs. Her face twisted into a bewildered mask. "But how? I mean, how could you, when the police and the sheriff's department drew nothing but zeroes the whole time? How did you find them?"

"Well, I knew almost for a fact they weren't from around here. So I thought of the state capital. It's the largest city closest to Rushton. I went there yesterday morning. I thought I might be able to get a lead on some motorcycle gangs and where they hung out."

When he paused, Peggy waited for a second. "And?"

"And I did." Judd poured two cups of coffee and set one in front of Peggy. Sitting down opposite her, he sipped his for a long-drawn-out moment. "I went to this motorcycle shop and found out that there are a couple of such gangs in the city. I simply drove by the first one until I was noticed. One of the members signaled for me to stop, and he asked where I got the bike and the clothes, since both were like theirs. I told him I was an admirer, and he took me into their headquarters and I was introduced. They thought I wanted to join them." He watched Peggy over the lip of his cup as he drank more coffee, to see if she believed his story.

"Just like that?" Peggy's eyebrows arched in surprise at the ease with which Judd had uncovered the gang. "Isn't that fantastic. Then what happened?"

"While I was in there, I happened to overhear two of them refer to the two girls they had raped and killed. The one told the other to shut up and motioned toward me. I guess he thought I might have heard him, which I had, of course. I did a good job of acting like I hadn't heard anything, and they just moved away."

"Oh, God, Judd! Call the police—right now. I'm so proud of you."

"*No!*" Judd slapped the table with his open palm, upsetting his cup of coffee, and jumped to his feet.

"What?" Peggy's face whitened. "But why? You've got them. Let the police do— What are you planning? Not your own brand of revenge or justice? Oh, please Judd. Don't."

"Hey," Judd said in a confused way, pacing up and down, wondering why he had reacted so violently to the suggestion. Had it been his reaction or was Bull back? He searched his inner being, mentally calling to the entity, but there was no response.

"Look, Peggy. Sure, I overheard them but I don't think that's admissible in a court of law. It would be my word against theirs. And they've got numbers to my one. There must be thirty or more members. They would all say they had nothing to do with it, and I'd say they did. Who would you believe?"

She thought for a moment, knowing his point was valid. "But if you don't have evidence, what *are* you going to do?"

"Go back. Maybe I can find something concrete—something that *will* be admissible.

"That's too dangerous."

"Nothing happened the first time," Judd lied.

"By the way, how *did* you get away from them?"

"Well, first of all, they weren't holding me prisoner or anything like that." He could imagine Peggy's reaction if he told her of the dark room, the terror when Mule entered it with the intention of killing him, and then carrying the befuddled man out and brazenly walking out of the warehouse.

"You walked in, talked a little, and walked out, just like that?" Peggy snapped her fingers.

Judd nodded. How could he tell her that the spirit of the dead gang leader had invaded his own soul and run the whole show? How could he expect her to believe that his own appearance had altered so much that some of the gang members had first thought he actually was the leader who had been murdered by Buckshot?

"Where is this warehouse?" Peggy had

no idea as to what she would do with the information if he told her. Would she call the police herself? It might be premature, and if that were the case, the gang might go unpunished. They would be free on some minor technicality and Judd would be furious. Judd might wind up hating her for acting in haste. He seemed to know what he was doing. She looked at him closely. His hair was still wavy, but she thought that perhaps it wasn't as bad as it had been. She covertly looked at his right hand. The long nail was still there, but his cheeks didn't appear to be quite as fleshy as they had been the last time she had seen him.

"A few blocks into the city, off to the right, there's a street that's lined with warehouses. I think the name of the street is Railroad Avenue. The warehouse the gang is in isn't used as a warehouse any-more. The front is rather narrow com-pared to the others, and it's the only one painted yellow. The name 'Holmes' is in faded black letters near the roofline. A person could hardly miss it. Of course, the yellow's pretty faded, but it's still notice-able."

Judd suddenly panicked. Would Peggy tell the law? "I hope you won't tell anyone this. Will you?"

"I'll be honest, Judd. At first I thought I would call the police. But if I did that, and the gang wasn't punished because the police really didn't have any legal right to arrest them, it might really hurt you. It could destroy you. Or it might make you hate me. I couldn't live with that. I would never run a risk of losing you, darling." Standing, she moved to him. They embraced.

When they parted, she said, "What *do* you plan on doing?"

"I don't really know. I've got to set them up somehow. So they outwit themselves, so to speak."

Peggy reached out, laying a hand on his arm. "You're no match for a gang like that. I'm really worried. I won't feel right until it's over or you agree not to do anything."

"I've got to do something. My God, Peggy. Cindy was my sister. My family. My only relative. I've got to do something. Besides, knowing what I do sort of balances things. I won't do anything foolish."

"How many members are there?"

He pursed his lips, picturing the gang in his mind as they stood huddled together when he left. A smile wrinkled his mouth when he caught the frightened expressions on most of their faces. He also had a few tricks up his sleeve. He had Bull. Or did he? Why didn't the spirit respond? "About thirty or so men and maybe fifteen or twenty women."

"You're outnumbered almost fifty to

one and you say you've got the balance in your favor with what you know? Are you crazy, Judd?" She instantly regretted her choice of words. When she saw no reaction to the uncaring question, she relaxed as much as she could.

Judd shrugged.

"You look tired." She reached out, touching his face. "Did you get any sleep at all last night?"

He shook his head. "I slept a few minutes but that's all. I really am tired. But I don't want to spend the whole day sleeping."

"You don't have to. It's going on eight-thirty. If you go to bed right now, you'll get five or six hours sleep and still have most of the afternoon and evening."

"Can you stay?" His eyes pleaded more than the words.

"I shouldn't, but if you want me to, I will. I can call Allan and tell him I'm taking the day off. All right?"

"That's perfect. You're perfect, too." He smiled and sat down heavily on a kitchen chair.

Peggy called her boss and then turned to face Judd. "Why don't I make breakfast for you? Hungry?"

"I hadn't really thought much about eating. Come to think of it, I didn't eat at all yesterday. I'm famished. I really am." He wondered how he could have gone the whole day, the whole night, and not once think of food. What had kept him going? Hate? Bull? What?

Peggy cocked and eyebrow. "All day yesteday and last night? Nothing? How many eggs do you want? A dozen?" She laughed.

It sounded so good, her laughter ringing in the kitchen. Judd thought that he hadn't heard such a musical sound in months. It was normal, healthy. "A couple of basted eggs will do just fine. There's some bacon in the fridge."

Smiling broadly at the opportunity to cook for Judd and make him feel at ease and relaxed, Peggy went to the refrigerator and got out the food. In minutes, the woody smell of bacon frying filled the kitchen.

Judd wondered why he didn't feel exhausted. Was he running on reserve strength? He felt just the least bit tired as if he had worked at the store all day and was home for the evening. If that were the case, in a couple of hours he would be tired enough to go to bed and sleep. Would he not be tired when he finished eating now? Or would he wait several hours, as seemed to be the dictate of his body at the moment?

When Peggy placed a plate with two eggs and four strips of bacon in front of him, he looked up, snapping out of his revery. "You're super. You know that? I love you."

She leaned down and kissed him, this time their lips doing more than simply brushing. Hers spoke eloquently of her desire, and his responded in imitation. When they parted, she smiled. "Eat your food before it gets cold. You can have dessert afterward if you want."

"That was a lovely appetizer," he said, biting into a strip of bacon. It tasted even better than it smelled, and he quickly satisfied his bodily appetite for food. When Peggy placed a glass of orange juice in front of him, he automatically picked it up, draining it in one motion. After he finished, he quietly drank a cup of coffee while Peggy cleaned up the kitchen.

Where was Bull? Why didn't he make his presence felt? If Bull were truly gone, Judd doubted if he wanted to run the risk of going back to the warehouse alone. Maybe he *should* call the police. He'd have to think on it once he had a few hours' sleep. Fatigue was beginning to take its toll on him and his eyelids were beginning to feel scratchy. He wanted to sleep. He needed sleep.

He stood. "I'm going into the bedroom." Without waiting for an answer, he left the kitchen and went through the small, formal dining room and into the living room. The master bedroom was the first one he came to after entering the hallway. Opening the door, he quickly stripped out of his clothes—Bull's clothes—and opened the bed. Lying down, he relished the coolness of the sheets against his nakedness. He pulled a sheet up, covering most of his lower torso. The bed felt good, relaxing. Once he slept, he would be able to think more clearly.

The door opened and Peggy walked in. She sat down on the edge of the bed and stroked his forehead. Bending, she kissed him, her tongue darting into his mouth, presenting her request.

Judd savored her taste before answering in kind with his own tongue. Then his eyes flew open and a low laugh rumbled in his chest.

Peggy stood, and quickly stripped before turning back to the bed. When she did, she screamed. It wasn't Judd lying on the bed. It was a different person. His face was fuller than Judd's—rounder—not triangular like Judd's. His hair was deeply waved and he appeared much beefier through the body. She struggled to cover her nudity but failed, and when he leaped from the bed, she found herself unable to make her body obey her command to flee. She couldn't move.

He grabbed her, wrestling her to the bed. When she resisted, he slapped her hard across the face and she screamed— both in terror and in pain. What was happening to Judd? Was it Judd? One minute he had been lying there, and when she turned around for a minute, Judd had either disappeared to be replaced by this stranger—or—she shuddered—Judd had changed into this man.

Judd, or whoever he was, clamped his mouth on hers, jabbing his tongue into her mouth. She wanted to gag but couldn't because the intruding muscle was in the way. She felt her stomach heave. What if she vomited? What would he do? His hardened penis pressed against her lower belly. It was hot—almost burning to the touch. Then she felt him raising his body and one powerful arm went to her legs, spreading them apart. Even though she resisted, the unbelievable strength in that one arm parted her legs as if she were cooperating and not resisting.

His mouth still covering hers, he penetrated her lower body and began rhythmically pumping. She felt a sob forming deep within her. She would have screamed but she couldn't. She wanted to cry but couldn't. All she could do was lie there and let the man—Judd—or whoever he was, fuck her—rape her. This wasn't the gentle lovemaking that she and Judd indulged in when they expressed their feelings. This was animalistic. It was barbaric. It was awful.

He finally released her mouth, and although she thought of screaming, she decided against it. The harm had been done. Why infuriate him and run the risk of being injured or possibly—killed?

His weight full upon her, he continued thrusting his blood-engorged member into her. She lay impassive, letting it happen, certainly not helping in any way.

Without stopping, he growled, *"Move. Move, goddammit. You're laying there like you're dead. Christ! Do something."*

She opened her eyes to see the wild stare and the saliva dripping from the corner of his panting mouth. *Oh, God,* she prayed. *Don't let this go on much longer. I can't take it.* To appease her attacker and keep him from doing anything more harmful to her, she moved her hips just a bit in unison with his savage attack. Who was he? Where had he come from? He couldn't be Judd. She was positive of that. Judd was gentle and loving. This man— this animal—was rough and uncaring. Besides, he looked nothing like Judd.

He leaned to kiss her again, and she moved her head to avoid the slobbering lips. His mouth struck her cheek and she winced. It hurt. He had slapped her there earlier. At first, she had thought nothing of it, being too shocked by the attack in the first place. Now, when he had touched her there, it had pained terribly. He *had* injured her.

His movement slowed, then he stopped, his breath coming in gasps while he lay heavily on her.

Peggy felt exhausted. Worn out. Limp. When he rolled off, she wanted to scream, relieved that he was no longer touching her. She wanted to get off the bed and run—run anyplace. Maybe next door to Zella's, but what would happen if she did that? The police would come? There would be a scandal of sorts. Judd might not want anything to do with her—ever again. She sobbed. The thought was overwhelming. Then she shuddered. What if, somehow, the man lying next to her *were* Judd. It was impossible, she knew. But it was just as impossible for Judd to have disappeared and be replaced by the animal who had raped her. What if he *were* Judd?

She half turned her head to look at him. The same fleshy face, the same wavy hair lay scant inches from hers. And he was falling asleep. A soft snore rippled through the room. Then a louder one.

Peggy froze. She had heard that snore before. The night in her apartment. When had that been? Not last night. Judd had been gone all of last night. When? It seemed so long ago. She mentally shook her head, when the truth dawned on her. It had only been the night before last. It seemed like ages ago. But it had been then, when she had heard the snore. And it had come from Judd. She shivered. Why hadn't Maceo Montgomery believed her? Maceo Montgomery. She had to call him. He had promised to help her if she needed help. And she felt she needed help of some sort now. She'd wait until the stranger—or should she call him Judd?—was more sound asleep. Then she'd convince Maceo to come over right away.

Her hips ached. Her genitals hurt. Her cheek throbbed. She felt like a mess. Still, as much as she wanted to get up and clean herself of the man's semen, she feared moving from the bed. What would happen if she woke him? Would he do it again?

He snored even louder.

In a few minutes she'd move. A few minutes. She closed her eyes to rest for those few minutes. And fell asleep.

16

Judd opened his eyes. Where was he? What had—? He looked around. It was a bedroom. His bedroom. When—? What had happened? Everything spun around in jumbled mental images. Nothing stayed in focus long enough for him to look at it, discover what it was, digest the fact, and come to a conclusion. What had he been doing? His body ached. Of course, why wouldn't it? He had not had much sleep in the last thirty-six hours or so. Where had he—? The state capital. The confrontation with the gang surged back to the fore of his mind. It all seemed so long ago. He had come home. Of that fact he was almost certain, since he lay staring at the ceiling of his bedroom.

He turned his head, just enough to

look at the curtains of the window, dancing in a gentle autumn breeze. Sunlight streamed in and without looking at the digital alarm clock on the bureau, Judd knew it was early afternoon. When he turned to verify his estimate, he saw her. Peggy. Peggy lying next to him. On her back. She was nude. What had—? Had they made love? As if viewing a movie from a long distance, the screen a mere postage stamp with figures barely discernible, he watched as a memory replayed itself. A vicious backhanded slap, the woman's head popping to the side. The man forcing himself on the woman, raping her in a vicious, hurting way. Suddenly the screen grew to a larger size and he could look over the shoulder of the man, directly into the woman's face. Directly into Peggy's face. And Judd wanted to scream, but his throat, constricted by terror, refused to cooperate.

Had he—? Had he raped Peggy? Not he. *Bull!* It had been Bull who had raped her, if what he was recalling right now proved to be a fact and not some awful dream. Good God! How could he possibly ever expect Peggy to forgive him of something so vile—so awful? He shuddered. They were through. They had to be. There could be no way Peggy would forgive him. Tears welled in his eyes. The last thing in the world he wanted was for Peggy to walk out of his life. And for what? A crime against her which he had had nothing to do with, but which she would think he was guilty of for the rest of her life.

Sitting up and dropping his legs over the edge of the bed, Judd rubbed his face. What could he do? Peggy would never believe him. Maybe the whole thing had been an awful nightmare. No, Bull had shown up. He had taken charge. *Goddamn you, Bull!*

He slipped off the bed and quickly dressed. He had to get away from Peggy. He couldn't think straight. Not here. Not in the room where he had either dreamt about raping the woman he loved or had actually done so. Before he tiptoed across the room to the door, he turned to look at her.

The bruise. The ugly purple bruise on her right cheek. It *had* happened. It hadn't been a dream, as he had so fervently wished.

"Goddamn you, Bull! You worthless bastard. You rapist. You dirty fucker! Get out of my life. I don't want you here anymore. Goddamn you to hell, Bull!" Judd's voice rose to a fevered, angry pitch with each word. "Jesus damn you to hell, Bull! I don't want you around me anymore. I never did. Get out of here. *Now!* Goddammit! Go to hell, Bull!"

Peggy opened her eyes, staring at him. Had he gone mad? At least he looked like Judd should. It wasn't the stranger who had—had—raped her earlier. "Judd?" Her voice croaked the one word.

He stopped, turning to face her. "Are—are you all right?"

She propped herself up on one elbow. "I—I think I am. I must have fallen asleep. How are you?" She wanted to scream out the fact that he had raped her. Or that someone who had somehow taken his place had raped her. But for the moment she fought to maintain her composure, her control. What would be gained at this late moment by screaming? For some reason, she felt that Judd had the answers to her unasked questions and she didn't want to drive a wedge between them that would prevent him from talking.

"If what I recall actually happened, I'm devastated. I—I—I'm—I don't know what to say, Peggy, other than I'm sorry. I—I had no control over what happened."

She looked at him. "No—no control? I don't understand."

He dropped his gaze from her and stared at the floor. He wanted to run to her but he had heard of women who would not allow anyone, most especially a man, not even their husband or lover, to touch them following a sexual assault. And that was exactly what he had done to her—to Peggy—to the woman he loved. Turning away from her, he clenched his hands into tight balls and screamed, "Goddamn you,

Bull!''

Peggy flinched. It had been something like that that had awakened her. What did it mean? Who or what was this Bull? ''Judd?'' She whispered his name. He had become violent enough to have raped her a few hours before and she had done nothing to warrant the attack then. Now, she certainly did not want to antagonize him further and set him off again. ''Judd, are you all right?''

He pivoted on one heel, staring at her, his eyes reddened from the sudden onslaught of tears running down his face. ''You ask me if I'm all right after what happened to you?'' He took a step toward her and stopped, even though Peggy had shown no signs of revulsion or retreat.

''I'm worried to death about you, darling. I really am. What's wrong? What happened before?''

''Before? When before? When I raped you? Well, I didn't. *He* did. I didn't.''

''*He* did? Who? Who are you talking about?''

''Bull! Bull, the sonofabitch. He raped you. Jesus! I'm so sorry, Peggy. If I had thought for a second that the bastard would have done to you what he did, I never would have asked you to come over here.''

Peggy's eyes widened. What was Judd talking about? He was acting as if he hadn't been responsible for the attack. In many ways, she could almost accept his plea that someone else had done it. Certainly, when he had been forcing himself on her, he had *not* looked like her Judd. He had looked like no one Peggy had ever seen before in her life. Who had he been? Was it someone other than Judd? She had asked herself that same question during the act. but if it weren't Judd, who could it have been? If it were someone else, as Judd was claiming now, how had he exchanged places with Judd in the few seconds she had turned her back to finish undressing? She had heard nothing—no bed springs—no rustling of bedclothes—absolutely nothing. Then when she had turned around, he had opened his eyes and was laughing. She shuddered at the recollection. The laugh had not been Judd's either.

"Judd. Who's Bull?"

He glared at her. "He's the one who raped you. I'm sorry, Peggy. You never should have come here today. I—I guess it's all over between us now, and it's his fault. Goddamn you to hell, Bull!"

He looked around the room, searching for something that Peggy couldn't see. "Judd, I love you. I want to help you. I can't unless you tell me everything. *Who's Bull?*" Her voice, edged with hysteria, rose in volume.

Judd turned to face her again. "The one thing I don't need is you patronizing me, Peggy. How could you still love me, after what's happened? Why would you still love me, after what's happened? Why would you want to help me after the terrible thing that happened? That goddamn Bull—he did it, and nothing will ever be the same between us again."

"Shouldn't I have as much to say about that as you?"

Judd stared into space, over her head, unable to look directly at her. "What—what do you mean?"

"I loved you before. I still love you now. I don't think you had anything to do with—with what happened. It certainly didn't *look* like you."

He dropped his line of sight to her face. "Oh, God, Peggy. I hope you mean that. I *didn't* have anything to do with it. I barely remember coming into the bedroom. When I awoke, I didn't remember anything at first. But then, as if I were remembering a movie or something, I began seeing what happened a way off in the distance. Then, all of a sudden, it came back to me. But I wasn't doing it. *He* was!"

"Judd, who *is* Bull?"

"You won't believe me."

"Try me."

Judd walked to the window. Zella was outside, raking up some leaves that had already fallen to the ground. The trees hadn't finished changing colors yet to any great degree. But keeping her lawn free of leaves would keep Zella busy. He wished that was all he had to worry about.

He cursed the day he had gone into the woods. Had he actually had anything to say about that? Looking back on it, he doubted it. The whole thing of going into the country ostensibly to search for clues, taking a spade with him for no known reason and then finding the grave of Bull and the motorcycle—it all had to have been out of his control. He remembered the notes and the dreams, all with the same theme: *"Help me! Come to me! Help me!"* It all seemed like a dream now when he thought back on it. But it had happened. He had found the motorcycle and then—and then—Bull!

"Goddamn you, Bull!" He threw his head back, screaming the words at the ceiling.

Peggy drew back toward the headboard. What was wrong with Judd? Could he be going insane? Mad?

"Come on, Bull. Goddammit! Face up to what you've done! Why'd you do it? Why'd you rape Peggy?"

When he paid her no mind, Peggy concentrated on watching him and forgot about worrying for her own safety. She felt safe. But her real concern was for Judd. He was acting as if someone else were in the room with them. She felt foolish when she looked about the room, searching the same areas with her eyes, without moving from the bed, that Judd had examined with his. What was he looking for? Who was Bull? Why didn't he answer her when she asked him?

"You might as well speak up for Peggy's benefit, Bull. You did it for the gang. Introduce yourself, you miserable bastard."

"Judd?" Peggy's voice cut through his last words and he turned to look at her. "Who is this Bull you keep referring to?"

"He's the sonofabitch who raped you. That's who he is. The dirty bastard. I wish he would get out of my life. Now. God-dammit, Bull, get out of my life. You're no better than that worthless bastard, Buckshot!"

Peggy's eyes widened. Judd had to be going insane. There could be no other logical reason for his actions or words. She had to get out of here and get to a phone. She had to call Maceo Montgomery. He was the only person she could think of who would be qualified to help Judd at this moment. She pulled her legs up closer to her body. Why couldn't she be dressed? Being naked would certainly do her own story no good when it came time to convince someone as to why she was running through the streets without clothing. Her slacks and blouse lay in a heap next to the bed where she had dropped them. She'd have to make a swiping grab at them, hope she got them, and dash through the door—all within the flick of an eye before Judd could do anything to stop her. She inched closer to the edge of the bed. Another second and she would try.

"That's a pretty low blow, comparing me to that scumbucket asshole, Buckshot!" The voice, a low growl, rumbled through the room.

Peggy froze. Now Judd's voice was different, and she suddenly replayed in her own mind the words *"Move. Move, goddammit. You're laying there like you're dead. Do something."* She shuddered. It was the same voice then as now. And it *wasn't* Judd's. She sensed her own panic growing in leaps and bounds. Perhaps it wasn't Judd who was going insane. It might very well be she who was losing her mind.

She had to stay calm, in charge of herself. If she didn't, both she and Judd could be in jeopardy. Why she believed that, she had no idea, but when she considered the events unfolding in the bedroom, she felt that one of them had to stay in charge of their emotions.

"What—what did you say, Judd?" She tried to sound normal, but when the words came out, they sounded hysterical.

Judd turned to her. "I didn't say anything. What did you hear?" His eyes flashed brightly as if to say he'd discovered something important.

"Something about *'buckshot'* or something like that."

Judd grinned foolishly. "Come on, Bull. She heard you. You might as well speak up."

Peggy swallowed the lump in her throat. Judd had lost it all. But now he was standing between her and the doorway to the hall, the only way out of the room except for the two windows. She waited.

"Come on, Bull. You can't hide anymore. You might as well speak up. The least you can do is apologize to Peggy for what you did to her."

A heavy quiet pressed in on the bedroom and the man and woman.

Then Bull spoke through Judd's unmoving mouth. *"So I tipped my hand, but you gotta admit it was a cheap shot, saying I was like Buckshot. Why'd you say that?"*

Peggy's eyes popped, her jaw hanging slack. There was a voice—a totally different voice coming from Judd, and he wasn't moving his mouth to make the sounds.

"Buckshot raped my sister. Now you did the same to Peggy. I wish you'd get the hell out of my life and go to hell."

"I hope I do go there. I've worked toward that end for quite some time."

Peggy's head spun. She had been wrong all along. It wasn't Judd who was going crazy. It was she. The last thing she thought she saw or felt was the bed, as she began gyrating like a bucking horse and then fell face down onto the cool sheets. A blackness closed in on her, wrapping her confusion in its embrace. Off in the distance she could hear voices. Voices talking. Voices talking about her. Calling to her. It sounded like Judd. Judd and another man. Wasn't she supposed to contact another man today about something? Yes. About Judd. But who was he? He was a black man. Tall, muscular, handsome, manly—Maceo. Maceo Montgomery. Perhaps that was the person with whom Judd was talking. Dare she open her eyes and look? She squinted. She saw no one. Was she imagining the whole thing? Then Judd moved into her line of vision. Judd. Dear, sweet, considerate, gentle Judd. His mouth was open a little. He was going to say something. Probably call to her.

"Wake her up. I'll help you explain things and set the record straight."

She wanted to scream but for some reason felt she shouldn't. It wasn't Judd's voice. And Judd wasn't moving his lips or mouth. Why couldn't Judd speak in his own voice?

"No thanks, Bull. You've done quite enough to Peggy already."

She relaxed. That was Judd's voice. And his mouth was working again.

"Peggy?" He wiped her face with a cold, wet washcloth he had gotten from the bathroom. "Are you all right? Can you hear me?"

Her eyes fluttered. "Judd? What happened?"

"You fainted. Are you feeling all right?"

"How did you do that?"

"Do what?"

"Make your voice sound different and not move your lips or mouth?"

"You saw?"

She nodded.

That much of it was over. Maybe since she had witnessed something as bizarre as Bull's voice coming from his mouth without any visible means, she might believe everything else that had happened to him in the last few weeks. The most he could do was try. The worst she could do was not believe and have nothing more to do with him.

"Do you remember the day I brought home the motorcycle?"

She nodded.

"That's when it all began. At least, that's when it happened. I guess it really began with the dreams and the messages." He told her of the words he had found in strange places, and the dreams in which someone had been calling to him. He told her of how he had found the mound and dug into it with the spade which he had taken along on what he thought had been a mere whim . . . of how he had passed out and thought at first he had been struck by lightning. Then he told her of how Bull had manifested in his mind.

"But why did he contact you?"

Judd shrugged.

"I picked up on his distress. I suppose it was over the death of his sister. But I grasped at his emotions like a drowning man grabs at straws. I called out to him, and when I finally got through enough to make him come out here with a shovel, I was able to move and cohabit with his spirit in his body."

Bull's voice fell silent and Judd merely gazed at Peggy. At first, when the strange voice spoke, interrupting their conversation, Peggy had wanted to scream, then run. But now she suddenly realized that all the things that had appeared so different about Judd did have an explanation. At least it did if she were willing to believe everything that Judd and this Bull person had just told her.

"But—why?" she persisted, wanting more evidence than just the simple statement as presented thus far.

Judd shrugged. "I guess two spirits—one bewildered, the other devastated—reached out and found something in one another. I don't know. I do know that since then, I've been able to do things I've never even tried before. Rebuilding the bike."

"Hog!" Bull corrected.

"Hog, then. Riding it. Being able to lift it onto and off the truck as easily as I did. I know that Mickey must have thought he was seeing things when I did that in the storeroom. I don't think I would have walked away from the Light Bearer's Chosen if Bull's spirit hadn't been with me."

"You *were* in danger, then, weren't you?" Peggy asked, her eyes widening.

Judd nodded.

"So what happens now? Are the two of you stuck together for eternity?" She studied Judd's face. He appeared normal. It was only when the other voice came through, and his face took on a rigid look and there was no muscular involvement in speaking, that she became upset.

Judd shrugged. "Bull promised to leave me if I helped him. I have. And now—"

"I know what you've got in mind, Judd. Don't even remotely think about calling the cops at this point. I'm not finished with Buckshot."

"Buckshot?" Peggy's confusion and inquisitiveness were summed up in the one-word question.

"He's the man who killed Bull. Bull wants his revenge on Buckshot."

"Then it isn't only to help you, is it?" An accusative look crossed Peggy's face.

Judd shook his head. "No. I promised, more or less, to help him if he led me to the person or persons responsible for Cindy's death."

"Oh, Judd." She reached out, caressing his hand.

"And there's no backing out. As soon as Buckshot is dead, I leave. That's the only way it'll be."

Peggy's eyes widened, filled with horror as the truth of the statement struck at her sense of understanding like a poisonous snake. "But—but that—that means that—Judd would have to—have to—kill this other man. Doesn't it?"

Judd didn't answer, nor did Bull.

"You can't, Judd. Bull would have his revenge, and you'd be punished for it. Don't you see? The victory for you would be hollow. You'd win the battle and lose the war. It's senseless."

"The gang wouldn't report the killing."

"What's that supposed to mean?" Judd demanded.

"They don't want any truckin' with the law. They'd just get rid of Buckshot's body like they done mine. You got nothing to worry about."

"I don't believe you, Bull," Peggy said defiantly, blinking her eyelids when she realized that she must be staring hatefully at Judd. "It's Judd's life on the line. Not yours. You don't have a life to worry about." She looked away. "My God, I don't believe I'm saying these things to you, Judd."

"You're not. You're saying them to Bull. And you're right. You know that, don't you, Bull? Peggy's absolutely right. You've got nothing to lose, and I've got everything to lose. You didn't think they'd do what they did when I—er—you—us—we walked into the warehouse. What makes you think you'll get away with this—using me to kill Buckshot and not having to worry about me getting into trouble because of it?"

At first there was no response. *"It'll work, goddammit. I know it'll work!"*

"Sure, it'll work," said Peggy, "but you don't know what the end results will be, do you? I think we'd better call the police, Judd." She reached for her slacks and blouse.

"I guess you're right, Peggy." Judd moved toward the doorway and stopped. "Hurry and get dressed. I'll call them right now."

When Peggy looked up, she found Judd still standing there, frozen in a step toward the door. "Judd? What's the matter? Judd?" Without waiting to button her blouse, she ran to him.

"Judd can't talk right now, Peggy. Sorry about earlier this morning. I guess I've been away from nice girls and women too long. I just forgot how to act. Don't

blame Judd. Not ever. He had nothing to do with it. Understand?"

She shivered when he grabbed her by the arms and gave her a little shake. "I—I understand. I love Judd. I don't want him to have to pay for your crime. Don't you understand?"

"Sure, I understand. But you gotta believe me when I say that I gotta kill Buck-shot. I can't leave Judd until I do. Get it?"

Peggy looked up into Judd's face, fighting to smother the scream of terror she felt building within her. His face was puffing up and his countenance took on the same lines and contours of the man who had sexually assaulted her that morning. "Let me go. I'm calling the police." She twisted free for a second, and just as she was about to flee the room, a rock-hard fist slashed out, catching Peggy on the point of her jaw.

The room flashed with brilliant brightness and equally striking blackness as pinpoints of light popped on and off. She felt something sagging—something a long way off—something almost completely separated from her. Then she realized that her knees were buckling and she sensed herself crumbling to the floor. Off in the distance she heard a voice dwindling into nothingness as it spoke.

"I'm sorry, Peggy. You're a nice broad. Sorry about everything. I'll take care of Judd."

Then the blackness closed in.

Judd hurried to the garage. Furious with Bull for having struck Peggy again, he chafed under the pressure he exerted without effect. "Goddamn you, Bull. If I could only put my hands on you, I'd kill you myself. What—"

"Cool it, Judd. We're going to the capital and that's that. Buckshot's a piece of dead shit right now. Only thing is, he don't know it yet."

"I'm going to fight you all the way, Bull. I really will. If there's a way for me to stop you, I'll use it."

"If you fight me, Judd, I'll not leave. Even after I killed Buckshot. Got it? I'll stay. I'll put your spirit right out of your body and take over completely. How'd you like that? Me and Peggy together. Not bad. Maybe—"

Judd threw open the double garage doors and mounted the motorcycle. "All right, you sonofabitch! You win."

"Now you're being smart."

Judd kicked the motorcycle's engine to life, revving it up, its throaty belch barking and backfiring as it roared.

Next door, Zella Ludinger, leaning on her yard rake, jumped. What was that awful noise? She thought she had heard a motorcycle earlier. Before she had risen for the day. Now it was back, and it seemed to be coming from Judd's back yard or garage, someplace on the far side of the Wellington house.

Hurrying to the front of her side yard, she crossed in front of the house next door and stopped just as the Harley-Davidson blasted down the driveway toward the street. Her heart pounding, she made a sign of the cross, even though she wasn't Catholic, and breathed a prayer of thanks. She had almost been killed by the maniac on the motorcycle.

Then her memory's eye replayed for her in slow motion the incident once more. She sucked in her breath when she realized that the man riding the machine somehow resembled Judd. He hadn't looked exactly like Judd, but for an instant she thought he might have been him, her neighbor. Hadn't he seen her? What was wrong with Judd that he would be so careless with a motorcycle like that? Perhaps she was mistaken, and replayed the scene again. This time the man didn't look much like Judd at all. Perhaps she had imagined it. Maybe it was someone who was visiting Judd. Maybe a cousin who bore a family resemblance. If that were the case, Judd would still be in the house, more than likely. She wanted to know, and she wanted to lodge her complaint about the main's carelessness as well.

Resolutely marching up the front walk and mounting the three steps to the porch, Zella rang the doorbell and waited.

17

Zella impatiently tapped her foot, waiting for some response to her short, staccato knocks, which sounded more like the drumming of fingers. No one—not even Judd Wellington, whom she admired in a motherly way—had the right to run down helpless senior citizens like herself. She had no idea what Judd, if it indeed had been Judd, might be doing with a noisy, smelly motorcycle in the first place. She had never seen him drive one before today. She had never heard him speak of one, before today. What had gotten into him to try to run her down like that? She clucked her tongue and knocked again.

For a split second before the lace curtain pulled back in the window of the door, Zella could feel eyes on her. Without hesitating, she knocked once more, and the inner door pulled open a few inches. Peggy looked out at her.

"Oh, Peggy, my dear. Is Judd at home? I'd like to speak to him." Zella smiled kindly. She didn't want to make a scene with Peggy. She didn't want to have an argument with Judd either, for that matter. She simply felt she had to lodge a complaint with someone. Judd seemed the most likely.

"Golly, Zella, he's not." Peggy stepped farther back into the shadows, turning her body so that only the left side of her face was exposed to the front porch.

"What do you know about that motor-cycle?" Zella defiantly thrust her chin forward. She wanted to have her opinion known. She stared at Peggy. Why was the girl acting so peculiarly? Peggy looked at her with a sidelong glance. It wasn't exactly haughty but it certainly bordered on it. Why didn't the girl simply look straight ahead and speak to her?

"Mo—motorcycle?"

"Yes, motorcycle. I think Judd was riding it, and he almost hit me when he came rushing like a fool headlong down the driveway and into the street. I want that sort of thing stopped and I want it stopped now. Suppose it had been a child? I don't think Judd would have been able to stop in time without hitting him or her."

Zella made the clucking sound with her tongue again for effect and waited for Peggy to answer.

"It—It wasn't Judd, Zella."

It was Zella's turn to wait before answering. If it hadn't been Judd, then who had almost killed her? Once more, she reran the event in her mind, slowing it to a virtual crawl when the motorcycle and its rider passed within two feet of her. Her heart pounded wildly as she relived the traumatic close call. The face was blurred. She backed the motorcycle up and ran it by again. As the machine bore down on her, she scrutinized the rider. He seemed to resemble Judd. But, if Peggy said it hadn't been Judd—"Who was it, then?"

"A—a friend—no—an acquaintance of Judd's. I—I'm sorry about it, Zella. I really am. So is Judd. I'll tell him when I see him. All right?"

Zella pouted. She liked Judd. She liked Peggy. Why make hard feelings between them when it was someone else who had tried to murder her just a few minutes ago? "I'd appreciate that very much, Peggy."

Peggy started to close the inner door, still holding the left side of her face to the porch.

"Is there something wrong, my dear?" Zella stepped closer to the screen door, peering intently in at Peggy, squinting her eyes.

"No. I—I've got some things to do. That's all, Zella. Really. There's nothing wrong. 'Bye."

The door closed and Zella stood for a moment, staring at the entrance. Turning, she walked down the steps. Something Shakespeare had written zipped through her mind, wondering just why the Bard had written it in the first place. Perhaps to take in situations like the one she had just experienced. When she reached the sidewalk, she mouthed the words in a soft mumble. "I think perhaps she protests too much." Shaking her head, she wasn't positive that was the way Shakespeare had stated it, but it certainly covered the situation now.

With little birdlike steps, she went back to her yard and began raking the intruding leaves once more.

Peggy leaned against the wall of the living room after closing the front door. The tears she had controlled for Zella's benefit freely tumbled down her cheek. Her face hurt in both places where Bull had struck her—once during his earlier attack on her and then when he punched her to keep her from interfering with his leaving. If it weren't for the fact that Bull was locked within Judd's body—she stopped. Could such things actually happen? She would be relieved once the monster was gone. But she loved Judd.

She loved the Judd she knew and recognized. Someone had stolen those looks and that body and was able to suppress Judd's spirit and soul until he seemed to no longer exist.

What should she do? What *could* she do? Call the police? *"Hello, police,"* she imagined the call. *"My boyfriend has another spirit in his head or body or wherever souls are located and he doesn't seem to be himself anymore. What can I do? Could you maybe arrest him and drive this awful thing out of him? Would you charge anything?"*

Running to the bedroom, she grabbed several tissues and dabbed at her eyes. Her cheek felt swollen, and she winced when she looked in the mirror on the dresser. An ugly bruise radiated outward from her high cheekbone. "Isn't that nice," she said aloud to her injured reflection.

Why had Judd struck her like that? That wasn't fair to Judd. He had not had anything to do with it. Of course, it had been his hand, but it had not been his mind controlling it. That had been Bull.

Bull. Did such a person or thing or—or ghost actually exist? How could—why did such a thing have to happen? And why to Judd, who had been through hell losing his younger sister in the violent way he had? How could she accept such a theory? Judd had been convincing when he told her everything connected with finding the motorcycle and all. But was any of it true?

She chastised herself when she doubted Judd's story. That wasn't too typical either, questioning something Judd had told her. He had never once tried to mislead her on anything. Why should he lie now? To cover his bizarre behavior? To keep her from knowing the truth about what was actually going on? If he was holding back, what had he not told her?

She came back to the thought of Bull. How could Judd have changed his voice and spoken the way he did, without moving his lips or mouth? He didn't know anything about ventriloquism that she knew of, and she knew just about everything concerning him.

"Oh, God, what should I do?" she cried aloud.

What options were open to her? Time was wasting away. Judd was probably on his way to the state capital right that instant. How long had she been unconscious? The digital clock read two-thirty-nine. She had only been out a minute or two, then, since Zella had awakened her by knocking on the door after Judd had almost run her down in the driveway. That meant he had really only been gone a few minutes. It would take him about two hours or so to get to the capital. Maybe she should call the police and have him intercepted. But they wouldn't believe her.

Besides, she felt that there had to be a more prudent way of getting to Judd and helping him.

Maybe she should follow Judd to the capital. She knew roughly where the warehouse was located. But what good would that do? If she caught up to him, what would she do then? Bull would simply knock her out again or rape her again or do something equally awful. Poor Judd had no say in anything his body did.

She could call Allan. But he would be as pragmatic as the police. In addition, she could not picture Allan ever accepting the wild notion that a dead motorcycle gang leader had invaded Judd's soul and was controlling him. Allan would be needed if Bull had his way and used Judd as the instrument of revenge, as he said he would. She knew enough about the law from having typed transcripts of trials and other legal documents to know such phrases as accessory before, during, and after the fact of a crime and willing participation. How would a court of law pass on the wild theory of two spirits, one good, one bad, inhabiting the same body and committing a crime? Who was guilty? The spirit inventing the crime or the body executing it?

Suddenly her mind cleared. Maceo. Of course. She had to call Maceo Montgomery. Why hadn't she thought of him immediately after waking up? Zella had taken up time and took her mind off the thing she should have been doing before. Then she had wasted valuable minutes thinking about the police and Allan, when all the time Maceo Montgomery held the solution to her problem. To Judd's problem. At least she fervently prayed he did. Or had he been humoring her when she told him of Judd's peculiar actions?

Where was the slip of paper with his telephone numbers? What had she done with it? Was it at her apartment? Or in her purse? She prayed that it would prove to be the latter and ran to the kitchen where she had left her handbag.

Maceo would know what to do. He said he held an interest in parapsychology, but had he said that in passing or was it true? Had anything he said been true, or was he simply trying to be nice? When she pictured his broad shoulders, his square face, the even white teeth flashing from his cocoa-brown face, and the steady gaze of his dark, piercing eyes, she knew Maceo Montgomery had not been anything but straightforward with her.

Opening her purse, she dumped the contents on the kitchen table. Nothing. Where was it? Pushing aside the balled-up tissues, the change, the ring of keys, her billfold, the small mirror, the comb and lipstick, she refocused her attention on the billfold. Opening it, she stuck her fingers into the bill compartment and pulled out the slip.

She looked at the clock over the sink. Two-fifty-seven. Where would he be? The numbers were for his home and the motel where he had stayed the previous night. It was Friday. Shouldn't he be at school yet? Where was the phone book? A quick perusal of the kitchen turned up the book in a rack below the wall telephone. Grabbing it, she thumbed through the pages. Under schools in the classified section, she found the number for the high school and quickly dialed it.

"Rushton Senior High School," the voice grated in her ear.

"Mr. Montgomery, please." She held her breath. How should she begin?

"One moment, please. I'm not sure if he's still here. I'll ring."

The humming buzz of the phone being rung in Maceo's office echoed in her ear.

She looked at the clock again. Two-fifty-nine.

Maceo shut his attache case and looked around his office. There was no reason to stay here in his office until three o'clock when the last period of the day and week finished. That was one advantage of being the psychologist for more than one school. He had much more freedom with his time and was his own boss for the most part when it came to determining working terms and conditions. If he had no student to deal with and it was a few minutes before school was finished, he could, if he wanted to, leave and not have to answer to anyone. He could be five minutes farther down the road at three o'clock.

Picking up his case, he strode to the door of the small office. Flicking off the light switch, he stepped into the hall and locked the door behind him. He liked the weekends and the complete absence of structure. If he wanted to sleep late, he slept late. If he wanted to go out of town for the weekend, he did. Being single, without responsibility to anyone other than himself, had its distinct advantages.

When he reached the main entrance to Rushton Senior High School, he pushed one door open and stopped. The cool air gushing in reminded him that he had worn his topcoat that morning and had left it in his office. He might have need of it over the weekend or Monday morning when he went to Travis City. It would be next Thursday before he got back to Rushton.

Turning on his heel, he bumped into Nancy Schumacker, the drama instructor.

"Hi, there," he said searching his memory for her name. That was one disadvantage in working three different high schools—it was difficult to keep track of the teachers' names, especially when he dealt with them very little.

"Nancy," she said, realizing he was unsure of her name. "You're Maceo Montgomery, aren't you?''

He nodded. ''Hey, I'd like to stay and talk, but I'm in sort of a hurry. Was there anything in particular?''

''No. I just wanted to say hello. We met in the treachers' lounge a couple of weeks ago. How's it going?'' She smiled, her blue eyes twinkling at him.

''Fine. Fine. I am, however, still in a hurry. Tell you what, why don't we have coffee next week? I'm here Thursdays and Fridays.''

''I know,'' she said. ''You buying?''

''Right. You got it.'' He turned and hurried down the hall. If he half ran, he might be able to beat the onslaught of students charging down the hall and into their two days of freedom. The last thing he wanted was to be caught in the tide of young bodies.

When he reached his office, he was fumbling with the key just as the phone started ringing. *Damn!* He wouldn't answer it. If he didn't answer, he wouldn't be detained. God only knew who or what problem was on the other end of that incessant ringing.

He opened the door, and the phone continued jangling as he grabbed his coat. Striding back to the door, he stopped. Not too professional. In fact, very unprofessional of him to even think like that. It wasn't anything, he was sure. So what if his plan for five extra minutes went down the drain? At least he wouldn't spend a lot of the weekend wondering who might have been calling him.

The phone rang again and he went to the desk. Picking up the receiver, he said, "Hello?"

"Mr. Montgomery? This is Peggy Dixon. Do you remember me? I've got an awful problem. It's Judd and the way he's been acting. He—well, not Judd, really—but it was this spirit in him who made him do what he did. He raped me, Mr. Montgomery. He raped me. And—and now he's gone and he's—he's going to kill someone. I—"

"Hey, wait a minute, Peggy. Slow down. I'm not getting half of what it is you're trying to tell me. You say you were raped? What happened? By whom? And what's this about killing someone?"

He heard her take several deep breaths before she spoke again. When she did, she told him in a slower, more controlled way the events of the day and what had happened since she went to Judd's house that morning.

When she finished, he paused for only a second. If she was that upset, and surely she had every right to be if what she had told him was the truth, he had best follow through on his offer to help her in the event she needed him.

"Where are you now, Peggy?"

"I—I'm still at Judd's house."

"Where's that?"

"It's only a couple of blocks from school. Let me give you directions."

When she had given him the simple instructions, he said, "I'll be right there. Hang tight." He hung up and left his office again. He'd have to start his weekend in another half hour or so.

Maceo winced when he saw Peggy's face. "You weren't kidding, were you?" He stepped through the doorway, and she closed the door after him.

"I thought you might think I was exaggerating and not come, if I told you everything. I was afraid you wouldn't after I hung up. What am I going to do?" Her voice cracked.

"Let me play back everything that you told me on the phone to make certain I understand. You said Judd attacked you—raped you—and took off. Right?"

She nodded.

"You said something about his spirit and that he was going to kill someone. Right?"

"Not exactly."

"Then," he said, sitting down on the couch in the living room, "tell me exactly what did happen."

"You won't believe me."

"Try me."

"I don't want you to humor me. I—"

"My profession is listening to people

tell me about their problems—sometimes they're rather mundane and sometimes they're rather preposterous—but I'm trained to listen and help—not, to use your word, 'humor' people. Understand? Just open up and tell me everything, Peggy."

She looked at him, averting her own gaze when she caught the intensity of his black eyes. He seemed to be staring right through her.

"Judd," she began, "has the spirit of a dead motorcycle gang leader in him." She waited to see what if any reaction Maceo might have to that statement. When he said nothing and continued studying her, she coughed once and told him everything that had happened that day, and everything that Judd had told her, in a slow, almost detached manner. She left nothing out. She felt she couldn't afford to do that. If Maceo was to help her, he had to know everything, no matter how illogical it might sound.

When she finished, Maceo stood, walking to the front window. He looked outside and then turned to face her. "Have you ever heard the term 'transmigration of soul'?"

Peggy wrinkled her forehead in thought. "No. Never. Why? What does it mean?"

"Exactly what it says. Transmigration. To cross over. To move across. The soul or spirit of a dead person, one who becomes disoriented at death, because of the trauma of death itself. Or because of a violent death or simply because of an unexpected death. Under those circumstances, a spirit can become confused at that instant and—well, to use a term you might understand better, become a ghost."

Peggy's eyes widened. "A ghost?"

"Let's use that term for now. You said that this Bull entity—this ghost of Bull—spoke through Judd?"

She nodded.

"If what he and Judd said is true, then when Judd went into the woods and dug up the motorcycle and the body of the rider, Bull latched onto Judd and the two became one, so to speak."

"Is Judd gone? Forever?" She looked at him through tears.

Maceo shrugged. "I don't know. It's been known for the spirit to leave voluntarily after a while. I don't think there have been that many well-documented cases."

"I read a couple of books about multiple personalities. Is it something like that?"

He shook his head. "That we could deal with in a studied way. More and more is being learned about that area every day. But the situation that Judd is in is completely different. The spirit of Bull is in

Judd, with Judd's spirit. From what you've said, Bull is dominating Judd at the present time. Or at least he was when he left here. That means the only way Judd can be made rid of Bull, if Bull doesn't leave voluntarily, is through hypnotism, long sessions of therapy or—" he hesitated, "are you religious, Peggy?"

She nodded, a quizzical expression crossing her face.

"Then, one other way open is exorcism."

"You mean like driving a devil out of someone?"

When he nodded, his head barely moved.

"I thought that was the sort of stuff Hollywood played up."

"They do. But it is a real thing. Today, there isn't as much of it done because of the vast inroads into that very subject that psychiatry has made. But psychiatry and psychology will not address the phenomenon of exorcism and possession."

"Why not?"

"Because there is no logical explanation for it. While both sciences are broad and great, they cannot acknowledge something they cannot see, or touch or cure.

"In other words, you can't help me or Judd. Am I right?" Peggy stood. Her last line of defense had suddenly vanished in a

339

sentence or two.

"I didn't say that. Therapy could help Judd, I'm sure. But I'm not certain what would happen where Bull is concerned. Hypnotism might be the answer, but again, Bull would be the question mark. Would he cooperate, or could the therapist control him?"

"Are you saying you can exorcise the—the ghost of Bull?"

Maceo shook his head. "No. That's the job of a religious person. A priest or minister. Someone like that."

"Then I was right. You can't help. Because you're a psychologist, you can't help. Am I right?"

"If I were just a psychologist, I would have to qualify my yes by saying only through extensive therapy. But I am interested in parapsychology and the occult in general. I find it fascinating. The first thing we have to do, if you want me to help, is catch up with Judd. Do you know where he was going?"

Peggy nodded. "To a warehouse, probably, in the state capital."

"A warehouse?" Maceo's brow furrowed.

"That's where this gang hides out. That's where Buckshot is. He's the man Bull wants to kill, using Judd's body."

Maceo frowned. "How long ago did he leave?"

Peggy looked at the clock on the living

room wall. It was going on five o'clock. They had been talking almost two hours. Judd could have reached the warehouse and Buckshot could already be dead. Or Judd might be dead. She hadn't realized so much time had gone by. "He left about two-forty-five."

Maceo shook his head. "He'd be in the capital by now, wouldn't he?"

Peggy slowly nodded.

"The best we can do is try," Maceo said, standing. "Let's go."

"Go? Where?"

"To the state capital. You do know where this warehouse is, don't you?"

"I—I think I do. I know the street—it's—" Her mind went blank. Then, "It—it's Train Avenue. No, that's not right. Railroad Avenue. There is a warehouse with the name of—of—Holmes on it."

"Come on." He grabbed her arm, steering her toward the front door.

"But why are you willing to do this for Judd and me?"

He opened the door, holding it for her. "Let's just say I'm interested and curious about the whole thing. Besides, from the way you talked about Judd, I think I want to meet him. He sounds like a nice guy. Come on, Peggy, we're wasting time."

He hurried her toward the black Trans-Am parked at the curb in front of the Wellington house and, after holding the door for her, ran around to the far side and got in.

The motor roared to life in a muffled, throaty growl, and Maceo spun the wheel, turning around in the middle of the block, and dashed down the street.

Zella Ludinger picked up the last armful of leaves she had managed to scratch together and dumped them in the half-full basket. She shook her head. What was happening with Peggy and Judd? Now Peggy ran out of the house with a black man and got into his automobile and sped away. It was getting so that a body was hardly safe in one's own front yard anymore.

Judd used to be a nice neighbor. Today, one of his acquaintances had tried to kill her. Now Judd's girlfriend was running around with a stranger—someone Zella had never before seen. Things could not be going well for Judd and Peggy, she surmised. She just felt it. And she was seldom wrong about things like this and matters of the heart.

Stooping, Zella picked up the basket and walked toward the back of her house. At least she had finished before the storm system, which the weather man had predicted would cover the state by nightfall, had set in.

18

Ugly gray-black clouds roiled angrily about, waiting for the correct moment to send torrents of rain upon the capital city below. An occasional flash of lightning seemed to warn anyone interested that the storm was about to begin and no consideration would be given to anyone caught in the open.

Irregular shadows moved along the dirt-encrusted clerestory windows of the yellow-fronted warehouse, projected from below by the evening fires dancing merrily in portable grills positioned in front of each motorcycle gang member's immediate quarters. Various smells of the cooking meals wafted about, mingling with the more usual, nauseous stenches that permeated the old building.

The normal carefree attitude of the Light Bearer's Chosen had evaporated and a complexion of gloom hung over the huge room like a shroud. The fires, the only source of illumination, failed miserably in seeking out the darkest corners, and the uncertain shadows of the gang members moved wraithlike in and out of the pools of light.

Gordo, who had no wife, always welcomed the presence of any of the mamas who wanted to join him for a snort of "coke" or for smoking up or simply for eating a meal. When Cow approached him as he lighted his fire, he broke into a wide grin, sending his face into greasy, convoluted folds of fat.

"Where's Buckshot?" He didn't want any sort of run-in with the leader. Not that Gordo couldn't have broken Buckshot in half if he so chose. It was just that Gordo didn't feel he could lead the gang in a successful way. Bull had been a good leader. Mean, rough, not afraid of anybody—not even the law. Gordo admired that in a man. But Buckshot was a coward. Everyone in the gang knew it, and it would only be a matter of time before someone got fed up with the inactivity and punched his lights out. Then they'd have a new leader and, hopefully, a new era of prosperity.

"Sleeping. The sonofabitch fucked Mink and then had the audacity to come back to our area and fall asleep. What are we going to do, Gordo?"

"We?" He didn't want to be sucked into some sort of liaison with Cow, although he wouldn't mind bedding her. He liked her body—especially her pierced nipples.

"Us. The gang. Buckshot is as worthless as tits on a boar. We haven't done a goddamned thing since he got rid of Bull. Everyone's sick of him for not doing anything."

"I know. It's a bad fix."

"We've performed exactly two rites since then, too. That bothers me. When Bull was around, we did our prayers to Satan and did the rituals and we had good times, didn't we?"

He nodded in answer to the question, but continued staring absently into the flames.

"Let me give you a good example of Buckshot's stupidity. When that guy came waltzing in here, acting like he owned the place, Buckshot just let him walk out again. The fucking wimp even fainted. I still don't know what was said to make him pass out like that. The guy sure didn't lay a hand on him. We'd have seen that."

"Yeah." Gordo nodded again. "Bull would've cut his balls off and handed them to him before he said 'hello.' "

Cow smiled, showing an even set of white teeth, which contrasted sharply with her sun-darkened skin.

"I wonder," Gordo continued, "who he really was. He *did* sorta of look like Bull. Don't you think?"

"Enough to have been a relative. But Bull never talked much about his family or his past. I don't know if he was hatched or was always an adult. I suppose the sonofabitch took off, and once he realizes that he got away will make trouble for us."

"How? Do you think he went to the cops?"

"I sorta doubt that. If he had, we'd have heard from them by now. I think most all of the gang members think he'll come back and try to take over."

"That wouldn't be too bad, would it?" Gordo stared at the woman, hoping she'd agree with him. It seemed most of the women agreed with him only when it involved fucking, or eating or getting high. When he wanted to give his opinion, they usually just walked away.

"We don't know him. If he wants to join, that's another matter. He'd go through the initiation rites and do what he had to. But we don't want no fucking stranger walking in and taking over. I'd rather see you be the leader than some guy off the street."

"What about Buckshot?" Gordo flushed when he realized that his own sense of leadership suddenly had awakened.

"Hey, why not you? Anybody'd be better than that asshole. All he can do is knife people and faint when the going gets tough." She shook her head. "He blows his nuts too quick, too."

"That's a horseshit way to talk about me," Buckshot said from behind Cow and, reaching out, pulled her to her feet. He backhanded her across the face, and she reeled toward Gordo and the fire pot. Gordo reached out, catching her before she collided with it, and steadied her.

"That's about your speed, Cow. Fat Gordo there and you'd make a good team."

"Shut up, Buckshot," Gordo growled. "Cow's right and you know it. You fainted and that's that. You can't change it."

Buckshot made a quick move with one hand, and the firelight reflected from the long blade of his switchblade.

"Go ahead, Buckshot. That's all you're good for, cutting people. You're no more of a leader than my dick is." Gordo pulled himself to his full height, trying to equal Buckshot's six-foot frame but failing.

"You want to be leader, Gordo? Come on. Come on." Buckshot waved the knife back and forth, motioning with his other hand for the fat man to come to him.

"What'll that solve?" Cow stepped between the men. "We can't be fighting and killing each other. There's no percentage in it. Besides, Gordo's a good man. He carries his end around here. Lay off, Buckshot. If you wind up killing every guy who crosses you, you'll be leading a bunch of thick-headed, stupid fucking mamas and nobody else. I sure as hell ain't going to hang around if that's the case."

"Shut up, you fucking witch."

"And another thing," Cow continued. "When are you going to start getting serious about our—the gang's—commitment? We ain't had but two rites since you took over. It's getting close to the autumn rite and we gotta get ready for it. Otherwise, I can't guarantee that we'll be all right."

"What do you mean by 'all right'?"

Cow glared at Buckshot. "That we're safe. You know, fathead. We ain't playing around with no invisible God who don't do much when he's prayed to. This is the Prince of Darkness that the gang is dedicated to, or did you forget?"

"Fuck the Prince of Darkness. That's a bunch of hocus-pocus bullshit."

"That's why you wanted me to sew the symbols on your jeans after you done Bull in, right? That's why you got '666' scratched into your Maltese crosses, right? Because it's bullshit? Right?" Cow's voice rose until she was shrieking, and Buckshot seemed to visibly wither under her verbal attack.

Cow caught movement out of the corner of her eye and, turning, found the gang closing in on Gordo's campsite. "There's your leader, people. He says that what you believe in, the very thing that got us whatever we wanted before, is so much hocus-pocus bullshit."

The ring of faces moved into the fire-light and stared at Buckshot.

"Come on, you guys don't believe in all that crap, do you?" Buckshot's voice whined, now that he realized that he had made a mistake.

"You'd better change your mind right now, dammit, Buckshot." Cow glared at him. Bull had made her the high priestess of the gang when he realized that her knowledge of the dark arts and witchcraft could stand the gang in good stead with the Prince of Darkness. As he had told her at the time, what better way to do your own thing than with the permission of Lucifer, who would help them acquire any end they might desire. Cow's position with the gang was unique, and not even a weak-minded leader like Buckshot dared make light of their religion and Lucifer. The other members had had too many good times result because of the rituals she had performed for them. Now, Buck-shot was making fun of them, and instead of it working for him, it was backfiring and working against him.

"What should we do, Cow?" Blaster

asked from the shadows.

"Hey, she's not your fucking leader. I am." Buckshot turned, challenging the voice.

"Some leader you are. Do you feel faint?" Armpit shouted.

Buckshot spun around to face the new voice.

"What do we do, Cow?" Gordo asked, without taking his eyes off Buckshot.

"We'd better perform a rite—a ritual that will appease Lucifer. When the gang took him as their spiritual leader, we were made his chosen ones. We can't turn our backs on him now. Can we?"

The heads shook back and forth in the shadowed golden glow.

"We've got to beg his forgiveness for this stupid asshole's remarks. And we'd better do it as soon as possible."

"What kind of ritual?" Mary Queen of Sots asked.

"A sacrifice. A symbolic sacrifice to appease Lucifer."

"When?"

"Now."

"But who or what will we sacrifice?"

Cow pointed to Buckshot, and the gang closed in on him.

Judd turned the motorcycle into Railroad Avenue, throttling down until its throaty roar mellowed to a muted purr. Idling along at a few miles an hour, he didn't want to announce to the Light Bearer's Chosen that he was arriving. It would be better to take them completely off guard. The gang was superstitious and easily provoked into doing almost anything if something bothered them.

A drop of rain hit him on the head, then another and another before it stopped. The storm's clouds rolled about overhead in the dark of early evening. It was only a matter of minutes before its full anger and fury would be unleashed.

Judd turned the ignition off and let the bike roll to a stop close to the entrance of the warehouse. Positive no one had heard him arrive, he kicked the stand into place and leaned the bike into it. He would have been there earlier but for the traffic on the highway, and now when he looked overhead at the encroaching blackness of night, he decided that a storm was the ideal background for his entrance. A wicked smile curved his lips into an angry scimitar.

When he reached the entrance, he stopped and peered into the dirty window next to the door. A flash of lightning overhead exposed his face and he winced. He didn't look like—like Bull or whoever it was he had resembled before.

"Bull? What's happening?"

"I'm here, Judd. I didn't change your body's appearance 'cause I think it'll shake them up even more if I speak to them in my

351

voice and look like you.''

"I—I don't understand."

"You're not supposed to."

"Will I be safe in there if I don't look like you? You're a lot stronger than I am, and if I have to defend myself, I won't stand a chance."

"What makes you think I could take on thirty guys and walk away untouched?"

"But I'm no fighter."

"And from what I picked up in your head, you ain't much of a lover either. Sorry about that."

"Why can't I just call the police and let it go at that?"

"Are you scared?"

"Of course I am."

"Things are tough all over."

"You make me sick. I wish you'd get out of my life and stay out."

"Geez, you're feisty. Still pissed about me clipping Peggy?"

"You know I am. I'll never forgive you for that. I'd never hit her."

"Shit. Makes a woman toe the mark to get a clop on the chops every once in a while. Believe me."

"Do I have a choice? I know what's in your mind in that respect."

"Come on. Let's get on with it. I don't want to debate philosophies here. Let's go."

Judd reached out, tentatively turning the knob to make certain it was unlocked.

When it gave, he pushed the door open and slipped inside. After his eyes adjusted to the darker dark of the building, he slowly moved ahead. Turning the corner that would take him into the warehouse proper, he stopped. In the center of the room he could see the gang converging on something or someone.

"Hey," he shouted, surprised at the sound of his own voice that spoke and that it wasn't Bull's. "Over here."

The gang stopped milling about and turned as one, to face him.

The TransAm's headlights sliced through the night, reflecting off the tiny daggers of rain. The traffic moved slowly, creeping maddeningly at fifty miles per hour.

Peggy wanted to scream. Why did they have to encounter this much traffic? Where could they all be going? It was Friday night. Certainly not to the state capital to be doing business? There had to be some other draw—some other attraction that was going on to have this many cars heading toward the same place she wanted to reach.

"How much farther is it, Maceo?" She fidgeted in her seat, trying to find a more comfortable position.

"As near as I can figure, about another eighty miles or so."

"Good Lord. That's another hour and a

half at the rate this traffic is moving. What time is it?" She ignored the digital clock on the dash.

"It's going on five-forty-five."

She heard a little moan escape her lips.

"Hang on, Peggy. We'll make it. We have to."

Half turning to face him, she wondered about this man. Why was he being so helpful? He had no obligation to satisfy. He didn't know her, and he had never laid eyes on Judd. Why? Why would he want to get involved? He seemed to be a nice enough person. He was handsome, but he could have had two heads and she wouldn't have minded as long as he was willing to help. But the one-word question hammered at her. Why? When she asked, he smiled.

"A long time ago, when I was growing up and found that not everyone in the world was going to be my friend or even act friendly toward me, I made up my mind that I would make myself available to anyone who needed help. I guess that's why, when I went to college on a football scholarship, I decided I could best help people by being what I am today—a psychologist."

Peggy digested that. It seemed a straightforward answer. And was, more than likely, the reason. Squirming in her seat to face him, she said, "Is there something you're not telling me? About Judd? About this—this, what did you call it?"

"Transmigration of soul?"

"Yes."

He pursed his lips for a second without taking his eyes off the road. "Not that I can think of. It is, of course, of vital importance that we get to him as soon as possible."

"What can happen if we're too late?"

Maceo shrugged. "I don't know. I do know that we've got to get to Judd and confront this spirit—this Bull person's spirit."

Peggy turned when he slowed even more and saw a car several hundred feet ahead preparing to turn off the highway. When it was off the road, the cars ahead of the TransAm picked up speed until the line of traffic was moving at almost sixty miles per hour. "I understand that we have to do this—confront the spirit—but why is it important?"

Maceo didn't answer immediately. Then, when he spoke, an ominous tone clung to each word. "Bull seems to be powerful. If he could influence Judd enough to assume a different appearance, you can put it in the bank that he's strong. Apparently, he's been gaining strength right along, while Judd, like any normal human being, has stayed at the same spirit level."

"I don't understand."

"Any changes we make, as people, as intellectual beings, are usually slow. Changes are very slow processes. For instance, a person who is going to be a super salesman acquires the ability to lead other people's minds in degrees. It doesn't happen overnight."

"Are you saying that Bull has completely overpowered Judd?"

Maceo shrugged. "I don't know. Maybe. Hopefully, he hasn't yet. But, if I'm right and Bull has been gaining strength right along, Judd is in danger."

"How much danger?"

He didn't answer.

"Maceo? How much danger could Judd be in?"

"I'm trying to remember if there has ever been an instance where a complete takeover has happened."

"What do you mean by a complete takeover?" Peggy felt her throat tighten and her mouth dry out.

"If a powerful enough entity encounters another spirit within a body, an eradication of the host spirit is supposed to be possible. But I'm not certain if it's ever happened." For a split second, he took his eyes off the road and turned to find Peggy weeping, tears running down her cheeks. He reached out and took her hand in his right and squeezed. "We're not going to let that happen. Y'hear?"

His hand felt warm on hers, and she felt the comfort and strength this man had to offer her. She took it, knowing she needed the additional support. "I'm not quite certain I understand. What would happen to Judd if that were the situation?"

"Bull would totally eradicate—get rid of—Judd's spirit. Drive it out. Judd's body would exist, but not Judd as you know him. He would in essence be Bull and maybe look like Judd. Or he could assume his own appearance."

"Is that really possible?"

"According to some experts, yes."

"There's no other alternative?"

"Bull could voluntarily leave, but from what you've told me, I don't think that's too likely."

She shuddered.

"I don't want you to be upset, but I think you should know this and be able to help me when we encounter Bull and Judd."

"What else is there that you haven't told me?"

"Bull could make Judd kill this man—"

"Buckshot."

"Yes, Buckshot, and then leave."

"Wouldn't that be all right?" To Peggy it sounded as if Judd would then be rid of Bull.

"If that happened, Judd would

357

probably be held responsible for Buckshot's death and have to pay the penalty. Bull, meanwhile, would get away with murder."

"But Bull or Judd, whoever," she said, "thought the gang wouldn't report the crime."

"I don't think we can count on such a thing happening. If it did, I think Judd would still be held accountable when and if the fact were ever uncovered."

Peggy dabbed at her eyes when she felt new tears forming. "Hurry, Maceo. Hurry."

The purr of the TransAm's engine filled the passenger compartment when the two people fell silent.

"Who are you?" Buckshot called out.

Judd moved forward, a swaggering confidence in each step.

When Buckshot and the gang got close enough to make out his face, puzzled expressions replaced the looks of surprise that had held there for a moment.

When Buckshot looked closer, he recognized the clothes. "Well, look who's back."

The gang instantly knew it was the intruder of the day before, and Cow stepped forward. "Who the fuck are you?"

"*Don't get too bossy, Cow.*" Judd threw his head back and Bull's laughter filled the room.

No one reacted other than to stare wide-eyed at the man who had spoken without using his mouth.

"How—how'd you do that?" Gordo asked, moving closer.

"Do what?" Judd's voice answered the question.

Gordo fell back.

"D'you know what you done to Mule?" Buckshot confronted Judd, pulling himself to his full height so that he could look down on the shorter man.

"No. What?"

"You made him into a raving madman. He's over in the corner there, someplace in the dark, blabbering and pissing in his pants and generally just going crazy. That's what you done to him. Why?"

"Better that it was you, Buckshot."

"You cocksucker!" Buckshot growled. "Get him, boys!"

No one moved.

When his order wasn't carried out, Buckshot turned to find the men of the gang glaring at him.

Judd smiled evilly. *"Get him!"*

Reacting instantly to the sound of their dead leader's voice, the Light Bearer's Chosen looked at each other for a split second and then grabbed Buckshot.

"Get your stinking hands off me. That's not Bull. He sounds like him, but he's not Bull. Bull was bigger. Heavier.

Wavy hair. More muscle. This wimp ain't Bull, I tell you. Let me go!"

The hands held fast and the gang laughed mirthlessly.

"Why the fuck do you think I passed out? I'll tell you why. This sonofabitch imitated Bull's voice and didn't move his mouth when he done it. I tell you, it scared the *bejeezus* outa me. Show 'em how you done it—guy—whatever your name is. Talk without moving your mouth."

"We already seen him do it, asshole," Gordo said. "Ain't none of us fainted, you fucking pantywaist." He pushed Buckshot's shoulder and Buckshot's head popped back, and then forward like a doll's.

Cow moved closer to Judd. "I thought yesterday that you looked a lot like my dead man Bull. Now when I look at you I see you don't. You got his clothes on, but the resemblance ends there.

"What's your name?"

"Call me Judd."

"You want in? You want to join the Light Bearer's Chosen?"

Judd wanted to scream but couldn't, nor could he keep his head from nodding to the question. How Bull was controlling his voice, making him say the things he did, escaped him. All Judd knew was that he was not in control of his body or voice, and his mind, although aware of Bull's presence, seemed to be weakening in its resolve. Suddenly all he wanted was to get out of the situation he found himself in and get back to Rushton and Peggy. He wanted to curse Bull for controlling him now and for letting him enter this den of snakes without any sort of protection other than the presence of the other spirit.

Gordo tapped Cow on the shoulder. "We gonna perform the ritual to bring him in?"

"Later. We got to perform the sacrifice before we do another thing. We'd best satisfy Lucifer or all our asses will be in a sling."

"Is Buckshot still going to be the sacrifice?" Gordo leaned forward with the rest of the gang to hear her answer.

Instead, she looked first at Judd, then at Buckshot, and smiled evilly.

Outside, the storm built in its intensity and the first crash of thunder was the only sound in the warehouse.

19

Slow. The traffic moved so slowly. Why couldn't the cars ahead realize that a life-and-death situation existed in the capital city and that Peggy and Maceo Montgomery had to get there as soon as possible? The tail lights of the car ahead wavered in Peggy's teary vision. She wanted to weep but knew it was pointless. Still, her instincts told her that if she wept, she would feel better—perhaps cleansed. Wasn't that the function of tears—to wipe away the soul's and spirit's trouble and pain?

The rhythm of the windshield wipers seemed to mock their impeded flight. *Slow-down. Slow-down. Slow-down.* She wanted to scream. Instead, she turned toward the dashboard and peered through her unshed tears at the digital clock. Almost seven-thirty. Would they be in time? Would they be able to find Judd? Had he even gone to the warehouse?

She pulled out a handkerchief and dabbed at her eyes. *Please, God, let us be in time*, she prayed silently to herself.

Maceo broke the silence. "Do you have any idea where this Railroad Avenue is?"

She shook her head. "I've been to the capital a lot of times but not to go to any warehouses. I think we'll have to ask for directions if you don't know where it's at."

"I'll stop at the first service station we see. Damn. I hate losing even those few minutes."

The storm continued to ravage the countryside, and the two occupants of the TransAm fell silent once more, each dwelling on their own thoughts.

Buckshot's eyes darted from one face to another. The ring closed in on him tighter. If he had bolted a few seconds before, he probably would have been able to break through. But now, their shoulders were touching and there was no way he would be able to get them off guard enough to let him break away.

"Get away from me! I'm your leader! You can't do this. Get the fuck away—do you hear me?"

Several of the members dropped out

of the closing circle and pushed together the crates which served as their altar. Mary Queen of Sots hurried over to Buckshot's camp area and fumbled through a set of saddlebags. A triumphant look crossed her face when she found the book she knew Cow would need.

When the crates were positioned and Mary returned with the book, the Light Bearer's Chosen closed in on their hapless leader. Cowering before they touched him, Buckshot screamed. "Let me alone. I ain't done nothing wrong. Goddammit! Let me go."

Cow glared at him, spitting in his face. "God will damn no one or anything for you, Buckshot. You've erred greatly in your execution of the leadership duties as they apply to the Chosen. You have insulted the Light Bearer. Lucifer will have his just due paid to him. We shall see to it. As high priestess of the Chosen, I shall see to it."

"What you gonna do, Cow?" Gordo's eyes glittered in the flickering light of the campfires.

"We'll kill two birds with one stone. We'll get rid of Buckshot and we'll initiate the new guy at the same time. He'd have to get rid of somebody anyhow before he became a full-fledged member. Who better than Buckshot? Besides, our asses will be clean if Judd here kills Buckshot. Right?"

"Right." Gordo smiled, a drop of

saliva oozing from the corner of his pendulous lips. "That's pretty good thinking coming from a cunt."

"This *cunt* has more brains than you guys are willing to admit to," Cow said savagely. "Whose idea was it to turn to Lucifer? Mine, when I joined up and became Bull's woman. Who's been running the rituals and getting the favors for the gang? Me. Who knows the rituals that have gotten us just about anything we've wanted? Me. That's who."

Gordo turned away, shaking his head. It wasn't right that a mere women have that much power in the Chosen. He wondered if things were changing too much. After all, the new guy, this Judd, had said two words, "Get him!" and the gang had reacted as if Bull had said them. Sure, it sounded like Bull, but the wimp wasn't Bull. Bull was over six feet and weighed damned near three hundred pounds. This guy was about five-eleven or so and maybe weighed in at one-eighty— wringing wet. Things were moving too fast for Gordo. He'd have to watch real close to make certain he didn't miss anything.

The gang pushed Buckshot to the side of the crates and waited.

"Strip him," Cow ordered.

Judd stepped through the circle of people, elbowing his way closer to Cow. When she sensed his presence at her side, she turned, smiling at him. He grinned, running his tongue over his lips. "It's great to be back here, Cow."

Her face blanched. "Just who the fuck are you?"

A sharp clap of thunder outside seemed to punctuate her question.

Maceo turned into the Shell station to the right side of the road. Stopping under the canopy, he waited, but no one came out. Then, realizing he had stopped at the self-service pumps, he jumped out and ran into the office where a pimply-faced teenage boy looked up from the girlie magazine he was reading.

"Yeah, what can I do for you?"

"Where's Railroad Avenue from here?"

The kid stood, moving from behind the counter, before dropping the magazine open to the centerfold displaying a large-breasted woman fondling herself as if she had just discovered her own sexual apparatus. "Okay, listen close. This isn't easy. You go two blocks straight down the street you were driving on if you came off the highway out there. You going that way?" He jerked his head in the direction of the TransAm.

Maceo nodded.

"Okay. Here's the tough part. You turn right and then you're on Railroad Avenue. Got it?"

Realizing the kid was obnoxiously insulting him, Maceo ignored the remark and said, "In which direction are the warehouses?"

"That's tough. Both ways. What are you looking for?" The young man's attitude changed from one of berating to helpfulness when he realized he had failed at upsetting the black man.

"I think the name Holmes is on it. The building is yellow—that's all I know."

The attendant shook his head. "Don't know of any that are yellow. Could be. I guess you'll have to look in both directions."

Maceo turned, hurrying back to the TransAm. Revving the idling engine, he slipped it into drive, and the black car roared out of the service station.

The attendant watched, a slight grin on his mouth. "Nice car," he muttered. "Always liked flesh tones for cars."

"Put him on the altar," Cow ordered. "You, Judd, stand by me." She turned, looking at the ring of faces surrounding the crude sacrificial table. "Gordo, get Buckshot's knife."

When he handed the weapon to her, Cow laid it on the altar and turned away. "Everyone stay where you are. I'll draw the circles."

Hurrying to the saddlebags from which Mary had obtained the book, Cow withdrew a large piece of chalk and drew two circles over the partially obliterated ones. When the altar and the Chosen were enclosed, she wrote the names of those devils and spirits she wished to invoke between the curved lines of the double circle. She finished by drawing the pentagram, making the members move out of her way when she had to move through them. Once she finished, she stepped out of the circle and then, satisfied that all was right, went back to her place at the altar.

The storm continued building, rumbles of thunder echoing around the long, narrow warehouse while pure white lightning flashed through the filth-encrusted windows, baring the most darkened corner of the room. In one corner, Mule lay on his back, his eyes wide open and rolling back and forth, his mouth flapping in a fevered gibberish that only he could understand.

"I invoke," Cow cried out loudly, "the Sons of Cham-Zoroaster—Cush, Mizriam, Phut, Canaan—the controllers of magic in Africa, Egypt, the deserts of the world and Phoenicia—my ancestors. I invoke the familiars of my mother, her mother and her mother and all the women who bore children in my line before me—Makeshift, Thief of Hell, Rago, Swein, Greedigut, Rapha, Littleman, Volon, Josaphat, Rory, Tissy, Freegmon and Dulios."

The thunder roared out in answer with

a crash that shook the building to its foundation.

Maceo slowed the car and moved into a U-turn. They had followed Railroad Avenue for six blocks. Little by little the buildings had gotten smaller and farther apart as Maceo and Peggy continued on their way.

"Keep your eyes open, just in case we missed it when we came down the first time." He started forward again, driving almost thirty miles per hour.

"I didn't see it. Maybe you'd better hurry and get to the other end where we haven't looked yet."

"I've never seen it fail. If one has a choice—left or right—up or down—in or out—and the choice is a critical one, it almost invariably will be the wrong choice the first time. Ever notice that, Peggy?" He grinned, trying to ease her tenseness.

"Yes. But hurry, Maceo. I feel that the more time we take, the more danger Judd is in."

He pressed the accelerator down a little farther and the TransAm leaped forward to forty miles an hour. When they reached the intersection with the street from which they had first turned, he slowed enough to see if any traffic was coming and shot across the intersection. Slowing to twenty-five, he peered to his left, and Peggy searched on the right side of the car.

The storm renewed its fury, sending tidal-like waves of rain over the car, its windshield wipers beating furiously to keep the window free of running water. A loud crash of thunder followed a fork of lightning that traversed the blackened sky overhead.

"I call on thee, oh, Prince of Darkness, ye who are the Light Bearer and who have chosen us to be his children. Come to us. Be with us as we wipe the slate clean of this human garbage lying before you. Come to us, Lucifer. Come to us, Beelzebub. Come to us, Satan. Come to us, Asmodeus. Come to us, Mephistopheles. Come to us, Mulciber. Come to us, Pentamorph—he of the five shapes. All of those who are the everlasting opponents of good, come to us. Help us. We invoke thee. We need thee. Come to us. *Now!*"

As if the storm were cooperating, another loud roar of thunder followed Cow's supplications.

"We beg thy forgiveness with these words that have been spoken to thee since the dawn of evil at the garden. It is not we, who have been faithful to thee, who must be punished. He will be offered to thee. His blood will flow for thee."

"No!" Buckshot screamed. "You can't do that. This is all a bunch of bullshit. You can't kill me! For Chrissake, listen to what you're saying, you bitch. You want to kill me to satisfy some fucking devil that don't even exist. What the fuck's the matter with you? All of you? Gordo? You can't believe in this shit. Blaster? Armpit? Come on, you guys. We ride together. Don't let her kill me. I don't want to die. Jesus! Come on, help me, you bastards!"

"Shut him up," Cow growled tersely, and Gordo stepped forward, clamping his hand over Buckshot's mouth. Buckshot struggled when his breath was cut off and Gordo's fat fingers partially blocked his nostrils.

Cow looked about the room and continued. "Help us, oh, Lucifer, the Light Bearer. Help us to attain our goals to become as much like you as possible. Make us devils and devilesses, clever devils and deceitful devils, lustful devils and sinful devils to better serve you in this, your princely domain."

Judd watched, his own perception of the incidents impeded by Bull's takeover. Nevertheless, he was able to witness to a full extent everything that happened within the range of his eyes, limited as if he were watching through sunglasses or a dark, thin material that covered his eyes. He wanted to run. He wanted to scream. He wanted in some way to resist witnessing this perverse behavior assaulting his senses and intellect. Try as he would, he could command nothing.

Cow turned to him. "Take this." She handed Judd Buckshot's switchblade knife. He didn't want that. He thought he knew what she wanted him to do, but he would not, he could not kill anyone. Sure, he had wanted revenge for Cindy's death. But at the last moment, he would never have been able to inflict any sort of mortal wound or real physical damage on anyone—even the person responsible for the death of his only sister.

"Cool it, Judd. I'll do it."

The instant Judd became aware of Bull's thoughts and intentions, he felt himself ripping apart as if someone or something had pulled his very soul from within him. His body felt peculiar, his face strange. His head itched, and for an instant he thought his hair was growing. Touching his face, he fingered a beard. His body felt fuller, thicker. His hands and arms seemed to be covered with sweat, and when he looked, he wanted to scream but could not. His hands weren't his hands anymore. They were much bigger. What was going on?

He turned to face Cow and tried to speak but was unable to do so. She was crouching or something. When he had looked just a few seconds before, her eyes were not that much below his own. Now, her head barely came up to his elbow.

When she turned to face him, she screamed.

"*Bull?*"

The one word brought the attention of the Chosen to him, and they all reacted as Cow had. Looks of astonishment, of fear, of disbelief, of horror filled their faces.

"It can't be."

"Who—?"

"Where'd he come from?"

"Where's the other guy?"

"How'd Bull get in here?"

"Bull's dead."

"It can't be Bull. It can't."

"It's Bull, all right."

The women screamed, and the men, backing off, could not tear their attention from the tall, bearded man standing next to the altar.

Cow remained rooted to the spot next to Judd, who now looked exactly like Bull. "Bull, how did—? I mean, where did—? What the fuck is going on? Are you Bull or aren't you?"

"Hey, Cow, who else looks like this?" He grinned, turning his attention back to Buckshot.

Buckshot's eyes hadn't blinked since Bull's transformation, and now that the apparition or ghost or whatever Bull might be had turned his attention to him, the bound man could do nothing but blubber.

"You ready to have the score evened

up, old buddy?'' Bull asked, running the tip of the blade down Buckshot's body toward his penis and scrotum.

"Hey, look!'' the voice of one of the members who had backed away from the altar cried out, and all eyes turned to follow the outstretched, pointing arm.

"There's the motorcycle,'' Peggy cried, pointing to the bike parked next to the loading ramp of a warehouse. An accommodating flash of lighting bleached the street and surrounding buildings in bright light for a split second, and both Peggy and Maceo could see the faded yellow coloring of the warehouse's front and the name "Holmes'' immediately below the roofline.

"This is it,'' Maceo said excitedly, slamming on the brakes. The TransAm fishtailed to a stop, scant inches from the back of the Harley-Davidson.

Both jumped out, running full tilt to the only door in sight, praying that it wasn't locked. Maceo reached out and gently turned the knob. It gave and the door swung in. Cautioning Peggy to be as quiet as possible, he stepped inside and held the door for her. She followed and the door was pushed out.

"Sh-h-h, listen,'' Peggy whispered.

The cries of astonishment and bewilderment from the Chosen rang through the building, echoing in macabre ways to accompaniment of the thunder.

"Don't make a sound," Maceo said, moving foward.

"Look," Peggy squeaked when they turned the corner and saw the gang backing off from the altar, away from the towering figure standing next to it. "Is that Judd?"

Maceo shrugged.

"He's wearing the same clothes. He's got wavy hair and the same fleshy cheeks. But the beard. Judd doesn't have a beard. He's not that tall. Where's Judd, Maceo?"

"Hey, look!" one of the members cried out.

The voice pierced through the gloom toward Peggy and Maceo. Unable to move, they stood, frozen to the spot. They had been discovered. They wanted to run but could not.

"Who the fuck let you two in?" Gordo demanded, walking toward them. The rest of the gang fell in behind him, leaving the circle, which had been broken by shuffling, retreating feet when they had backed away from the sight of Bull.

Then a new sound could be heard over the thundering storm, over the voices, over the babbling duet of Mule and Buckshot. It began as a low moaning whistle and quickly grew until everyone in the warehouse was aware of it. Wailing, undulating, piercing, it rose only to fall, growing louder with each passing second.

Gordo stopped, and the Chosen did likewise. They looked about.

"The cops!" one yelled.

"The fucking fuzz!"

"No. It's something else."

"It ain't the cops."

"What the fuck is that?"

They threw their hands over their ears trying desperately to shut out the painful sound as it continued growing in volume. Unable to hear Cow screaming, the gang milled about, their eyes wide with terror and horror as they felt their eardrums bursting.

"Get back in the circle, you fools! It's Lucifer! Get back in the circle." The screaming sound stopped.

Bull turned to look at Peggy and quickly turned away when an astonished look of recognition crossed her face. Redirecting his attention to Buckshot, he raised his arm, the knife blade flashing in the firelight, as if it held a life of its own.

"My God, that's Judd, I think. It's just the way he looked in the bedroom, but then he didn't have a beard. Maceo. Stop him! It's Judd. He's going to kill that—"
She stopped when Bull's hand swept down, slicing through Buckshot's unprotected neck, severing the windpipe and jugular vein. The blood spurted out in quick jets, and the only sound besides the rain beating on the roof was the slurping sound coming from Buckshot as he des-

perately tried to retain his life for one more second of time.

Then the wailing cry began again, louder than before. Creating its own sound waves, the scream rose and fell, fanning the flames of the fire. The tires on the motorcycles burst, sounding like small cannonfire. The gang ran about, hands over their ears again, trying to escape the fury of the noise. No matter where they ran, the sound followed them. Only Bull stood in the center of the room, unaffected. Peggy, her hands clamped over her own ears, turned to Maceo, and they both ventured farther into the cacophony. When Bull saw them coming, his shoulders slumped and he turned to face them.

Cow, her hands covering her ears, screamed, "It's a miracle. It's a miracle. Bull has come back. He's beaten death. Lucifer has given him back to us. Thank you, mighty one. Thank you, Lucifer. Thank you!" She fell to her knees, kissing the floor.

"Judd?" Peggy shouted above the din.

Bull looked at her blankly.

"Judd, come with us," Maceo said, reaching out to take his arm. At first Bull resisted, but then allowed the black man to guide him from the room.

The noise swelled to a decibel level beyond the range of human ears, and, just as it disappeared, the windows in the clerestory began shattering, showering the milling Chosen below with shards of glass.

Peggy led the way from the room, turning the corner to the short hall that would take them to the door and the outside. When she stepped through, she waited for Maceo and Bull.

Maceo stepped through and then brought the man following them into the rain. It was Judd.

"Judd!" Peggy screamed, throwing her arms around his neck.

"Where am I?" He looked about, the rain washing down his face. "What happened? What's going on?" Looking dumbfoundedly at Maceo, he said, "Who are you? Peggy? What's going on?"

"We'll tell you in the car," she said, pulling him toward the TransAm.

The car roared down the highway toward Rushton. Judd and Peggy, sitting in the back, their arms around each other, listened intently as Maceo explained what had happened.

When the psychologist finished, Judd said, "The whole thing seems like a dream. I sort of remember digging up the motorcycle, but then it becomes a mishmash of bits and pieces of scenes that seem to be real and then just as quickly are more like dreams."

"I suppose that would go with the

territory," Maceo said from the front seat.

"Look," Peggy said, holding up Judd's right hand. "Your little nail is normal."

"What's that mean?" Judd looked at her, his face reflecting his question.

"It's a long story. I'll tell you everything when we get home."

"You know, that's quite an experience." Maceo leaned back in the driver's seat and patted the steering wheel. "The mentality of a gang like that motorcycle bunch is fascinating to me. Their hell-bent-for-leather attitude toward life, not caring about society and its mores, doing whatever they want to do without worrying about the consequences—all of it is really fascinating. It's as if they have their own society in their own world and don't give a particular darn about anything or anybody outside their circle."

"You can have them," Judd said.

"I agree with that a hundred percent." Peggy smiled, snuggling closer to Judd.

"No, really, from a professional viewpoint I think it would be fascinating to study them sometime. I could write a book or something. It would really be interesting."

He tapped his right hand on the steering wheel again, unmindful of the long nail on his little finger. Reaching up with it, he jabbed it into his ear and wiggled it about.

"Yeah, really fascinating," Maceo

said, smiling benignly into the night.

The TransAm continued down the highway toward Rushton.

Epilogue

Two Days Later

Peggy watched Judd wolf down his breakfast of bacon, eggs, and waffles. They had slept until eight, deciding to go to a later church service. She reflected back to the day before when they had talked about Judd's experience and whether or not he should go to the police. They had had a heated argument until they both began laughing.

"It's so silly for us to be angry about it," Peggy said.

"I know. I'm just thankful that I came out of it in as good shape as I did. At least, I hope I'm all right."

"You do feel all right, don't you?"

He nodded. "You know, if the gang doesn't report the murder of Buckshot, and you claim that it was Bull who was standing there and who cut Buckshot's throat, I think I can live with not reporting it, too."

"Why do you say that?"

"As I recall everything that happened after I went into the warehouse, it all seems like a television program or movie. I'm just watching—I'm not in the picture, so to speak. It's Bull—all the way."

Snapping out of her revery, Peggy found he'd finished eating. She took his dishes away and laid the morning newspaper in front of him. "Here, you read this while I tidy up the kitchen. Then, after we shower, we can go to church."

He grabbed her around the waist before she could move away. "Who says we'll want to go to church if we start showering?"

"I do. I don't know about you, but I've got an awful lot to be thankful for right now."

He released her and nodded. "Yeah, I guess I do, too."

He opened the newspaper and froze. The headlines reported the discovery of a body in a deserted warehouse. "Look at this!"

Peggy came back to look over his shoulder. "Oh, no. What's it say?"

Judd began reading: "Capital Dateline: City police are investigating the murder of a 33-year-old man whose body was found in a deserted warehouse owned by Allenede Industries, Ltd.

"The body of William Everhart was found lying on two packing crates in the center of the warehouse.

"Lieutenant Jacob Reisen, who is in charge of the investigation, says that it 'will be only a matter of time before we apprehend the murderer.' Reisen says that the knife, which was used in the slaying, was found next to the body and that a clear set of fingerprints has been identified.

"An all points bulletin has been issued for James Sterling, 38, whose fingerprints were found on the handle of the murder weapon. Sterling, who goes by the name of Bull, is the leader of a motorcycle gang called the Light Bearer's Chosen.

"It is believed that Sterling was out of town when he was sought for questioning in a double murder in September. Sterling is about six feet, two inches tall, weighs well over two hundred seventy-five pounds, and is believed to be without transportation. His motorcycle was found in front of the abandoned warehouse.

"Police are also searching for the members of the Light Bearer's Chosen for questioning."

Peggy hugged Judd. "It's all over. It's really all over, darling."

Judd smiled. At least Bull had done

one right thing during his stay by leaving his fingerprints. Judd pulled Peggy down on his lap and kissed her.